Jane held Sofia's wedding dress in front of her and looked at herself in the mirror.

The huge room was now empty. Voices faded in the background. Instead of the wedding march, there was the sound of a haunting Greek song somewhere in the distance. Jane twirled around on the pedestal, holding the dress to her shoulders, hearing the satin *whoosh* as she moved, and wondering—was she destined to be a bridesmaid forever and never a bride?

She was suddenly aware that she wasn't alone. Someone stood in the shadow of the doorway, feet crossed at the ankles, shoulders braced against the woodwork.

"Watch out." Alex winked at her. "Somebody might mistake you for the bride and kiss you." He turned and walked out, leaving Jane alone again, her cheeks burning and her hands shaking.

———

"Grace takes readers on a lively journey to Italy's spectacular Amalfi coast and spins a funny, sexy tale of intrigue and romance. A light, thoroughly entertaining read that should do wonders for the Italian tourist business."

—*Library Journal* on *That's Amore*

This book is a work of fiction. Names, characters, places and incidents
are products of the author's imagination or are used fictitiously. Any
resemblance to actual events or locales or persons, living or dead, is
entirely coincidental.

An *Original* Publication of POCKET BOOKS

 POCKET BOOKS, a division of Simon & Schuster, Inc.
1230 Avenue of the Americas, New York, NY 10020

Copyright © 2004 by Carol Culver

All rights reserved, including the right to reproduce
this book or portions thereof in any form whatsoever.
For information address Pocket Books, 1230 Avenue
of the Americas, New York, NY 10020

ISBN: 978-1-4516-3190-6

First Pocket Books printing May 2004

10 9 8 7 6 5 4 3 2 1

POCKET and colophon are registered trademarks of
Simon & Schuster, Inc.

Cover design by JungMin Choi
Cover art by Jae Song

Manufactured in the United States of America

For information regarding special discounts for bulk purchases,
please contact Simon & Schuster Special Sales at 1-800-456-6798
or business@simonandschuster.com

This book is dedicated to the Kings Mountain Book Club—lovers of good books and good food—with thanks for throwing the biggest and best book signing bash in history!

An Accidental
Greek
Wedding

Chapter 1

She was seasick. Her first trip to the Greek Islands, and Jane Atwood's stomach was pitching and rolling along with the blue Aegean Sea. She leaned against the railing of the ferry, wedged among the tourists oohing and ahhing over the view of the island with its white, sugar-cube houses that clung to the lush green hills and the rocky cliffs that plunged into turquoise bays. As the waves slammed against the hull, Jane kept her eyes on the horizon and did not look down.

Sofia had warned her the seas could be rough in May. But Sofia wanted her wedding to be in May on the island of Mios, and she wanted Jane to be her bridesmaid, and Sofia Leonakis always got what she wanted, including the smartest, sexiest, most ambitious man in the world—Alex Woods.

Jane thought she'd either have to throw up or leap overboard and take her chances of being washed up on one of the island's sandy beaches. With any luck she'd be rescued by one of those handsome Greek fishermen Sofia told her about.

A familiar deep voice said in her ear, "Welcome to Greece. Are you ready to face the madhouse?"

Alex had snuck up on her before she was prepared to come face to face with six feet two inches of all-American masculine charm, dammit. To imagine that he'd gained weight and had sagging jowls since she'd last seen him was wishful thinking. No, he was just as gorgeous as ever; lean, tanned, fit, and smiling. And he had the same effect he'd always had on her: he left her breathless, tongue-tied, and awkward.

"Oh my God, Alex, what are you doing here?" she blurted. "You were supposed to be on the island days ago getting ready for the wedding."

"I know. I got held up in Seattle, then I missed my connection in New York. But I'm getting there as fast as I can. Calm down, Jane. Haven't you heard the saying, 'Siga, siga'?—'Slowly, slowly'? This is Greece. They have a different sense of time here."

"Sofia has the same sense of time she always had—she wants everything done yesterday. She must be going crazy that you're not there. But you always did like to make her crazy."

"Me? She's the one who makes *me* crazy. This

wedding has turned into a circus. It's not until Saturday, you know. Plenty of time to get ready."

"She wanted you here last week for the parties and the baptism and everything else that goes into it. Sofia does everything on a grand scale. You should know that by now. She's been planning her wedding for years. Why do you act surprised?"

"I'm not surprised, I'm just on edge." He rubbed his chin. "Bad food, no sleep, jet lag, culture shock. You name it, I've got it."

"And pre-wedding jitters?" Jane suggested. Though at the moment she was the one with the jitters. Seeing Alex again, his hair windblown, the shadow of a beard on his jaw, and that cleft in his chin, made goose bumps break out on her arms despite the warm Greek sun.

"Real men don't get jitters," he said with a wry smile. Then he turned and looked out across the water toward the island. If they listened hard enough, Jane was sure they could hear Sofia's voice giving orders, venting her frustration, and ranting about her absent bridegroom. "Though this is not the way I would have planned it," he added under his breath.

Jane followed Alex's gaze to the red terra-cotta roofs that peeked above the treetops. She wondered which was the villa that belonged to Sofia's family.

"How would you do it?" she asked.

"Go down to city hall, pay the two dollars or whatever it is, break out a bottle of champagne, and be done with it. I wouldn't have phony posed pictures, snarky hand-written poems to each other, a sky-high wedding cake frosted with wallpaper paste, and an elaborate baptism ceremony for the groom. Why does everything have to be such a big deal?"

"It's a once-in-a-lifetime event," Jane said. "Did you tell Sofia your idea of the perfect wedding?"

He shot her a look that said, *Are you kidding?*

Jane could just imagine Sofia's response. Either she would have had a tantrum or laughed herself silly. "I understand about the cake and the poems, but the pictures? Wouldn't you want a photo album to show your grandchildren?"

"Grandchildren?" He threw up his hands. "Good God, Jane, I'm only twenty-eight, even though today I feel at least fifty-eight. Don't worry, there *are* going to be pictures and cake and flowers and whatever else she wants. It's Sofia's show and I'm just the guy in the suit.

"I know I sound annoyed, but you're the only person I can tell what I really think. You always were, ever since the first day we met. Chemistry 101, remember?"

Remember? As if she could forget. He was her lab partner who never blamed her for that unfortunate explosion that singed her eyebrows and blew him across the room. He'd told the professor it wasn't her fault.

She agreed. It *was* his fault, for making her so nervous she'd misread the formula for ammonium dichromate. Was that the day she'd fallen in love with him, when he'd taken the blame for her mistake?

"If it weren't for you, I wouldn't be here on my way to marry Sofia," he continued.

That was true. Jane had brought Alex back to the dorm to study and introduced him to Sofia, her gorgeous Greek-American roommate. In one fell swoop she'd lost her best friend and the man of her dreams. She'd turned her energies to studying and graduated with honors. No boyfriend, but a Phi Beta Kappa key.

"I owe you big-time, Jane." Alex leaned over and kissed her on the cheek. Just a friendly kiss, but it made her heart thud so wildly she was afraid he could hear it.

"About the wedding," he said, oblivious, as always, to the effect he had on her. "I'm really fine with it. While she was working on it, I was free to work on other things. So it took six months out of her life and God knows how much of her parents' money—if she's happy, then I'm happy." He smiled, a perfunctory smile that was gone as fast as it had appeared.

Still, Jane felt relieved. However he felt, however late he was getting there, everything would be fine once they arrived. Sofia would understand that maybe real men did get the jitters. She'd understand that Alex was late because he had other things to do, and she wouldn't lose her cool when he showed up.

The boat rolled. Jane's stomach lurched.

Alex stepped forward and looked at her with concern. "What's wrong? Are you okay? Your face is green. You look awful."

She swallowed hard and clamped her lips together. Her knees wobbled and she reached out for something for balance. She grabbed Alex's arm, then she leaned over . . . and vomited on his shoes.

"Oh, God, look what I've done!" Though her stomach felt better, she'd ruined his shoes. "I'm so sorry."

"Don't mention it," he said, looking down at his feet as if they belonged to someone else. He probably wished they did. "I think I have another pair."

Shocked, she asked, "You mean you're wearing your wedding shoes now?"

"I might be. I packed in a hurry. Who's going to notice what I'm wearing on my feet, anyway?"

"Sofia will." Jane took a deep breath and felt much more steady, more sure of herself. She was no longer that impoverished, insecure college girl who blew up experiments. She was a CPA with an excellent job, a good future, and a man who wanted to marry her. She was a woman who was up to any emergency. She reached for her large leather purse. "I have a spot remover right here."

"Wait a minute." He took the spray can out of her hands and read the label. "That'll take the skin off my feet. Save it for the next catastrophe. Knowing you, I'm sure there'll be one." His teasing grin mitigated his remark.

She stuffed the spray can back in her purse, but before she could find a package of Tidy Wipes, he'd cleaned his shoes with his handkerchief.

"Sometimes I think you create disasters," he said, "because you're so good at fixing them."

"That's not true." She wasn't sure if he was referring to the lab fiasco, or the time she spilled coffee on his computer keyboard and then spent all night reinstalling his software, or the time . . .

"Little Ms. Fixit," he said dryly. "You look better now." He tucked a wisp of her hair that had blown across her cheek behind her ear, then he let his gaze drift down from her pale blond hair to her low-heeled sandals. "A lot better."

"Not so green?" she asked, fanning her flushed cheeks and popping a breath mint in her mouth. "That's a relief. I wouldn't want to clash with my hot-pink bridesmaid dress."

She knew she looked better now than she had in college, and even better than the last time he'd seen her while visiting Sofia in San Francisco.

Her hair was styled differently now—not that it did any good today, blown around by the sea breeze. And she had an elegant wardrobe of basic beige, white, and black tailored clothes that were right for the cool, foggy city she lived in.

Of course, it didn't matter how much better she looked when Sofia was around; all eyes would be on her, she thought with a pang of envy.

"Hot pink? That doesn't sound like you."

"It isn't me. But this isn't my wedding."

"I know how you feel," Alex said. Then he turned around. "Here we are. We'll be docking any minute. Get your bag."

Jane glanced toward the island as the tiny port came into view, its shore lined with pink and white tamarisk blooms. Crowds of people were waiting to greet the passengers who disembarked at Mios, but Sofia was not among them.

"She's not here," Jane said, pulling her suitcase behind her as they walked toward the street lined with taxis and tour leaders holding signs that said AMERICAN EXPRESS, SILVIA PARTY, and ARGO TOURS.

"Frankly," Alex said, "I didn't expect her."

Jane half expected him to say, "Frankly, my dear, I don't give a damn." But of course he gave a damn; he was getting married in a few days!

Alex hailed a taxi for the short ride, and they sat in the backseat with Jane's capacious purse between them. She turned her head from side to side to take in the rocky cliffs and the clear, azure water of the Aegean on their right, and the green fields dotted with wild red poppies on their left. Alex was staring straight ahead of him, oblivious to it all. Of course, he'd been there before. But Jane was enthralled with the views and the smell of the cypress trees that lined the road.

"I was hoping Nikos would meet me," he said at last. "I wanted to talk to him before things got too hectic."

"Oh?" Jane said. She wanted to say, What about? But it was none of her business. An awkward silence followed. "It's so exciting about your being made vice president," she ventured.

Alex turned to stare at her, his mouth open in surprise. "What?"

Jane could have kicked herself. Sofia had told her in confidence about Alex's promotion a few weeks ago, so she assumed he'd been told by now. When did they plan to tell him?

"I thought you knew," Jane said. "You can't be too surprised, right?" *Please say you're not. Please say you're happy about it.* "I mean, Sofia's father thinks you're the best. Why shouldn't you be vice president?"

"Because it smacks of nepotism—promoting me, his son-in-law, ahead of other guys who've been there longer. Besides, I have other plans. I can't work for Nikos anymore. I can't design another office building or a warehouse store. That's why I need to talk to him."

"Does Sofia know about this?"

"I've told her, but she doesn't want to hear it. She won't believe I'm actually going to quit."

"I'm sure she'll be supportive of whatever you want to do," Jane said primly. What else could she say? *It better be something lucrative, because Sofia has certain standards, certain expectations?* If Alex didn't know that by now, it was too late to inform him. "What do you want to do?"

"What I've always wanted to do," he said with a faraway look in his eyes. "Start my own business. Use my own designs."

Jane knew he'd had student loans to pay off, and that the Leonakises had made him an offer he couldn't refuse when he graduated. "But how will you . . . ?"

"Support Sofia in the manner to which she's accustomed?" he asked dryly. "It won't be easy, at first. I've saved some money so we won't starve, but we won't be dining out on king crab every night, either."

But Sofia's parents had always made sure she had the best of everything. They'd bought her a condo, a car, and still supplemented the income from her job so she could dine at a five-star restaurant every night if she wanted to.

Looking at Alex leaning back in the seat, his eyes half closed, his forehead creased with worry lines, Jane wished she hadn't spilled the beans about the promotion. She squelched a desire to reach over, put her hand on his shoulder, and tell him everything was going to be all right. But he'd just laugh at her concern and ask her why she thought he was worried. Alex was not the type to admit to weakness, jitters, or worries, even to her. She suspected it was the stiff-upper-lip attitude he'd used to cope with his childhood. She decided to change the subject, but the only subjects that came to her mind were connected to the wedding.

"Will your family be there for the wedding?" she asked brightly.

Alex shook his head. "I think I told you once that my dad walked out on us early on, and he died a few years ago. My mom is remarried. It's too far and too expensive for them to come."

"Who's your best man?"

"Sofia's brother George," he said. "He's here and it saves one of my friends from making the trip. I know what you're thinking; that I'm not taking this wedding thing seriously. But it's a guy thing."

"I understand that. It's just the contrast. Sofia's been planning her wedding on the island since she was old enough to dress her Barbie dolls in white and parade them down the imaginary aisle with her Ken doll waiting at the altar. And you show up with no extra shoes, no family, and no best man. It blows my mind." But maybe contrast was what it was all about—opposites did attract, after all.

Jane knew Sofia's goal in college had been to find a husband. She was smart enough to finesse her classes and graduate, even though she'd often spent her time sketching bridal dresses instead of taking class notes.

Jane was relieved when the taxi pulled up in front of the villa. There was no more time for conversation. No more time for her to say the wrong thing, no more time to hear any more of Alex's secrets, or worry about what would happen when the Leonakises learned them, too.

They got out of the taxi and Jane stood gaping at the big house with the cream-colored facade and twin towers flanking a huge set of central windows. All of the doors and windows were open to the sea, and the driveway was full of cars and delivery trucks.

Alex bounded up the stairs with Jane behind him. A man with an armload of flowers brushed past them, and three women in black dresses and white aprons came rushing down the circular staircase carrying stacks of towels.

Sofia and Alex dropped their bags in the vestibule and walked into the high-ceilinged living room. Sofia stood there on a pedestal in her white satin wedding dress, like a queen surrounded by her ladies-in-waiting.

"It's ruined," Sofia moaned loudly, staring at her reflection in a full-length mirror that shared the pedestal with her. "My whole wedding is ruined. Why is this happening to me? Why can't anything go right for a change? First the flowers, then the caterer, now the dress. Worse, the wedding is Saturday and my bridesmaid and my groom aren't even here yet!"

The women's voices sounded like birds chirping, bright, cheery, and soothing at the same time.

"Now, Sofia . . ."

"Everything's going to be fine."

"Hold still. Let me fix it."

Jane stared at the dress with its high neck, the row of tiny buttons marching down the front of the bodice, and the acres of shimmering satin that cascaded to the floor. It was exquisite, and Sofia looked like a dream with her long, dark curly hair brushing her shoulders and framing her face. What could possibly be wrong with her dress?

Suddenly Sofia saw them, and she turned pale. "Alex, stop!" she shouted, holding her hand out like a traffic cop. "You can't come in. You can't see me in my dress. It's bad luck."

All heads turned in his direction. Female voices rose and swelled. "Get out, get out! You can't see her. It's bad luck. No, no, no!" The women rushed at him, grabbed his arms, and though they were half his size, pushed him out of the room. The ridiculous sight of a big, broad-shouldered man being shoved out of the room by these determined little ladies brought a smile to Jane's face.

As Alex passed her, he winked and muttered just loud enough for her to hear, "See what I mean? I'm irrelevant. I told you it's a circus."

"Jane!" Sofia got down from her pedestal and crossed the room, her train billowing behind her, to hug her best friend. "I'm so glad you're here. We have to talk," she added urgently under her breath.

Everything was urgent with Sofia. Everything was a drama, and she was indeed the drama queen. "Look at my dress," she said, pointing to an infinitesimal spot on the skirt.

"That's nothing. I can fix that." Jane opened her purse and pulled out her tube of Zout, the miracle spot remover.

"See? I told you Jane would fix everything," Sofia announced to everyone with a bright smile.

Sofia's grandmother closed her eyes and crossed herself. Sofia's aunts gathered around Jane and kissed her on both cheeks. Sofia's mother came down the stairs, followed by a man in a black suit, and pressed Jane to her large bosom. Then she held her at arm's length.

"Look at her. She's so thin. And so pale. We have to put some color back in those cheeks to match her dress." She turned back to Sofia. "The caterer called. So far she hasn't been able to find caviar anywhere. And the florist phoned to say there are no lilies on the island for your bouquet. What about roses?"

"Roses?" Sofia's voice was full of disbelief, as if her mother had suggested cactus. "Roses are so common." She sighed loudly. "Honestly, if one more thing goes wrong . . ."

Jane held her breath. What *would* she do if one more thing went wrong? What would she do when she found out Alex was serious about going into business for himself?

Sofia waltzed out of the room to change so that Jane could fix her dress.

Apollonia, Sofia's mother, guided Jane to a damask-covered love seat in the corner and sat beside her. "I feel so much better now that you're here," she said in a confidential tone. "You have a good effect on Sofia. A calming effect. Without you, she . . . well, you know how she is. I hear Alex is finally here, too. Nikos wants to talk to him. He has a surprise for him—a wedding gift."

Jane could only hope Alex would pretend to be surprised about the promotion. Though maybe it was best that he was prepared.

"He loves Alex," Apollonia said. "We all love him. He's like the son we never had."

"But you do have a son."

"Yes, of course, but George is not like Alex. Alex has a head for business. Nikos trusts him."

And why not? He was loyal, dependable, hard-working, and he'd had the good sense to fall in love with their daughter, Jane thought.

"He'd never think of retiring, if it weren't for Alex," Apollonia continued.

"Mr. Leonakis is going to retire?" *Now* what would Alex do? Not only was he going to be the vice president, he was going to inherit the business. When he heard this, he might change his mind.

"Not now," Apollonia said, "but someday. And when he does . . ."

Jane nodded. They thought Alex would take his place. But he wasn't going to. Should she warn Apollonia? No, she should not. She should keep her mouth shut.

"Have I told you how glad I am that you're here?" Apollonia beamed at Jane as if Jane could make everything right. But she couldn't. She couldn't find caviar for the reception or lilies for the bouquet. She could clean the dress, though, and that's what she would do. "Your being here helps make up for the wedding being in May. You know this is the month the dead souls return to earth to do their mischief. It's bad luck to lend anything or to be married. I told her that, but . . ."

But Sofia always gets what she wants. Apollonia sighed loudly, patted Jane on the hand, and went off to the kitchen to see about the food.

Jane sat on the love seat and watched while the

aunts and uncles, cousins, and local people came in carrying vases of fragrant freesias, trays laden with nuts and candies, and packages wrapped in gold ribbons and white paper, and then went out talking and laughing. She felt invisible. For all anyone noticed, she could have been part of the furniture. A string quartet set up their instruments in the far corner and began tuning up. She knew Greek wedding festivities went on and on, building and building until the ceremony and continuing on afterward, but the wedding wasn't until Saturday. How much more festive could things get?

Sofia came back in low-rider jeans hugging her curvy hips and a tight T-shirt, transformed from a Greek princess to a hip American twenty-something. She laid the dress in its plastic bag on Jane's lap and sat down next to her.

"So much has happened," Sofia said in a low voice, leaning toward Jane. "I don't know where to start. First, Daddy is giving us the most wonderful wedding present."

"I know. You told me about the job."

"That's not a present. That's something that Alex deserves, and that he's worked for."

"But does Alex want the job?" Jane asked carefully. Now was her chance to plant the seeds of doubt in Sofia's mind.

"Of course he wants it," Sofia said breezily. "Oh, he has some crazy idea about going into business for himself, but when he hears what Daddy has to say, he'll be all for it. If he'd gotten here on time,

Daddy would have told him yesterday and everything would be settled. Because he was late, Alex also missed the baptism we had scheduled for him. He missed the engagement party the town people threw for us, too." Her voice quivered. "You have no idea how hard this is for me. I've been waiting all my life for this. I thought my wedding would be all about me, but it isn't. Mother is worried about Yaya making it through the long ceremony. Daddy's worried about the business. No one's worried about me, except for one person."

"Alex."

"No, not Alex. He hasn't even been here. It's someone else. That's what I need to talk to you about. I've had no one to talk to except . . ."

"Yes?" Jane said, on the edge of her seat.

Sofia gave a furtive glance over her shoulder. "I can't talk now, but just imagine how hard it's been when everybody is constantly asking the same questions: Where's your fiancé? What's keeping him? When is he getting here? Are you sure he's coming?"

"Now, Sofia, you know how hard Alex works. He probably had things to do."

"What things? Leonakis Construction Company has been closed all week because of the wedding."

"I don't know." But Jane had a pretty good idea. He was probably setting up his new business, which Sofia had just dismissed as a crazy idea. "Shopping for your wedding present maybe, or packing. But he's here now and everything's going to be fine." She put one hand behind her back and crossed her fingers.

"I hope so." Sofia sighed. "Sometimes I think Mother was right that getting married in May is bad luck. Sofia glanced out the doors to the terrace. "Look, there's Daddy and Alex—they're probably discussing the job right now."

Jane noticed that neither of the men was smiling. Nikos was gesturing wildly, and Alex had his hands stuffed in his pockets.

"Or the present," Sofia continued. "Daddy's giving us a house."

"A house?" Jane's eyes widened. What more could Sofia want? A house, a honeymoon in the Greek Islands, and a husband who adored her. "Where's the house? In Seattle?" That was where Alex had been working for the past three years.

"No, silly, here on the island. It's a vacation house. Daddy knows how much I love this island. Now it will always be a part of my life."

"That sounds wonderful." Jane shouldn't have been surprised at the size of the gift; the Leonakises were the most generous people in the world. She had been on the receiving end of many gifts herself over the years.

"I have something to tell you." Sofia's dark eyes shone with excitement. "You're the only one I can tell, the only one who can keep a secret."

Jane tensed. "Maybe you shouldn't. I'm really not good with secrets."

"You are, too. You're my best friend. If I can't tell you, who can I tell? Definitely not Mother—she'd have a fit if she knew. And Daddy? Never."

"Sofia, come quickly," her mother called from the other room. "Look what just arrived."

Two men in overalls were walking up the driveway carrying a huge crate labeled LIVE ANIMALS. Sofia jumped up and went running to the door.

"It's the doves," she said. "Finally something is going right. Don't go anywhere, Jane. We have to talk, about . . . you know." She shot Jane a dazzling smile and went out the front door just as her father came into the living room through the French doors.

"Jane," he said. "Welcome to Greece." He leaned down to kiss her on her cheek. His face was lined with wrinkles; his eyes looked sad and tired. Alex must have told him his plans, but he seemed to be taking it well, all things considered.

"Thank you, Mr. Leonakis."

"This is a happy time, and a sad time, too. Losing your daughter . . ." His eyes filled with tears. They were an emotional family, wearing their feelings on their sleeves, and Jane didn't know what to say to comfort him. "I see you're working on the dress," he said, making an effort to control himself. He took the seat next to her that had previously been occupied by his wife and then his daughter. "I have a favor to ask you. Sofia says you can fix anything."

"Oh, no, not really." *Here it comes. I want you to fix Alex for me. Make him take the job. You can do it.* "I wish I could, but—"

"It's a small thing, but it's important to me."

Nikos reached into his pocket and pulled out a small jeweler's case. "These are my cuff links for the wedding. They belonged to my grandfather, and I want to wear them for this special occasion. The stone came loose in one of them. I was wondering if you could fix it?"

Jane almost laughed with relief. "Of course I can fix it," she assured him. "I have a tube of Krazy Glue in my purse here and I'll have it repaired in no time."

He smiled and left the jeweler's case in her lap. "Thank you so much. I knew you could do it. And Jane? We're so glad you're here."

Jane nodded and tucked the cuff links in her pocket. Then she set to work removing the spot from the dress. It came out easily, and she carried the dress up to the pedestal, where a rack held a long white silk slip and a padded satin hanger for the dress. She held the dress in front of her and looked at herself in the mirror.

The huge room was now empty. Voices faded in the background. Instead of the wedding march, there was the sound of a haunting Greek song from somewhere in the distance. Jane twirled around on the pedestal, holding the dress to her shoulders, hearing the satin *whoosh* as she moved, and wondering—was she destined to be a bridesmaid forever and never a bride?

She was suddenly aware that she wasn't alone. Someone stood in the shadow of the doorway, feet crossed at the ankles, shoulder braced against the woodwork.

"Watch out." Alex winked at her. "Somebody might mistake you for the bride and kiss you." He turned and walked out, leaving her alone again, her cheeks burning and her hands shaking.

Chapter 2

$\mathcal{I}$n typical Leonakis style, the whole town was invited to a dinner party at a taverna at the beach that night. After a few hours of drinks and toasts to his health and to their everlasting happiness, Alex's head felt as if it were caught in a vise and his vision was blurred. He was surrounded by Leonakises. He danced with Sofia's grandmother, talked with her aunts, kissed her mother, and held hands with Sofia under the table. One of the things he'd always loved about her was how close she was to her family. Growing up with an absentee father and a working mother, he'd missed out on the kind of all-encompassing love and affection Sofia took for granted from her big, demonstrative family. But tonight, after he hadn't slept for twenty-four hours, he felt as if the Leonakis walls were closing in on him. He glanced at the door and saw Jane sneaking out. He'd give anything to do the same, for a few minutes, for a breath of air. Fat chance.

Loud conversation swirled around him. The traditional island songs, played by the clarinet, mandolin, and the bagpipes, made it necessary to shout if he wanted to be heard. He didn't. He had only one thing to say, and this was not the time or place.

He'd planned to tell Nikos this afternoon, but he quickly realized it wasn't the right time. Not with the excitement of the wedding coupled with Nikos's heart condition. He might even have to wait until after the wedding. Once he got over the shock, Nikos would understand. After all, he'd done the same thing—started his own business, worked hard, and made it a success. The only problem was convincing Sofia it was a good idea to work for himself. So far, she'd been less than enthusiastic.

He hoped Jane was right when she said Sofia would support him in whatever he wanted to do, but he wasn't completely sure about that. There was only one way to find out. Tell her what he'd decided. Tell her how his plans were going. Tell her now.

"Sofia," he said. "I'm suffocating in here. Let's go outside where it's quiet."

"What for?"

"I have something to tell you."

"What is it?"

"Not here."

She stood and held out her arms invitingly. "Let's dance. I love this song."

He followed her to the dance floor. She put her arms around him and they swayed to the music. He was glad it was a slow song so he could close his eyes and drift off. But as luck would have it, the tempo changed abruptly. The band was playing the *nisiotika,* the traditional wedding and festival music, and suddenly the dance floor was crowded with wedding guests and locals, stamping their feet and holding hands at shoulder level. Each time someone's boot hit the floor, it was like a hammer pounding a nail in his head.

"Where's Jane?" Sofia shouted in his ear.

"She went out."

"Go get her. She has to dance with us."

He didn't hesitate. Not even when a rugged-looking guy in a fisherman's cloth hat and tall boots grabbed Sofia's hand and jerked her out of his reach. He headed for the door like a drowning man swimming to the surface.

The air was fresh and cool and laden with the pungent smell of fishing nets. Alex crossed the street to the beach. In the bright moonlight he saw Jane leaning against the hull of a small boat, facing the water. The wind was tossing her skirt above her knees and molded her simple, dark dress to her body. She didn't look as thin as she used to. He wondered if she had a man in her life.

Sofia thought Jane spent too much time working and not enough time socializing, but that didn't mean she hadn't found the right man. Someone serious and focused. Someone who'd appreciate her for what she was—sensitive, trustworthy, kind, and best of all, a good listener.

Seeing her with Sofia's gown this afternoon had made him wonder if she was planning a wedding of her own. Why not? Out of Sofia's shadow, she could be very attractive.

The tang of the salt air filled his nostrils, and he longed to be off across the water, headed for the islands. He'd thought they would sail away on their honeymoon after the ceremony on Saturday, but Sofia had informed him that the feast and the dancing could last another five days. Why had he ever agreed to this extravaganza of a wedding? Why hadn't he insisted that they elope? The waves rolled onto the beach, and the moon made a wide river on the sea.

"Couldn't take it, huh?" Alex asked, leaning against the boat next to Jane.

She inched away from him as if he had an infectious disease, and turned her face to look out at the sea, and at the smattering of stars overhead. "I needed some air," she said. "What about you?"

"It's too nice outside to stay in a noisy, crowded room, but Sofia sent me out to bring you back in to dance."

"Tell her you couldn't find me, and go back in and do the Zorba dance thing with the guys," she said firmly.

"Call me a crazy American, but I'd rather be out

here, and I'd rather dance with girls." He held his arms out.

"No, thanks. I don't dance."

"You dance, I know you do. I remember dancing with you somewhere."

"The freshman mixer. I stepped on your toes."

"I lived. Let's give it another try." He put his arm around her waist and pulled her toward him. She stiffened.

"Don't worry," he said. "I won't hurt you."

"Even if I step on your wedding shoes?"

"Even if you vomit on them again. Believe me, it's not the worst thing that's happened."

"What is?"

"It's this business with Nikos. I think he'll understand, but I don't want to hurt him. He's been good to me, treated me like a son. Better than he's treated George. And that's the problem: George should inherit the business, not me." It was so obvious. Surely Nikos would understand.

"I thought George wasn't interested."

"Only because they haven't given him a chance. After I'm gone . . ."

"So you're really going to quit."

"Nothing could stop me." Not Sofia begging, pleading, or throwing a tantrum. He'd made up his mind.

"Good for you. Now really, Alex, I don't want to dance." She tried to slip out of his arms, but he pulled her back.

"I'm sorry, but what you want and what I want

are not relevant tonight. Sofia wants you to dance, and since she always gets what she wants, you're going to dance." Jane gave a rueful smile and he smiled back. "Hey, that's twice you've smiled today. That must be a record."

"What are you talking about? You haven't seen me for months. I smile all the time. I even laugh when something's funny."

"You used to laugh at me," he said. "Remember the homecoming parade when I wore a monkey suit and threw bananas at the crowd?"

"I remember. I caught one. You looked ridiculous." The corner of her mouth quirked in a smile.

But that was before he'd hooked up with Sofia. Things were never the same after that. "I've missed you, Jane," he said soberly. "I've hardly seen you at all these past few years."

"That's what happens when you move to Seattle," she said lightly.

"Even when I'm back in town, you never seem to have time to get together, even for a drink."

"I'm sorry, but I have a busy schedule, especially during tax season."

Was she really that busy or had he said or done something to alienate her? He wished he knew.

"Some people say a platonic friendship between two people of the opposite sex can't work, but ours did. I've never had a friend like you before or since," he said. It was true. They'd had a great relationship, but somehow after graduation, it had slipped away completely. Sure, they both had busy lives, but that was no excuse.

"Right," Jane said. But she didn't sound very sure about it.

"After the wedding, we'll get together more often. Count on it."

Holding her, he could feel the tension in her muscles and see it in the way she held her shoulders. "What have you got to be so tense about?" he asked. "You're not marrying into a huge, ethnic family with expectations, customs, and rules that crop up when you least expect them. You know about the custom where the guests spit at the bride when she goes down the aisle, to fool the devil into thinking she's worthless, don't you?" he said, hoping they could share a laugh over it.

Jane only shrugged. "I gather you haven't broken the news yet," she said. Despite her reluctance to dance, she put her hand on his shoulder, and he caught the scent of some light fragrance which might have been her perfume or some wildflowers on the shore.

He guided her across the sand to imaginary music that had nothing to do with the raucous noise coming from the taverna.

"Not yet. Nikos didn't look good today, and I was afraid I'd trigger another attack of his tachycardia, so I'm going to wait until things calm down a little."

"You wouldn't want to spoil the atmosphere tonight."

"The atmosphere," he repeated, thinking of the noise inside the restaurant and the thick cigarette smoke that stung his eyes.

"Later," she said. "You'll have time."

"Yes, although I can't wait too much longer. I'm getting older by the minute. Just in the last few hours I've aged at least five years. Look at these wrinkles." He raised his eyebrows to make the lines in his forehead appear deeper. He meant it as a joke, but she drew her eyebrows together. He didn't want anyone to worry about him or feel sorry for him. He was getting married to the most beautiful, most desirable woman in the world, and he had a career ahead of him that was full of exciting possibilities. "I can't stall any longer. If I have to design one more parking garage or shopping center, I'll be a candidate for the loony bin."

"What do you want to do, design houses?" Jane asked.

"Sure, or museums and libraries. Leonakis Construction Company doesn't do that kind of thing. What about you?" he asked, remembering how she'd looked up there with Sofia's dress. He let his hand drift to the curve of her hip. "Any wedding plans of your own?"

"Not yet. There is someone, but—"

"Want my advice? Wait. Everybody ought to wait at least ten years to be sure."

"Like you did?"

"I wasn't ready ten years ago. I wasn't even ready

a year ago. We had some problems to work out, as you probably know."

"Well, I can't wait ten years. By then I'll be a withered-up prune."

He looked at the curve of her pale cheek in the moonlight and the sweep of her eyelashes, trying to imagine Jane in ten years. He realized how much better looking she was than in college. She'd been a skinny kid then, and she'd turned into a slender but curvy woman. "I wouldn't worry about that," he said. "You'll probably improve with age, like fine wine. You're a late bloomer." As opposed to Sofia, who was in full bloom ten years ago. Not that she'd faded any; she was still a beautiful woman. But in ten years? Who knew? He didn't care. He loved her for her spirit, her vivaciousness, her spontaneity, and those wouldn't fade.

"There," she said, dropping her hand from his shoulder. "You've done your duty. Go back to the party. Tell Sofia I'm going to walk back to the villa."

"Now?" He stared at her, feeling as if she'd just splashed a glass of cold water in his face. He was enjoying her company, but obviously the feeling wasn't mutual. He'd found the one person he could talk to who wasn't a Leonakis, and she apparently didn't want to listen any longer.

"Yes, now," she said, reaching for her shoes, which she'd left on the sand.

"I'll walk you back," he offered.

She shook her head. "Go back in. It won't make

Sofia happy to have you dancing out here instead of inside, where you belong. Sofia is like the Energizer bunny: she can keep going and going until everyone else is worn out—except you, of course. You could always keep up with her."

"Yeah," he said, "I could." But right now, what wouldn't he give to go AWOL and walk back to the villa, stretching his legs and taking in some fresh air with only the sound of their footsteps crunching on the gravel road? Being alone with Jane was relaxing and stimulating at the same time. He wasn't surprised to hear someone wanted to marry her.

"It's not that far," she said. "And I need the exercise."

"Are you sure?" If he walked fast, he could be back with a clearer head before he was even missed.

"I'm *very* sure," she said so emphatically, he was taken aback. Where was good old Jane who never complained, never asserted herself, and always did what she was told? "I'm tired of dancing and I'm tired of talking and I'm just, just . . . tired." Her voice quavered and he could have sworn she was on the verge of tears.

Alex watched her pick up her shoes and walk away. He would never understand her.

The brisk walk back to the villa was just what Jane needed to erase the memory of dancing on the sand with Alex. It was ridiculous, the way he made her feel giddy and light-headed, with her stomach doing flip-flops. So like the first time she met him and he'd chosen her to be his lab partner, and like the time he'd danced with her at the freshman mixer, and like the time he'd kissed her on New Year's Eve—along with every other girl at the party. She'd thought she was over him. She *had* to be over him.

At least she'd had the sense to get out of there before she fell apart completely. *Like fine wine . . . a late bloomer.* The words reverberated in her head. She told herself Alex was just being polite. *Forget it, forget him.* He was getting married in a few days.

But what if she had to kiss the groom?

She groaned out loud, but nobody heard her but the nightingales singing in the juniper trees that lined the road. It was May, their mating season. Everybody's mating season, she mused—everyone but her.

Jane felt sure Sofia hadn't missed her when she left, since her family and Alex and half the island of Mios were at the taverna. Still, she sat by the window reading her book on mythology, waiting up in case Sofia wanted to talk before she went to bed, and tell her what the big secret was. Jane was more than a little curious.

But when they did come home, well past midnight, no one knocked on the door of the peach and pale green guest bedroom. There was the murmur of voices below, then footsteps on the stairs, doors opening and closing, and finally everything was quiet, except for the sound of the waves washing against the shore.

The balmy air, laden with the scent of fresh

thyme and rosemary growing wild below the house, wafted in the open window. Jane decided to go to bed, too. Someone had already unpacked her bridesmaid dress and shoes, and the items she'd brought along in her carry-on bag for the week: two pairs of pants with comfortable elastic waists, shorts, a crisp cotton shirt, a tailored jacket from Talbot's, her favorite store, a swimsuit, a white linen dress, and a few T-shirts. Since she had to be back at work next Monday, that was all she'd need.

After a shower with lavender-scented soap, Jane sank gratefully between her satiny sheets and turned out the light. Just five more days until Saturday and the wedding she'd been dreading since Sofia picked a date a year ago. In five days the happy couple would be sailing off into the sunset.

Then the fighting started—or continued. It came from the room above her—Sofia's room. It came from the balcony above hers—Sofia's balcony. Sofia's voice rose; Alex's voice deepened. They were arguing; they were shouting. He must have finally told Sofia about starting his own business, and now they were having it out.

Jane buried her head under her pillow, but she could still hear them. She stuffed her fingers in her ears, but it didn't help. She got up and went to the window to close it . . . but paused with her hand on the wooden frame and listened shamelessly for a moment, overcome with curiosity.

"I can't believe you're telling me this tonight!" Sofia cried.

"I've been telling you for the past six months!" Alex shouted.

"I didn't think you were serious. I thought you'd come to your senses."

"I have. I finally know what I want to do. We might have to make a few sacrifices at first, but when it works out—"

"*If* it works out."

"It *will* work out. But I need you on board, Sofia. I need you on my side."

"You need me, but my father needs *you*. This is not a good time to quit the company."

"When would be a good time?" he asked calmly.

"Never, if you ask me."

"I did ask you, but you weren't listening. All you've been thinking about, all you've been talking about for the past six months, is the wedding."

"Someone has to think about it," she snapped. "You couldn't even get here in time for your baptism or the parties! If you loved me, you'd forget all this ridiculous business."

"If you loved *me,* you'd want me to follow my dream. You'd understand why I'm doing this."

"Oh, I understand," Sofia said. "I understand that your work comes first, ahead of me and ahead of my family."

"Family is important. But marriage means putting each other ahead of everyone else."

"You say that, but you're putting your job ahead of everything else. I don't think you even love me."

"Then why am I marrying you?"

"I don't know. Why are you?"

"Because I love you, dammit!"

"You have a strange way of showing it."

Jane shivered in the warm night air and finally closed the window. Mercifully their voices faded, but then the thumping started. *Bang. Thud. Bam.* Jane imagined Sofia stamping her feet. She could picture her throwing vases across the room, and Alex ducking while the pottery shattered against the wall.

"You'll be sorry!" Sofia shouted.

Then it was quiet. Jane waited. Ten minutes went by in blessed silence. She heaved a sigh of relief and went back to bed.

Jane drifted off to sleep, but something woke her up. She jumped out of bed and stepped out onto the balcony that overlooked the manicured grounds and the sea in the distance. She saw two figures on their way out of the gate toward the sea. Sofia was in a long white nightgown, her hair tossed by the wind. It was so romantic, it made Jane's throat clog with tears and her heart ache. They were holding hands and running off toward the water. Probably going for a moonlight sail on one of the Leonakis boats docked at their own private pier. This is the way they'd always been—they'd fight like cats and dogs, then make up. Jane knew she ought to be used to it by now.

On her way back into the bedroom, Jane stubbed her toe on a terra-cotta pot filled with pansies. She closed the French doors and hobbled back to bed, her toe throbbing along with her heart. She lay on her bed staring at the ceiling, fruitlessly waiting for sleep until she gave up and turned on her light.

She reached for her book again and read what happened to mortals in ancient Greece who succumbed to jealousy. They were sent to the underworld, or scorched by the sun, or struck by Zeus's thunderbolt. It was a grievous fault, no doubt about that. Finally she fell asleep with the book open on her stomach and dreamed she was Athena, the virgin goddess of wisdom. But if she was so wise, how could she be stupid enough to love the one man she couldn't have?

The next thing Jane knew, it was Tuesday morning. Bright sunlight was streaming through her window. But it wasn't the light that woke her. Loud shouts filled the air, there were footsteps pounding on the stairs, and someone was banging on her door.

"Jane, wake up," Alex called. "Sofia's gone!"

Chapter 3

$\mathcal{J}$ane jumped out of bed and opened her bedroom door. Alex stood there wearing wrinkled shorts and a polo shirt, his face drained of color, his brow furrowed with worry lines. She heard bells ringing, the banging of pots and pans coming from downstairs, and frantic shrieks and cries in the distance.

"Have you seen her?" he asked.

"Not since last night," she said, her heart pounding. "When I saw the two of you going out the front gate."

"What are you talking about?" he asked. "We didn't go out the front gate."

"I saw you," she repeated numbly. "It was around two o'clock and Sofia was wearing her nightgown.

You were holding hands. At least, I thought . . . Who else could it have been?"

"We had a fight and I left her in her room," he said, running his hand through his hair. "She was angry. The last thing she said was—"

"You'll be sorry," Jane said.

"You heard that? Yes. Then I went to bed. That's the last I saw of her."

"Have you searched her room?"

"Yeah, and I found this." He held out a piece of paper. It said, *I'm leaving. Don't try to find me.*

Jane looked at Alex. His mouth was set in a tight line, as if he was trying to hold in his feelings as well as his words.

"She doesn't mean it," Jane said quickly. "She wants you to find her."

"Don't worry, I'm going to," he said grimly. "I just wish I knew where to look."

"What about Nikos and Apollonia?" Jane asked anxiously. "Do they know?"

"They're hysterical. They have no idea where she went. I showed them the note so they wouldn't think she'd been kidnapped. You'll have to tell them you saw her out there with some man."

"What will they think?"

"What do *you* think?"

Jane's brain was racing. *You're the only one I can tell, the only one who can keep a secret. . . .* But Sofia had never told her her secret. Jane could only guess.

Before she could come up with an answer, Sofia's mother and father appeared at the door.

"Jane, Jane, have you seen her?" Apollonia cried. Her face was pale, her eyes were red and swollen from crying. "Do you know where she's gone?"

Helplessly Jane shook her head.

"She's gone." Her father buried his face in his hands and sobbed. "Why would she go? Where could she be?"

"I don't know," Jane said, putting her arms around him. She took a deep breath. "But I saw her going somewhere last night, in the middle of the night."

"Going somewhere?" Apollonia repeated. "She wouldn't go anywhere. She's getting married in five days."

"I know." She shot a glance at Alex. He shrugged as if to say, *Don't press the issue. If they don't want to believe you, they won't.* "We'll find her, I promise. Hold on, I'll get dressed and come out."

When she came out, only Alex was waiting for her. "They've gone to ask the servants and to search the grounds," he said.

"What about the police?" she asked.

"They don't want to involve the police. The next thing you know it'd be in the papers, and they hate that. Besides, they think the police are incompetent."

"I want to look in her room," Jane said. "In case there's something, some clue, anything . . ."

The high-ceilinged room with the white carpeting and the four-poster bed was as pristine as if the maids had just cleaned it. Maybe they had. Maybe no one had told them it was a crime scene.

Crime scene? Now she was being melodramatic. Hadn't Sofia just gotten mad and left of her own accord? It had certainly looked as if she was leaving because she wanted to. But who was the mystery man?

Jane turned down the comforter and lifted the pillows. Sofia's unmistakable scent filled the air from a sachet. Alex looked in the walk-in closet, though Jane was sure he wouldn't know if anything was missing. Most men were clueless about women's clothes, and Alex was no exception. Sofia often complained that he didn't notice a new dress, paid no attention to her latest fur jacket, leather pants, or boots.

"I know she was mad, but I didn't expect her to leave," Alex said from the doorway.

Jane heard the anguish in his voice and her heart went out to him. "You can't take this personally."

"How else can I take it?" he demanded. "The last thing she said to me was 'You'll be sorry.'"

"I know, but that's not the same as goodbye. Whatever happened to her, it isn't your fault," she said. "You know she's just trying to scare you. It's like her to take off for a while, cool down, and then when she's good and ready, she'll be back, all smiles." Jane smiled reassuringly, but Alex didn't look convinced. He went to the window while Jane went through Sofia's dresser drawers.

Damn Sofia for acting like a spoiled brat! So she was mad at Alex for quitting his job, but did she have to run away only days before her wedding?

Worrying not only him but her whole family, too? This was beyond anything she'd done before. Angry, Jane slammed the drawers that were full of Sofia's beautiful, expensive clothes. "Let's go look outside, where I saw her last."

"Are you sure you weren't dreaming?"

"This was no dream," she insisted.

"But who was the guy?"

"I don't know. I told you—"

"You thought it was me. I know."

In case Alex hadn't checked it, Jane went to Sofia's small white desk in the corner and opened the top drawer. There was a matchbook from a hotel called Cavo d'Oro on the island of Andros.

"Is that where you were going on your honeymoon?" she asked, holding it out in her hand.

Alex shook his head. "I don't know; Sofia made the reservations." Now he was sorry he hadn't listened to her when she talked on and on about the details of the wedding. Just the way she hadn't listened to him for the past six months. They'd had a monstrous disconnect going, and now he was paying the price. When she came back, he vowed he'd listen to her.

Alex felt as hollow and haggard as he must look. Sofia was really gone and it was his fault, no matter what Jane said. Part of his brain said she was right—Sofia ran away because she wanted to scare him into agreeing to stay with the company. Once she realized he was serious about leaving the business and that she wasn't going to get her own way, she'd be back. She always came back.

Or maybe Jane had imagined it, or maybe the guy drugged her or sweet-talked her into going out for a sail, and she was using him to get even with Alex. He took the matchbook and pocketed it. "I'm going to the beach."

"I'll meet you there," Jane said. "I want to look in her closet just in case. . . ."

When Alex left the room, he ran into Apollonia, who was standing in the hall sobbing hysterically. Her sister was hugging her and wailing loudly. Alex stopped to tell them how terrible he felt, how sorry he was, and how he was going to find Sofia, but they waved him away with matching white handkerchiefs as if he were a pesky insect. Never had he felt more like a *zeno,* a non-Greek in a Greek world.

Next he bumped into a maid in a white apron carrying a platter of baklava in the direction of the buffet table in the dining room, and his stomach clenched. He hadn't eaten much in the past twenty-four hours. But the maid and her platter were gone before he could grab one of the pastries drenched in honey and nuts.

He still couldn't believe Sofia would walk out on her own. It was one thing to worry him, but her whole family? And yet . . . and yet . . . She'd done it before. More than once. The last time they'd been skiing at Lake Tahoe, she got mad at him for not waiting for her at the lift. She'd stormed off and driven back to the city without a word. She'd expected him to come after her. He hadn't.

But if she'd changed her mind and was ready to

come back, she would expect Alex to rescue her, and he wouldn't let her down.

Hang on, Sofia; I'm coming. I'll find you.

He'd bring her back and do whatever it took to make her happy, except give up his dream of starting his own business.

When he got to the gate, he stood there staring across the road, trying to imagine Sofia running off with another man. The pain was like a knife in his heart. In a few minutes Jane joined him.

"Any luck?" he asked. "Any clues?"

"It doesn't look like she took anything, not even her purse. To me, that means she didn't intend to go anywhere except for a walk."

"Or a sail. So why isn't she back?" He didn't wait for an answer; there wasn't one. "Let's go down to the beach."

They crossed the road and went to the boathouse and Leonakis's long, white painted pier, where a small boat was tied up. Alex's heart sank at the sight of the gleaming white cabin cruiser anchored in the bay, the one they planned to take on their honeymoon. If she came back. If she had a good explanation. If she still wanted to marry him.

"Alex, look," Jane said, pointing at footprints in the wet sand. "Are these . . . Could they be . . ."

"They're not Sofia's," he said, putting his shoe down next to the prints. "They look like boot prints."

"Of course," Jane said. "Most of the local fishermen wear boots."

"Probably nothing to do with her," Alex muttered to himself while Jane went down on her knees and started searching the sand, tossing shells from one side to the other as if she had nothing better to do than play.

"We're wasting time," he said, his impatience and irritation growing. "I'm going to look for her."

She looked up. "Where?"

"Isn't it obvious? At the Cavo d'Oro on Andros."

A moment later she gasped and held a small object up for him to see. It was Sofia's necklace, a gold chain with a diamond heart hanging from it. The clasp was broken.

"Now we're getting somewhere," Alex said, taking the necklace out of Jane's hand.

"So she did come down here," Jane said, blinking rapidly. "And she wasn't alone. I know she wasn't."

"Wherever she went, whoever she went with, it doesn't matter. I'm going to take the boat and find her. I'll start with the Cavo d'Oro on Andros. If she's not there, I'll keep looking until I find her."

"I'm coming with you," Jane said.

"No, you're not," he said tersely. "I'm sorry, Jane, but you'd get seasick and you'd get in the way. She's my fiancée and she's my responsibility. I'm going alone."

"She's your fiancée, but she's *my* best friend." She stamped one foot in the sand. "I'm coming with you, but first I'm going up to the house. Maybe they've heard something by now. Another clue or a message." She glanced back at the villa. "She could even be back by now, you know."

"All right," he said. "But hurry."

Jane ran back to the house, her heart pounding, her face perspiring from nerves, exertion, and the heat of the morning sun. She hoped Alex wouldn't do anything rash, like taking off without her. After all, she was worried, too.

He'd always been a good influence on Sofia. It was always Sofia's idea to dance on the tables, to wade in the reflecting pool, and to stay up all night partying before exams. Now what had she done? Had she run away with someone or by herself? If it was with someone, who was it and what did they want? If this was a kidnapping, then why didn't they leave a ransom note?

The first person Jane saw was Nikos standing on the terrace pacing back and forth. "Have you seen Alex?" he asked, his face ashen, his eyes sunk deep in their sockets. "I need to talk to him."

Jane squeezed Sofia's broken necklace in the palm of her hand. "He's going to find Sofia," she said. "And I'm going with him. We think she's gone to Andros."

"Andros, why?" He looked bewildered.

"Because we found a matchbook with the name of a hotel on Andros in her desk," Jane said.

Nikos seemed to be in a state of shock. At this moment it was hard to believe he was the head of a huge company, someone who made important deci-

sions. All the life seemed to have drained out of
him. She could see why he needed Alex and why he
wanted him to be his successor.

"We'll call you as soon as we find anything. Don't
worry."

"Bring her back. Just bring my baby back," he
said as a tear rolled down his cheek.

"We will," she said. "In time for the wedding."
She wished she felt as confident as she sounded;
she didn't even know where Andros was. But they'd
find out and they'd find Sofia. They had to.

He nodded. "Godspeed."

Jane felt tears come to her eyes. She hugged him
and ran up the stairs two at a time to the guest
room, where she grabbed her purse and repacked
her small valise. It might only take a few hours to
find Sofia, but maybe it would take days.

Jane hurried down the back stairs and through
the kitchen, where the cook was stuffing vine
leaves with rice and a lemon egg soup was simmer-
ing on the stove, then she ran down the path to the
gate. At the gate she paused and looked over her
shoulder.

The next time she saw the villa, she vowed that
Sofia would be with her. Her parents would be sobbing with relief and happiness. Alex and Sofia
would say their vows, there would be pictures and a
cake and music, and they'd parade through the village in their wedding clothes, guests would spit on
the bride to ward off the devil, if that's really what
they did here, and they'd live happily ever after. She

turned and ran across the road and down to the beach, her shoulder bag banging against her hip, her valise swaying against her legs as she ran.

When she got to the beach, she stopped abruptly. Alex was gone. Was he already on the yacht, getting ready to take off without her? She should never have left him here! She dropped her bag and stamped her foot in the sand and cursed in Greek just as she'd heard Sofia do one hundred times. *"Skata, skata, skata."* She wasn't sure what it meant, but it made her feel better. It also attracted the attention of a fisherman who appeared from out of nowhere, wearing hip boots and carrying a bucket in his hand.

"Miss?" he said. "Something is wrong, yes?"

"Yes, I need to go to that boat out there." She pointed to the Leonakis cabin cruiser. "Right now. I can pay. Do you have a boat? Can you take me there?"

He nodded and pointed in the direction he'd come from.

"You going with the man out there?" he asked, gesturing at the yacht.

"Yes, the man out there. How did he get there? Did you see him leave?"

"Oh, yes, I see him. I take him."

How dare he leave without her? He *knew* how much she wanted to go.

"Did you see anyone else leave from here?" she quickly asked. "I mean last night. A man and a woman. Did you see them?" Her words tumbled out as she grabbed his shirtsleeve.

"Last night, yes, the lady and the man in the boat."

"The lady with the long hair and the long dress?" she asked breathlessly. "Where did she go? Who was the man?"

He shook his head. "I didn't see. Too dark. But he was this tall, a fisherman in a fishing boat."

"And the woman, what was she wearing?"

"A dress, yes, a long white dress."

"And she was beautiful, wasn't she?" Jane asked eagerly.

He nodded. "Oh, yes. He got himself a beautiful woman, that one."

"Oh, God," Jane whispered. Did that mean the fisherman had stolen Sofia, or had she taken off on her own volition to teach Alex a lesson? "Do you know where they were going?"

He pointed out to sea. "That way. Toward Andros."

"Andros," she breathed, her heart pounding. That confirmed it. "How far is it?"

He shrugged. "Not far. A few hours. Depends on your boat. That one—" He pointed to the Leonakises' thirty-foot cabin cruiser. "That one— very fast. Very nice boat."

"But in a small fishing boat, how long would it take? Would they be there by now?"

"Neh," he said. The Greek word for yes. "The woman is the bride, yes? No good. May is no good for marrying. Bad luck."

Jane was beginning to think he was right. It was

bad luck to get married in May. It was also bad luck to quarrel with your fiancé right before the wedding. It was even worse luck to run off with some other man before your wedding, if that's what Sofia had done.

"Can you take me out to the boat now?" She pointed to the Leonakises' gleaming white yacht.

The fisherman nodded, and she followed him down a path that bordered the water, stumbling over fallen branches as she dragged her suitcase behind her. She kept her head turned to where the boat was still anchored, praying she'd make it in time.

At last they came to a small fishing boat with poles extending out at a 45-degree angle from both sides. The man took her bag and dumped it in the stern, then took her hand and helped her to a rough wooden seat in the center. He shoved off from the stony beach until he was knee deep in water, then he jumped aboard and went to the stern to start the motor. It sputtered and she held her breath. When the engine turned over, she breathed a sigh of relief.

Jane craned her neck around. The yacht was still there. But was that the sound of a motor in the distance or just her imagination? *Hurry, hurry, hurry,* she murmured, biting on a fingernail.

The noise was getting louder; the engine on the yacht was definitely running. "Can you go any faster?" she yelled, half standing, half sitting.

He shrugged and raised his arms as if to say, you

want to go faster? Why didn't you say so? They were close enough now that she could see the name on the stern, *Aphrodite*, and the port, *Mios*. She couldn't see Alex, but she knew he was there. He'd be at the helm, sitting in the captain's chair, looking at the charts, having a cold beer and getting ready to sail without her. How could he? How *dare* he?

She couldn't wait to see the expression on his face when she burst onto the bridge and demanded to know why he'd left without her. Didn't he realize he couldn't drive this boat and find Sofia all by himself? Didn't he know he needed a second mate, a friend? Someone who cared about Sofia as much as he did?

As the fishing boat edged close to the yacht, the yacht's engine turned over. Jane's heart lurched. Damn, damn, damn! He was going to leave without her.

"Stop!" she yelled. But he wouldn't be able to hear her over the roar of the motor. Well, she'd just climb the rope ladder hanging down the side and surprise him. The fisherman drew up to the yacht, his boat bobbing in the choppy sea, and he skillfully nudged the side by the ladder.

Jane gave the man a handful of euros from her purse, then reached up and grabbed the bottom rung of the ladder. It swung wildly. She gripped the rope so tightly her knuckles were white. She looked down at the water some six feet below her, and a wave of dizziness hit her. She told herself that if she fell in, it would be no big deal. She'd be soaked and humiliated, but the fisherman would pick her up and she'd start all over again. If only her heart would stop pounding. *Don't look down.* She *would* board this boat. Only four rungs, and she'd be on board.

She made it. Putting her hand on the smooth mahogany railing, she felt the vibration of the engine. She swung her leg over, put one foot firmly on the teak deck, and then the other. She heaved a ragged sigh of relief and grinned, pleased with her success. She'd done it, and her trusty purse was still hanging from her shoulder. But . . . where was her suitcase?

She got to her feet and yelled down to the fisherman. He yelled back something that sounded like *"Opa,"* which meant look out, then turned his boat and headed back to shore. Above the rumble of the yacht's engine she heard the burble of the exhaust pipe and puff of gray smoke filled the air. Weak-kneed, she leaned against the railing and stared off in the distance as the boat started moving, and the shore and her suitcase grew farther and farther away.

Alex had a map of the islands in front of him and he'd pinpointed Andros. As soon as he got there, he'd call the Leonakises and tell them where he was and what he was doing. He didn't know how they'd react to his taking the boat without asking, but he sure knew how Jane would react. Right about now she'd be standing back on the pier, stamping her feet, mad as hell.

But he couldn't wait another minute. Not after hearing what the fisherman had to say. Sofia was his responsibility; he was the reason she'd left and he'd bring her back. Jane meant well, but she'd be much more useful to the family back at the villa. She was calm, quiet, and resourceful, just the kind of person you wanted around in a crisis. He hadn't been kidding when he complimented her on her ability to fix things. She was amazing. But this was a one-man job, and he was the man to do it.

He heard the sound of footsteps over the rumble of the engine, and whirled around. It wasn't possible, but there was Jane, windblown and pink-cheeked, her enormous, ever-present pocket book hanging from her shoulder. He must be hallucinating. It was the lack of food and sleep.

"How did you get here?" he demanded. If she was an apparition, she wouldn't answer. She would fade from view.

Jane put her hands on her hips and glared at him. "The same way you did," she said. "We could have saved a few euros if you'd waited for me."

"I didn't know how long you'd be, and I couldn't wait any longer. The fisherman told me he'd seen Sofia take off in a small fishing boat last night."

"He told me the same thing. Do you believe him?"

"Why would he lie?" Alex asked.

"Why would Sofia go off in a boat with some fisherman right before her wedding?"

"Probably to get me to cave, but I'm going to find out."

"We're going to find out," she announced.

"Look, Jane, I appreciate your trying to help, but—"

"Don't 'Look, Jane,' me. I'm here and I'm staying. Now, what can I do?"

"Nothing. Finding Sofia is a one-man job. She's my fiancée, after all."

"And like I told you before, she's *my* best friend and it's *my* job to find her, which is what I intend to do. If you want to help, we can discuss it." She folded her arms across her chest.

Alex felt the blood rush to his face and his head started to throb. "There's nothing to discuss. I'm at the helm, I'm the captain, and you are a stowaway." He was tired of being reasonable; reasonable no longer seemed to be working.

"If I'm a stowaway, you're a thief. If I'm not mistaken, this is *not* your boat."

"No, but as soon as I get the ship-to-shore radio hooked up, I'm going to call the family and tell them what I'm doing."

"I already told them what *we're* doing," she said.

Alex shook his head. "I should have known. Look, if I needed help, I'd hire someone who knew something about boats and who didn't get seasick."

"I'm not going to be seasick anymore. I have my pills here." She tapped her purse.

"I don't care if you have a whole pharmacy in there. You still can't stay." Alex stood to face her.

Jane planted her feet firmly on the deck and put her hands on her hips. "What are you going to do, throw me overboard?"

It was a tempting thought. He pictured the shocked look on her face as she sputtered furiously, her pale hair floating in a halo around her head.

"Don't be ridiculous. I know you mean well, Jane," he said calmly. "But don't you see, they need you back there to comfort them and keep their spirits up. This may just be a wild-goose chase. Sofia may have had her little adventure and just walk in the door of the villa anytime now."

"If she does, they'll call and tell us, and we'll turn around and go back," she said.

"You have it all figured out, don't you?" He almost wished Jane wasn't so damned sensible and reasonable. She was the complete opposite of Sofia, which was probably why the two were such good friends. "Okay," he said, throwing his hands in the air. "You win." He sat down again.

She nodded as if there had never been a doubt in her mind, then leaned over his shoulder to look at the map in front of him. "So that's Andros. Once we get there, we just have to find the Cavo d'Oro."

Her hair brushed his cheek, and he tried to ignore the tantalizing effect it had on him.

"*If* she's gone there. It was just a matchbook," he reminded her.

"It's our best clue," she said. "Now, what can I do to help? Drive the boat?"

"Have you ever driven a boat?"

"No, but it doesn't look like rocket science to me."

"No? Then take over." Alex got to his feet. God, she could be maddening. "I'm going below to check out the bilge pump. I heard some sloshing when I started the engine."

"How do you know about bilge pumps? And how do you know how to operate this boat?" she asked.

"When Nikos bought it, he took me out for a trial run. There are no sails to fool with, just an engine, and everything in it is the best money can buy. I also have a friend with a boat like this in Seattle, though not as big or luxurious." He moved aside and she slid into the captain's chair.

"Wait," she said, her voice betraying a touch of anxiety. "I . . . uh . . . what do I do?"

"Keep steering toward the island there ahead of us, and keep an eye on the gauges." Let her realize that though it may not be rocket science, it wasn't all that much fun to sit there and steer the boat and hope nothing went wrong.

He'd just lifted the hatch to the pump compartment when he heard a loud warning buzzer go off. Alex let the hatch cover slam shut and took the stairs two at a time to the deck. Jane was standing at the controls, looking petrified as the buzzer continued its loud warning and a red light flashed on the console.

"Oh, my God!" she yelled. "What happened? What did I do?"

The arrow on the water temperature gauge was in the red, and Alex reached down to turn off the engine. Then there was no sound at all—no engine, no alarm, only the waves slapping against the hull.

"Looks like an engine problem," he said. "I'll go check."

"Can I come?"

"Sure, and if you've got a torque wrench in that purse of yours, we can take the heads off."

He meant it as a joke, but from the look on her face, her purse was off-limits for jokes. Of course, if she did have a torque wrench, he'd be more than happy to eat his words.

She followed him aft to the back of the boat, where he lifted a hatch and backed down a short ladder to the engine room. She came down almost on top of him, and they stood wedged together in the small space.

Water was spraying out of a split in a rubber hose.

"Damn," Alex said as he grabbed the hose and squeezed it.

Jane leaned over to look and the hot water sprayed her face, her shirt, and her shorts.

"Ouch!"

"Are you okay?" he asked, brushing the water off her shirt. As his hand came in contact with her breast, he heard her suck in her breath. He hadn't meant to shock her. And he wondered briefly if she was a virgin. She hadn't had any boyfriends in college that he knew of.

"I'm fine." She simply wiped her face with the back of her hand, rather than screaming and running upstairs to change clothes, as any other woman would have done.

Jane's shirt was now plastered to her body, and Alex felt an electric jolt race through his body at the sight of her small, round breasts and nipples that beaded as the water cooled on her body. He dragged his gaze away. What in hell was wrong with him, leering at Sofia's bridesmaid while the boat drifted toward the rocks?

"That was the cooling hose that split," he said. "I hope you didn't get burned."

She shook her head and shivered. "Is it serious?"

"Serious enough. It's the link between the engine and the heat exchanger."

"Can you fix it?"

"Maybe temporarily, if I had some tape."

"I have some. It's in—"

"Your purse." He grinned. "Where else?"

When she came back waving a small spool of narrow black tape, his mouth fell open.

"Electrician's tape," she explained.

"I know what it is," he said. "But I don't know what you're doing with it in your purse."

"It comes in handy. Just yesterday I had to repair my purse strap. You never know when you're going to need it."

He nodded. She never ceased to amaze him. Her and that purse of hers.

Their repair held for about an hour, then the engine faltered and Alex sent Jane running back down to retape the hose. They did this over and over for another hour. They didn't get very far toward the next island, but at least they weren't drifting, either.

Then the red light started flashing again, which meant things were not going well down there. Alex was about to go below when Jane came up from the engine, her face flushed, her hair damp and her clothes still clinging to her body. She pushed a strand of blond hair behind her ear and held out her empty roll of tape.

"All gone," she said. "Is there a Plan B?"

"There's always a Plan B," Alex said, thinking fast. "I'll get into the dinghy tied up at the stern, hook it to the front of the boat, and tow us to Andros, where we can get a new hose."

"That little boat can pull this big boat?" Jane sounded skeptical.

"It has a smaller motor, but it will work," Alex said with more confidence than he felt. But what was his choice? Call the Coast Guard? The Leonakises? Not until he either had everything under control or had failed completely. And he was not in the habit of failing.

"What will I do?"

"You'll steer this boat, right here."

She nodded calmly. Alex wondered what Sofia

would have done, and realized he hadn't thought about her for the past hour—though that was due to this emergency, of course.

"I'm going to get the dinghy," he said. "Do you want to change or anything?"

"I can't change. I left my suitcase in the fisherman's boat."

"You mean you don't have a change of clothes in that purse of yours? A poncho, some sandals, your yellow polka-dot bikini?" he teased. "You can go below and find something in Sofia's suitcase. She had our bags brought out to the boat yesterday. They're in the stateroom."

"Sofia's trousseau clothes are here already? I guess I shouldn't be surprised. She's always so organized." So organized and so determined that this would be the "perfect" wedding. No hitches, no forgotten items. Just one missing bride! "No, I couldn't wear something of hers. Not now."

Alex shrugged. "Suit yourself. I'm going to get the dinghy. You go to the bow, and when I come around I'll toss you the rope. You'll knot it around the cleat, then come back here and take the wheel. There's an on-shore breeze, so we have to be careful we don't go on the rocks."

Jane gave a glance at the rocky outcropping and imagined the Leonakis yacht smashed in pieces. How would they explain that? *No, we didn't find Sofia, and we wrecked your hundred-thousand-dollar boat.*

Well, she'd done a pretty good job so far, if she

did say so herself. She'd gotten on board, and her tape had enabled them to put a few knots between them and Mios—which was more than Alex would have done without her.

Now there were bigger challenges. Knot the rope securely, the way sailors did, so that it wouldn't come loose. Then steer this boat away from the rocks and into a harbor. She had to; Sofia needed her.

Chapter 4

Despite her sweaty palms, Jane had managed to knot the rope around the cleat, and so far it was holding. Back at the helm, she gripped the wheel tightly. She kept her eyes on Alex ahead of her in the dinghy. He was now shirtless, with his hair blowing in the wind. Despite her preoccupation with the boat and her missing best friend, Jane had to say, objectively speaking, he was one great-looking man, with his broad shoulders, his bare chest, his strong jaw, and laser-blue eyes. Of course, she was hardly objective. He could still give her heart palpitations with just a look. But looks weren't everything, she told herself sternly. It was more important to find someone who was steady, who would put her first, and who adored her the way Alex adored Sofia.

Was that someone Warren? Her mother thought so. Her mother was impressed with his job, his background, and his plans to buy a house and pay off Jane's school loans. But wasn't it just as important that Jane adore him? Maybe it would happen if she just gave it enough time. Maybe that would happen after this wedding, after she finally let go of her fantasy about Alex.

After ten years, wasn't it about time? Yet she still sizzled from that brief touch down in the engine room. Her breasts were still tingling, more sensitive than she'd ever realized. She had to face the depressing possibility that she'd never get over him, married or not. Then the best she could hope for was that he would never know how he affected her.

Every few minutes Alex would turn and look at her and his lips would move, but she had no idea what he was saying. The rocks receded in the distance, so worry number one was gone. Still, she wished that he'd give her a sign that she was doing the right thing and things were going as planned. Just a thumbs-up would be nice.

Her shirt and pants had dried in the wind, and now the sun was so warm she wished she, too, could toss off her shirt and let the sun beat down on her bare skin. She imagined the look on his face if he turned around and saw her in her demi-bra. Would that warrant a thumbs-up? Not likely with her barely-a-B-cup.

He probably wouldn't even notice. After all, he

had Sofia on his mind. But what if she tossed her bra aside and sat there brazenly half naked at the helm? She giggled at the outrageous idea—the shock and disbelief on his face, his jaw dropping, his mouth falling open. Somebody else might be able to pull it off, but not her. Still, she felt her nipples bead as she imagined the warm air on her bare skin.

Her imagination was running away with her. It was just her way of coping with the problems at hand. In reality, there was no way she was going to remove one stitch of clothing with him or anybody else around. Sofia called her Ms. Modesty. Sofia— who might be lying bound and gagged somewhere, while she was entertaining improper thoughts about her best friend's fiancé.

They were slowly approaching Andros, and she picked up a pair of binoculars to survey the port. Bigger than Mios, its harbor was full of boats. What if she ran into one?

At that moment Alex turned his head toward her, and through the binoculars she could see the lines etched in his forehead, the set of his mouth, and the well-defined muscles of his chest. He seemed to know she was studying him, because his mouth quirked at one corner, and he gave her the thumbs-up she'd been wishing for.

Her mouth went totally dry and her pulse raced. Just from a smile and a simple gesture. Just from a look at his bare chest. She was in worse shape than she thought. Jane put the binoculars in their leather case and snapped it shut. She'd seen too much already.

Soon they were entering the harbor, and Alex began waving frantically to her from the dinghy.

"Yes," she muttered. "I know we're here; what am I supposed to do, besides the impossible? Steer the boat in, and drop anchor—I can't! I can't," she wailed.

But she did. Somehow she managed to navigate among the boats crowded in the harbor, and the next thing she knew, Alex had tied the dinghy to the yacht and was back on board in the rear, dropping the anchor.

"Good job," he said, giving her a brotherly pat on the back.

"Thanks," she said, as the anchor hit bottom with a clank of the anchor chain. If she could keep her voice steady and her face from turning red, he'd never know what his touch did to her. "What next?" she asked.

"Next I'll take the broken hose and get a replacement. There has to be a boat repair place nearby."

"And I'll go look for Sofia at the Cavo d'Oro," she said.

"You're not going alone. Do you think Sofia's going to pop out of one of the rooms and turn herself in because you show up?" he asked.

"Why wouldn't she? I *am* her best friend."

"If you know her so well, tell me, why did she leave?"

"Because she was mad at you for refusing to

work for Nikos. She wants you to come looking for her. And she wants you to give up your idea of working for yourself. Don't you think that's why she left?"

"I hope that's all it is," Alex said.

"Of course it is."

Alex put his hands on her temples to frame her face, his thumbs pressing against her jaw, his eyes burning with a blue flame. "Jane, I know what the fisherman said, but I trust you more than him. Are you *sure* you saw her leave with a man last night, or could it have been your imagination at work?"

"Yes, I'm sure," she said, biting down on her lower lip to stop it from trembling. "And no, it couldn't."

As much as she wanted to spare him from the pain of thinking Sofia had run off with someone else, she couldn't lie to him. He dropped his hands and she looked down at her polished toenails, trying to ignore his rock-hard, muscled chest covered with a fine pattern of dark hair. Suddenly another wave of seasickness hit her, even though they were moored in calm waters. She closed her eyes, but the rocking didn't stop.

"What's wrong?" Alex asked. "Oh, no, you're not sick again."

"Move out of the way, if you value your shoes."

But he didn't. He didn't even get on her case about being a poor sailor. Instead he steadied her with his hands on her arms. "Take a deep breath. I've got you. You're going to be fine."

Her eyelids fluttered. She did what he said.

Took a deep breath, swallowed hard. She let him hold her, support her. And she was, miraculously, fine.

"I'm okay now," she murmured, stepping back. "Let's go."

He grabbed his shirt and yanked it over his head. They got into the dinghy, and Alex started the motor. In minutes they were in the harbor and tied to the dock. Even though they were on solid ground, Jane felt as if the pier were rocking under her feet. It was bad enough to feel seasick on dry land, but she also had to try to conceal it from Alex. She didn't want him to think she couldn't hold her own.

She made herself think about Sofia and how they'd have a joyous reunion while the hose was being fixed. Alex and Sofia would settle their differences, the way they always did. Jane would tactfully disappear to some beach, where she'd sit under a beach umbrella and sip an iced frappé while they made up in a room at the Hotel Cavo d'Oro. They'd all go back to Mios, have the wedding, and they'd live happily ever after.

The thought should have made Jane's heart lighter, but she found herself dragging her feet as they walked to the end of the pier. She told herself once again to get over it. Sofia and Alex were destined for each other, since the first day they'd met. They were cut from the same cloth—both fortune's children, so good-looking that as a couple, they got second looks from everyone around. It didn't matter that Sofia came from a rich family and Alex didn't. They were even now in looks and education, if not in accomplishments—there, Alex had pulled way ahead of Sofia.

It was Jane's job to help bring them back together, as she'd brought them together some ten years ago. Alex might think it was up to him, but Jane knew he couldn't do it without her.

As if to prove her point, she was the one who saw it: a swatch of pale silk georgette wedged between two boards on the pier. She reached down and pulled it up, ripping it in half as it snagged on a nail.

"Alex, look! This is from Sofia's nightgown. The one she was wearing last night."

He stopped and rubbed the fragile silk between his fingers. "How do you know?" he demanded.

"I remember when she ordered it from Victoria's Secret. 'White silk georgette with etched roses, a flounce, and a bias-cut hem.' Wasn't she wearing it when you saw her last night?"

"I don't know. I don't remember."

Jane sighed. How typical. "She's here. She must be here. She ripped this off her gown and left it for us as a sign."

At the end of the pier they saw a fisherman with a bucket in hand. They asked about boats from Mios.

"Many boats from Mios," he said.

"We're looking for a woman," Jane said. "About my height." She held up her hand.

"No women on fishing boats," he said with a frown. "Women bring bad luck."

They went on to a boat repair shop at the end of the pier, where the clerk said he'd try to find a replacement hose for them. It could take hours or days.

"Can't you just repair it?" Alex asked.

He shook his head and told them to come back that evening. Evening? Then Jane remembered that stores closed for the siesta and reopened in the late afternoon.

They found a cab and told the driver to take them to the Hotel Cavo d'Oro.

"Cavo d'Oro?" he repeated and scratched his head.

For one terrible moment Jane thought they'd made a mistake and there was no such place on this island. But after repeating the name a few more times and asking another driver, he finally quoted an exorbitant price. They nodded and then they were off, driving on a winding road through cypress forests, past steep ravines and rocky grottoes, passing white windmills that were turning briskly.

"Where is this place?" Jane asked Alex. "No wonder it costs so much to get here."

"We should have rented mopeds," he said. "It would have been cheaper and faster."

Alex was staring out the window, probably thinking of what he was going to say to Sofia. Hoping she'd forgotten how mad she'd been at him the night before.

By the time they found her, Jane thought Sofia would be so happy to see him, she'd throw herself in his arms, sorry she'd ever left. When they asked who the man was, she would simply shrug and say, "No one." And that would be the end of it.

The road led to a small village on the sea, and the driver stopped to ask directions of an old woman in black who was crossing the street in front of them. She pointed in the distance, and they were off again, past houses and hotels facing the sea with decorative painted balconies. The driver pulled up in front of a large, Neo-Venetian palazzo across from a crowded white pebbly beach. The name was in large letters—Hotel Cavo d'Oro. They'd found it.

Jane jumped out of the taxi while Alex paid the driver. She caught a glimpse of herself in the mirror behind the front desk and was sorry she hadn't changed her clothes as Alex had suggested. She looked like a *Survivor* finalist, someone who'd been on the island for weeks without bathing, with her sunburned nose, hair hanging in limp strands, and wrinkled shorts and camp shirt stained with rust-colored spots.

The clerk told them an American couple had checked in last night. Jane's heart stopped beating for a second as she scanned the guest list. Their name was listed as Jones. She and Alex exchanged a look.

"Was Mrs. Jones . . . did she have long, dark curly hair? Was she about my height?" Jane asked.

The desk clerk nodded.

"And was she American? Was he?"

"They spoke Greek together, but she . . ." He nodded. *"Neh.* She may have been American."

Jane braced her elbows on the desk and leaned forward. "Was she beautiful?"

He nodded solemnly. "Very beautiful."

"It's her," Jane murmured. "It's them."

Alex drummed his fingers on the front desk. "Would you ring their room?"

"They are not here. They have gone to the nudist beach." The clerk waved his arm in the direction of the sea. "At the end of the beach, behind the rocks."

Jane felt deflated as they walked out of the hotel. "It couldn't possibly be her. Sofia wouldn't go to a nudist beach."

"We have to check it out anyway," Alex said.

"Why? This is a married couple we're talking about. Their name is Jones."

"Do you really think every couple who signs in as Mr. and Mrs. Jones is married?"

"Of course not. But if it is Sofia, who's the man who's with her?"

"I don't know," Alex said grimly.

Jane had the feeling he didn't want to know. It would be bad enough to find Sofia with another man, but at a nudist beach with another man? That would be terrible.

"The clerk said they were speaking Greek," Jane said, "so that means—"

"It means nothing." Alex's voice was tense and

edgy. "Except that I'm going to the beach to have a look."

"A look at a lot of naked bodies," she murmured.

"One of those bodies might be Sofia. You can wait here if it makes you uncomfortable," Alex said.

"Why don't you wait here and I'll go look?" That way if Sofia was there and she was with another man, God forbid, Jane would bring her back and Alex would never have to know. It wouldn't be easy to walk naked down a beach, but she'd do it for Alex. At least then he wouldn't have to come face-to-face with the other man, if there was such a person.

"You?" Alex couldn't imagine buttoned-down Jane disrobed in front of strangers. But Sofia? That was another matter.

"Yes, me," she said. Her chin was stuck out in that stubborn way she had, but he thought her face was a little pale under her sunburn.

"Then we'll go together." Despite the fear in the pit of his gut that Sofia might be consorting with some stranger in the buff, he couldn't help being amused by the expression on Jane's face. Going to a nudist beach together was a lot different from going alone. She couldn't back out now, after what she'd said, but she was clearly worried. He could tell by the way she gnawed on her lower lip, the way her eyebrows were drawn together.

"Okay," she said.

He raised his eyebrows. Maybe he shouldn't be

surprised. Ever since they'd started this trip, Jane had shown her determination and her willingness to ask hard questions. She wasn't bad at the helm, either. But a nudist beach? He'd bet his last dollar she wouldn't go through with it.

They walked in silence toward the rocks at the far end of the beach, toward a sign warning of the nature of the beach ahead and the price of entry. Alex paid for two admissions, and the guard gave them each a basket for their clothes and gestured toward the dressing rooms. Alex looked at Jane. She didn't meet his gaze and he sensed she was wavering.

"You don't have to do this," he said.

"I know. I suppose it doesn't bother you, being nude in front of strangers," she said.

It didn't, but suddenly the thought of being nude in front of Jane bothered him more than he'd bargained for. He really wished she'd stay there. "There's no need for both of us to go," he said, making one last try. "It won't take that long to see if she's here."

"And if she is?"

"Then I'll bring her back."

"What if she won't come?"

"If that's the case, let her stay. I'll wish her a happy life and go back home."

"You don't really believe that," Jane said, shifting from one foot to the other on the warm sand.

"I don't believe she's here, either, but I have to check it out."

"I do, too," she said stubbornly. "I have to see for myself."

"Fine," he said.

Jane walked into the tiny canvas cabana and pulled the sliding curtain shut behind her. She stood for a long moment staring at the brightly striped fabric that surrounded her, wondering how she was going to get out of this.

"Wait," Alex called.

She slid the curtain back. He was still dressed. He'd changed his mind; thank God. "What happened? Did you see her?"

"I just want you to know you can't bring your purse with you."

"I wasn't planning to. I think you can check your belongings with the guard."

"Right," he said.

She closed the curtain again.

Oh, God, what was she going to do? Well, she'd just avoid looking at him, because she couldn't back out now. She unbuttoned her shirt, took it off, and folded it carefully. Then she unhooked her bra. It was suffocatingly hot inside the little dressing room, but she was shivering all over. She took off her shorts next and her cotton bikini panties, and put them in the basket. Then she stood there waiting, hoping, praying for a miracle.

Maybe Alex would clear his throat to let her know he was right outside, and he'd say, "Jane, you go. I've changed my mind. I'll wait for you at the public beach." Or "Jane, there's a tidal wave coming. They're evacuating the beach." Or maybe, "Shark attack! Head for the hills!" She'd just have time to get dressed and start running.

But the only sounds were shouts from far away where nudists frolicked on the sand. Her throat was dry. She tried not to think of the acres of naked bodies. She especially tried not to think about Alex's naked body. The nude statue of *David* kept popping into her mind.

She closed her eyes and tried to think about the changes to the tax code she'd been reading before she left home. Then she made a mental list of her clients and their deductions. Rivulets of sweat dripped down her temples and between her breasts. How much longer could she endure this torture? What had happened to him?

She pushed the canvas curtain open just enough to peek outside. Alex was standing a few feet away from her, completely nude. She thought she might faint. The walls were pressing in on her. She took a deep breath and closed her eyes.

"Jane?"

Act casual. Pretend you didn't see him. Pretend you can breathe normally. "Yes?" Her voice came out as a squeak.

"Let's go."

She carried her basket of clothes in front of her, her eyes straight ahead as if she were in a military parade. She handed the basket to the bored guard and pivoted on her heel.

They walked side by side down the beach without speaking. Jane crossed her arms over her breasts, but that felt awkward and probably made her look ridiculous, so she dropped her arms and swung them at her sides. She kept her gaze level, repeating over and over to herself, *Don't look, don't look, don't look.* But she hadn't banked on her excellent peripheral vision. Even without looking, she could see. She could see way too much. She yearned for sunglasses. She yearned for blinders. She had nothing to shield him from her view. Nothing but her own willpower, which was fading fast.

Alex, on the other hand, was strolling the beach as if this was no big deal. Not a hint of embarrassment on his face, from what she could see out of the corner of her eye. Seeing her and all the others on the beach without clothes obviously meant nothing to him, whereas her face was burning. Of course, that could be the effect of the brilliant sun overhead.

She wondered how many women he'd seen nude. In the long periods of time when he and Sofia had broken up and gone their separate ways over the past ten years, Sofia had had other boyfriends and he'd undoubtedly had his share of girlfriends. No wonder he could carry this off so well, while she was wishing she could be buried up to her neck in sand.

Jane sternly reminded himself why she was there, and she scanned the crowd for a woman with long, curly hair and a birthmark on her hip. A few yards away there was a game of volleyball going on. Muscled men with uniform tans were running to catch the ball and falling head over heels in the sand. Women without tan lines were shrieking with enthusiasm as they spiked the ball over the net, their breasts bouncing when they jumped for the ball. Sofia was not one of them.

There were whole families with little naked kids wading in the water. There were even wrinkled old people with leathery skin and sagging bellies. There was a man doing a handstand in the sand while his girlfriend stood by watching with admiration. Jane had to admit the place had a sort of wholesome atmosphere, rather than the sleazy ambience she'd imagined.

Another plus, objectively speaking, was that her body compared well with most of the others on the beach. At least she didn't sag. Not that anyone noticed her; not even Alex. He hadn't given her a glance since she'd come out of the dressing room. Or if he had, she was unaware of it. Not that she wanted him to.

"We should have split up," he said.

Something in his voice made her glance in his direction—not quite carefully enough, because she saw his physical reaction to the naked women on the beach. She shouldn't be surprised, but she was. And she shouldn't be upset, it was just a guy thing; but she was.

"It's too late now," she said. Too late for a lot of things.

All she could think about was how gorgeous Alex looked. He really did have the body of that famous Italian statue, with muscled thighs, a strong chest, and broad shoulders. It was no surprise that he was in good shape. He'd played soccer in college and was a member of the sculling crew. Sofia had told her he still rowed regularly on Lake Washington in the mornings before work. That explained his beautiful upper body. And his lower body? She didn't want to go there . . . but her eyes did.

She was very much aware that he was only a foot away from her. Way too much aware of how much better looking he was than any other man on the beach. She was not there to gawk at her friend's fiancé. After all, he wasn't looking at her. But if he did, she wondered how he'd think she measured up to the other women on the beach. What a ridiculous question! They'd just passed one who was stunning, with big breasts, a small waist, and generous hips. No wonder Alex was turned on. Yet, whatever their shape, no one looked the least bit self-conscious. If only she could take this all in her stride the way they did.

The sand was warm between her toes. The sun was hot on her bare shoulders, and her skin prickled all over her naked body. The silence between her and Alex became more and more awkward. Jane was dredging her mind for something to say, anything to lighten the atmosphere, when she suddenly she some flamingos wading in the shallow water, tall and gangly, their skinny legs glistening pink in the sun. It was a rare sight, surprising and delighting her. She quickened her step. "Look!"

"Flamingos. Where did they come from?"

"They're native to the eastern Aegean, but I never dreamed I'd get to see them. And a whole flock! I wish I had my camera so I could show my bird-watching group."

"No cameras are allowed here," Alex said. "How would you like somebody taking your picture without your clothes?"

"I guess I wouldn't mind if I had feathers."

She felt his eyes on her, and she wished the earth would open up and swallow her. She kept her eyes on the birds.

"You'd look good in feathers," he said. She didn't say anything, he quickly continued. "I didn't mean you need feathers to look good."

"Thanks, Alex, but after two days of travel and not much sleep, I know how I must look. Please, let's not make this any harder than it is."

"Any harder than it is?" he muttered. "That's not possible."

She told herself to focus on the birds. Fortunately, the birds were cooperating. One was prancing around on the sand while the others watched. "Another mating dance," she said. "The second one since I've been here. Last night it was the nightingales in the trees. And yet they say May is an unlucky month to mate."

"If you'd stayed at the party last night, you would have seen another mating ritual. All the women watching those macho men kicking up their heels." He went down on one knee and stretched his arms out to demonstrate. He seemed to have forgotten he was nude, and she envied him his savoir faire.

"Did you join in?"

He stood up. "No."

"Why didn't you? You're a good dancer."

"Thanks, but after two days of travel and not much sleep, I wasn't in the mood."

Jane nodded sympathetically. "There sure are a lot of couples here," she noted, shading her eyes with her hand. It wasn't brilliant conversation, but it was better than silence. "Why couldn't Mr. and Mrs. Jones, whoever they were, have gone to an ordinary beach?"

"Maybe they thought it would be exciting," he said. "We don't have many nudist beaches in America. Or if you go to one, you might see some-body you know. It could be embarrassing."

She didn't ask if he'd been to one, or whom he'd gone with. She didn't want to know.

There was another long silence as they walked toward the breakwater. The birds had flown away, and Jane looked around, desperate to find some-thing to say.

"The tide's up," she remarked as the water splashed her ankles.

"That's not all that's up," Alex muttered. "I'm going to cool off." He turned sharply, waded out, and plunged headfirst into the cool, clear water. She watched him swim out with an expert stroke.

He came up for air in deep water and shook his hair out of his face. He looked at her, but didn't beckon her to come in.

So what? She didn't need an invitation to join him. She ran into the water, splashing and submerging her body as soon as she was knee deep. It was glorious to feel the cool, clear water ripple over her naked body. She didn't want to get too close to Alex, even though she didn't have much left to hide. If he'd been interested, he could have seen all five feet eight inches of her naked body. When she got within a few feet of him, she stopped swimming and treaded water. Unfortunately, the water was so clear she had a perfect view of his body. And vice versa.

"This is great," she said, tossing her hair back behind her ears.

"Never been skinny-dipping before?" he asked.

She shook her head. "I thought it was decadent, but it feels . . . I don't know, natural."

He grinned at her.

"Just because I've never been skinny-dipping doesn't mean I've never been to a nudist beach," she said. "In case you were wondering."

"I was. So how does it compare?"

She shrugged. "Once you've seen one naked body, you've seen them all, right?"

"Sure. For me, it's a first for the Aegean and my first nudist beach with flamingos."

He didn't say, *First time with a girl who's not a girlfriend,* but she imagined he thought it.

"You've been hot-tubbing too, right?" he said. "I remember when we all went up for ski week and stayed at that hotel. There was a hot tub. Didn't you . . . ?"

"Of course." Jane had worn her bathing suit, but she wouldn't remind him. He already thought of her as a classic geek, the girl who spent her Saturday nights in the library, an image she'd be happy to shed. "Anyway," she said, remembering why they were there. "Sofia's not here. We'd better get back."

"We can check on the hose and ask around the dock for her," he said.

"I'll go on ahead." She dived under the water to swim to shore.

Alex watched her swim away from him with neat strokes. This had been the most frustrating, maddening day at the beach he'd ever had. Even in the water he was hot and bothered by the sight of Jane in the nude. What in hell was wrong with him? He told himself his erection was due to all those naked bodies, but he knew better. It was due to just one naked body. Jane's naked body.

He watched her walk out of the water, her legs long and shapely, her narrow hips, her cute little butt, and once again his body was out of control. How could this be? Jane was his friend, Sofia's friend. That was all.

As she walked down the beach, other men were looking at her, too. Even though it wasn't cool to ogle, they were doing it. Among all the other bodies, she stood out, tall and well-shaped. Small breasts, but not as small as he'd pictured. Nipples like ripe berries. Disturbing. Tempting. All the cool water in the world couldn't stop him from reacting to her.

Alex swam parallel to the shore until he saw the gate and the sign and the bright dressing rooms. He dashed across the sand, ducked into a dressing room, and when he came out, she was back in her wrinkled travel clothes, waiting for him. She looked relieved to see he was fully clothed, and sighed loudly as if she was glad to have that ordeal behind her. He couldn't agree more.

Chapter 5

"Men," Jane muttered as they stood in line at a souvlaki stand across from the hotel. "I'll never understand them."

"What's not to understand?" Alex asked, handing her a barbecued lamb sandwich wrapped in pita bread and dripping with a spicy *tzatziki* yogurt sauce.

"How you get excited about a beach full of naked strangers."

"That surprises you?" he asked, biting into his sandwich and waving to a taxi with his free hand.

"I guess it shouldn't, but it does, yes."

"Are you saying all those young, muscled men out there didn't turn you on?"

Jane ate hungrily. No, they didn't turn her on.

Only one man did. "For women it has to be more than muscles, more than just another pretty face."

As they finished eating a taxi pulled up, and Alex told the driver to take them back to the dock. He got in beside her in the backseat and said, "Tell me about it. I want to know. What turns you on?"

"This is not about me personally," she said, already regretting she'd started this conversation.

"Why not? We're old friends."

"I'd rather not talk about it," she said, turning her head to look out the side window.

"What would you rather talk about? Your bird-watching? I guess you could tell me how many blue rock thrushes you've spotted, but I'd rather hear how many men you've fallen for and why."

"Why?"

"Yes, why."

She turned to face him. There was a smudge of sand on his cheekbone, which she longed to brush off. "And then you'll tell me about the women in your life other than Sofia?"

"If you like."

"No, I wouldn't like."

He smiled warmly. "You're so loyal. That's what I love about you."

She *wasn't* loyal. If he only knew how she felt . . . If *Sofia* knew.

"I'm waiting," he said with a nudge of his elbow.

She was tired of being good old boring Jane. He wanted to hear her story? Fine, she'd give him a story. When he found out it wasn't true, she'd just laugh it off, if she wasn't already long gone. She took a deep breath and plunged in. "Okay, in college there was Professor Goodrich."

His eyebrows shot up. He grabbed her by the arm and turned her to face him. "The classics professor with the long hair who rode a motorcycle to class? No way."

"Yes."

"You had an affair with Professor Goodrich? No wonder you didn't date fraternity boys. My God, Jane, you know he could have been fired."

She smiled. "I know. He said it was worth it."

"There was a rumor about him and his students, but I didn't believe it."

"Believe it." Jane smothered another smile. This was fun. She'd never done anything like this in her life; she'd always told the plain truth. But the old Jane would never have gone to a nudist beach, either.

"Did Sofia know?" he asked.

"Of course. We told each other everything."

"She never said a word."

"I made her take a blood oath," Jane said solemnly.

"Go on," Alex said with a slight frown.

"The next man in my life who meant anything—"

"You mean there were some who didn't mean anything?"

Jane tossed her hair out of her face. "A few."

"I thought your point was that men were shallow and women were not."

"I said that for women, it has to be about more than a face and a body. It has to be about soul. What do the Greeks call it, *kefi?*"

"For your information, Jane, men are just as interested in soul. Maybe not all men, but—anyway, you were saying . . ."

"After college I went to work for a small accounting firm. My boss was young and attractive and very idealistic."

"An idealistic accountant? What a combination. Of course you couldn't resist," he added with a twist of his lips.

"I tried, because there was a company policy against interoffice dating, but . . ."

"But you caved. What happened? How did you keep it a secret?"

He was leaning toward her, so close his thigh was pressed against hers. So close, she could see flecks of green in his blue eyes, as changeable as the Aegean. For a moment she lost her train of thought. All she could think of was how he'd looked in the nude. Muscles, skin, and . . .

She licked her lips. "How? Uh, let's see, it was a long time ago. Oh, it was those long lunches in his office."

His jaw dropped. "You made love in his office?"

She nodded. "On his desk. Until one day the door flew open and it was his secretary. He'd forgotten to lock it. Or maybe he wanted to be found out; maybe he wanted the world to know. I don't know; I don't understand men. Which is where this all started." She leaned back against the seat and closed her eyes. She was tired from the sun and the sea and the search for Sofia, and she was tired of pretending she was a player on the stage of love, tired of denying there was only one man on that beach she found attractive, the one she could never have.

The next thing she knew, her head was resting on Alex's shoulder and they were back on the other side of the island.

She jerked away from him as if she'd been leaning against a cactus. She could still smell the salt water in his hair and feel the warmth of the sun on his skin.

"I fell asleep," she said, blinking rapidly. How long had she been snuggled against his shoulder?

"I noticed. Bringing back old memories must have been tiring." His head tilted at an angle, he studied her as if she were an insect under a microscope. An insect with a strange and active sex life. "Speaking of old memories—remember the time a bunch of us drove to Mexico in a jeep for spring break? You fell asleep on my shoulder on some bumpy road along the coast."

"That's right." It all came back: the warm, dry air, the starry skies, and Alex without Sofia for a whole glorious week on the beach. "Where was Sofia, again?"

"She'd gone to Palm Springs with her family. Now, go on with your story. What happened next?"

"Where was I?"

"The accountant."

She glanced out the window. They were headed down a narrow street, passing shops with their doors wide open, filled with bright blue and white ceramics and postcards with scenes of Greek islands, square, hand-painted tiles, woven linens and pottery. The siesta was over, both hers and the town's. "Let's get out and mingle. She's got to be here somewhere. We can walk to the dock from here."

They wandered down winding streets, brushing elbows with tourists in bikinis and diaphanous dresses or white slacks and blazers. Jane turned her head from side to side until she was dizzy. She was looking at faces and figures, listening to the conversations in British English, German, and French that wafted from sidewalk cafés. Sofia spoke some Greek, but would she be speaking English? To wander around, she would have to have bought some new clothes. But how, without her purse?

They returned to the ship supply store, where the clerk told them he'd have a hose by tomorrow afternoon.

"That will give us another day to search the island," Alex said.

They really couldn't waste a minute, they should be out actively looking, but Jane felt weak and in need of a boost. "I'm going to get something to eat. I'll be next door." She entered a small candy shop and pointed to a bar of bittersweet chocolate laced with almonds.

The shopkeeper handed it over and smiled at her. "Happily, you didn't ask for the chocolate-covered cherries," he said. "I sold out this morning."

Jane's heart beat faster. "Sofia's favorite," she murmured. "Was the customer an American woman?" She held her breath while she waited for the answer.

He shook his head. "He was Greek, a tall man with boots. A fisherman, I think."

Jane turned and looked at Alex, who was standing in the doorway. A current passed between them, part hope and part fear.

"It's possible," he said. "Let's go to the docks."

Jane stuffed her candy in her purse, and they half ran to the stone jetty where dozens, if not hundreds, of fishing boats were tied up. It was seeming more and more obvious that Sofia had gone off with a fisherman. How many times had Sofia talked to her about the sexy, strapping fishermen on the island, rolling her eyes and giggling about them? But to run off with one a few days before her wedding? Sure, she might have been convinced to go out for a moonlight sail . . . but all the way to Andros?

Up and down the piers they went, looking into fishermen's boats filled with fresh octopus and squid. There were many tall men in boots hauling crates of black-shelled mussels as they shouted to one another. But there was no Sofia.

Alex stopped one fisherman after another and asked if they'd seen any boats from Mios or any American women. Some laughed, some just shook their heads, which may have meant no or maybe that they didn't understand English.

Jane looked at Alex. "I wish I knew what to do," she said. "Even if one of these men gave her a ride here, they wouldn't admit it, would they? If only we knew how to say, 'Have you seen an American woman in a negligee wandering around?' in Greek."

"We're getting nowhere," Alex agreed. "If anyone had seen her, they'd remember her. She's so . . ."

"Beautiful," Jane said.

"Unforgettable."

"Stunning."

Alex lapsed into silence. Not that he couldn't think of more words to describe Sofia—like *exciting, fun-loving, exuberant*—but his heart wasn't in it. He watched while Jane retrieved her candy bar from her purse. She held it out, but Alex shook his head.

"I need a drink," he said.

They walked back through the docks, looking automatically at the boats, scanning their names and their home ports, but all they saw was Rodos, Syfnos and Criti; not one boat from Mios.

They sat outside at a small, round table of an *ouzeri*—an ouzo tavern—and in a few minutes they each had a glass of clear 48-proof ouzo and a glass of water in front of them.

"Isn't this the strong stuff?" she asked, sniffing the scents of anise and fennel.

"Don't drink it straight. You dilute it with the

water," he said, pouring some water into her ouzo and watching the drink turn milky. "Like this." He glanced up and saw there was chocolate above Jane's mouth from her last bite. He reached over and wiped it off with his finger. Her face paled, then turned pink under her sunburn. What had he done? What was wrong with her?

"It's the candy," he explained, licking his finger. "Are you sure Sofia likes chocolate-covered cherries?"

"Of course I'm sure. I thought you'd know that. What did you give her for Valentine's Day?"

He shrugged. "I don't remember."

Jane took a sip of her drink and coughed. "No wonder she ran away."

"I sent her roses and chocolate-covered strawberries. Strawberries, cherries—don't tell me that's a reason to run away."

Alex waved to the waiter and ordered a plate of *mezedhes* to tide them over until dinner. Jane swirled her ouzo around in the glass.

"Just like a native," he told her approvingly.

When the waiter came back with a plate of cheese, cucumber, tomatoes, olives, and a couple of small fried fish, he was accompanied by an older man in a flat hat, his dark pants covered with an apron.

"I am Kostos," he said, pulling a string of amber beads from his pocket to click them together. "You're American, yes? Where do you come from?"

When he heard they were from California, he sat

down at their table and told them his brother lived in Sherman Oaks. He himself had visited there just last year. California was a wonderful place, full of wonderful people. "How did you come here to Andros?" he asked.

Alex told him they'd come by boat.

Jane got up to use the bathroom, and Kostos leaned forward and peppered Alex with questions while they sipped ouzo. Then the older man lowered his voice. "You are married, yes?"

"No, not yet. But I will be on Saturday." Think positive, Alex told himself. Believe it and it will happen. Sofia wouldn't miss her own wedding, even if she was still mad at him.

"I thought so. I can always tell when love is in the air. Tonight you must come to my house for dinner, to celebrate. You like Greek food?"

"Yes, very much, but . . ." Alex stumbled, trying to choose the right words. He'd heard about Greek hospitality, he'd certainly experienced it with the Leonakises and their friends back home, but this invitation caught him off guard. How did one celebrate one's wedding without the bride? How did one explain her absence without getting into a messy, gray area? "Thank you, but we couldn't impose."

"I insist. My wife and daughter will be so happy to meet some Americans from California."

"We'd like very much to come, but I'll have to ask Jane."

Kostos looked up to see Jane making her way through the tables crowded with people drinking and talking and laughing. "Ah, Jane, what a beautiful name. And a beautiful lady."

While Kostos drew a map to his house on a napkin, Alex watched Jane walk toward them. Her cheeks were lightly sunburned, her clothes were shapeless and wrinkled, and he wondered . . . beautiful? Jane? He didn't see it. She was attractive in her own way, but he wouldn't say beautiful. Sofia was beautiful. Jane was . . . well, Jane was Jane. No pretensions, no illusions.

With Jane, what you saw was what you got. It must be that straightforwardness that attracted all those men in her life—as well as her subtle but sexy physical attributes. The combination had turned him on today, but that was just because it was a nude beach. It wasn't going to happen again.

Kostos repeated his invitation to Jane. When he said, "to celebrate your wedding," she shot a surprised look at Alex, opened her mouth to protest, then closed it. A few minutes later, after she'd had more ouzo, she said they'd be delighted to come.

Alex had never thought of her as the sociable type, but he was beginning to think he'd never really known her at all. That story about Jane and the professor—could it be true? It must be; Jane would never lie.

They finished their drinks, Kostos gave them the map to his house, and they said they'd see him later.

Back in the dinghy on their way to the Leonakis

yacht, Jane shot a sideways glance at Alex. "He thinks you are I are getting married, doesn't he?"

"It's a logical conclusion. We're traveling together. You're obviously crazy about me." He grinned at her.

"Hah! Just crazy is more like it," she sniffed.

"If it bothers you, you can explain the whole situation tonight."

"I guess it doesn't matter. After tonight we'll never see him again." She sighed. "I don't know why I said yes. I'm too tired to go anywhere tonight."

"You can't be too tired for an authentic homemade Greek dinner. You slept in the taxi, remember?"

He certainly remembered her head on his shoulder, the smell of her skin, and the way her hair had brushed against his face. Just as it had so many years ago when they were packed in somebody's jeep. It was the first time he'd seen her relax and let her guard down since they'd met on the ferry. He'd almost hated to see her wake up and put her defenses back in place.

"We have to go," he said. "Besides, Sofia may still be on the island. It's another chance to look for her here."

"That's true," she said.

Dusk was falling over the harbor, and the fishing boats were coming in for the night loaded with smelt and cod and mullet. Colored lights from the tavernas facing the sea were reflected in the water. The ocher-colored buildings turned orange and crimson in the fading sunset. Well-dressed tourists sat out on the boat decks, talking and laughing, their voices carrying across the water. It was a beautiful night for a honeymoon, just the way he'd pictured it. Except it would be him and Jane on the yacht, not Sofia. Would Sofia really be back in time for the wedding? Where was she tonight, Alex wondered, overcome with a feeling of melancholy.

He pulled up to the Leonakis yacht, and Jane scrambled nimbly up the rope ladder ahead of him as if she'd been doing it all her life. He followed her down to the wood-paneled forward cabin.

Jane sank down on the padded sofa bench and looked around at the brass fittings, the colorful deck chairs, and the mahogany table. She'd just had the most exhausting day of her life, both emotionally and mentally, but she wasn't too tired to appreciate the luxury of her surroundings. "This is beautiful," she said.

"Wait till you see the stateroom."

The stateroom—where the honeymoon couple was supposed to sleep. Who would sleep there tonight, and where would the other person sleep?

Alex sat across from her and propped his feet on the coffee table, his expression unreadable. He looked just as fresh as he had this morning. A little rumpled, maybe, but that just made him look even sexier. And she wasn't the only one who thought so. She'd seen women casting glances his way today, in the café, in the streets, and on the beach. Oh, yes, definitely on the beach.

"There should be enough water in the tank for us both to take showers," he said.

"And if there isn't?" Jane asked.

"I guess we'll have to shower together," he said with the sexy grin that had hooked her ten years ago.

She gave him a disapproving glance, though he was probably—had to be—kidding.

"Oh, come on, Jane," he teased. "We've already seen all there is to see of each other. Unless you didn't look?"

Chapter 6

*J*ane stood in the small fiberglass shower by herself, letting the hot water beat on her shoulders and down her back, her mind spinning with all the things she should have said a few minutes ago. Why did it take her so long to come up with a retort? The man was outrageous and just a little too sure of himself. He needed someone to put him in his place.

She should have said, "Why would I look? I'm not that hard up for cheap thrills." But then he would have said, "Those weren't cheap, they were free."

But they weren't free. Those thrills cost her plenty in lost composure. She only hoped he hadn't seen her face turn scarlet.

Conscious of the scarcity of hot water, she washed her hair quickly with Sofia's herbal shampoo and conditioner and got out of the shower. She wrapped her head in a thick white towel and borrowed a terry-cloth robe from an open shelf. Then she stuck her head into the cabin.

"I'm through. It's your turn," she said.

He looked up. For a long moment he didn't say anything; he just looked at her as if he were trying to place her.

She tightened the sash on her robe. "What's wrong? Did you forget I was still here?"

"Nothing," he said at last. "Before I shower, we'd better call the Leonakises." He picked up the cell phone that was mounted on the wall.

She stepped inside the cabin. "I'm surprised they haven't called us."

"I just turned the phone on."

"Oh. What will we say? We don't want them to worry, yet . . ."

"We won't tell them we went looking for her at a nudist beach," he said.

"No. But we have to give them some hope. We should mention the ripped piece of her nightgown."

He picked up the phone. "Nikos? It's Alex, I'm calling from Andros." There was a pause. "What? She did? What did she say?"

Jane sat down on the edge of the cushioned bench and unwrapped the towel from around her head. She strained to hear the voice on the other end of the phone.

"What did she mean? . . . Yes, all right. We'll leave here tomorrow, as soon as possible. Don't worry. We think we know where she is." He looked at Jane and she knew what he was thinking. "Or was."

"How are you holding up?" Alex asked his future father-in-law. "How is Apollonia?" Jane could hear a murmur from the other end of the phone, but she had to wait another five minutes to find out what Nikos had said.

After Alex hung up, he ran his hand through his hair. "Sofia called this afternoon. He couldn't hear her very well, but at least they know she's alive."

"Of course she's alive," Jane said, clenching her hands. "But where is she?"

"He doesn't know. She was being vague, but said not to worry. She doesn't want anyone looking for her. She said she's fine. Then she said something to him about an oracle, something like, 'Ask the oracle.'"

"Which oracle? The oracle of Delphi, the oracle of Zeus, or what?"

"Nikos said it's the oracle of Artemis."

"The goddess of the hunt. Maybe she said that because she knows we're hunting for her. Well, she hasn't lost her sense of humor. And what do we ask the oracle: 'Where's Sofia?'" Jane buried her head in her hands.

"At least we know she's able to get to a phone and call."

She looked up. "Why doesn't she come home?"

"Don't ask me," he said grimly. "Ask the oracle."

"I will." As she stood up, her robe gaped open in front.

"For God's sake, Jane, put some clothes on." Alex walked out of the cabin.

Jane stared at the door he had just closed behind him, her eyebrows raised. "What happened to 'We've already seen all there is to see of each other?' "

She went to the stateroom and noticed there was only one suitcase—Sofia's new Italian designer bag with the silver handle and the butter-smooth natural leather trim. Alex must have taken his bag to wherever he had gone to change. She could hear the shower running now, and she knew how he'd look with the water running down his chest, the drops catching in the light dusting of hair. Even though she'd already seen all there was to see of him, the image flustered her and she fumbled with the catch on Sofia's suitcase.

A pang of guilt hit her at the thought of even touching Sofia's things. After all, this was her trousseau. She told herself Sofia would want her to wear her clothes. She was always trying to talk Jane into wearing brighter, bolder colors and more up-to-the-minute styles, and always offered Jane her hand-me-downs. But it was different, wearing clothes Sofia had never worn. Clothes she'd picked out for her honeymoon.

Clothes shopping gave Sofia a high. "It's cheaper than therapy," she told Jane when they went shopping together. But not much—she certainly couldn't afford to buy at the boutiques Sofia frequented. The way Sofia saw it, when she dressed well, she added beauty to the world. How could anyone object to that?

Jane gently lifted the lingerie out of the suitcase, bras and panties that were beyond anything she'd ever seen before in Sofia's wardrobe. Whisper-soft, delicate fabrics in mauve and pink and pale blue. Next were her casual clothes—bright, patterned linen pants with shirts and tank tops to match. Miniskirts, sandals, low-rider pants, and a caftan dress. A bandeau bikini, a strapless white dress, and a black maillot. Sofia must have been planning for a honeymoon that included swimming, sunning, dancing, and dining.

At the bottom were clothes she could wear to a party. There was a wrap dress, wide-leg pants, and plunging halters, all in bright colors with splashly prints. Fine for Sofia with her dramatic coloring and her natural flair, but what about Jane?

She finally chose a yellow halter dress with a bold print. It wasn't her; none of these clothes were her. But what did it matter? The Greek family didn't know her, and Alex really didn't know her, either. He really only knew the old Jane, and that was quite enough.

The trouble with a halter dress was that one couldn't wear a bra with it. But with her body, who would notice? Now, if she were Sofia, she would be noticed.

Jane found a pair of matching yellow sandals in a

shoe bag, clipped a stunning coral and turquoise starfish pin to the front of the dress, then stood in front of the full-length mirror on the back of the door.

"Who are you kidding?" she asked herself. "You are not the halter type. Face it, you're an impostor."

She realized the shower water had stopped running some time ago, and there was no sound below deck other than her own voice. She walked carefully in the yellow sandals up to the deck, where Alex was standing looking out across the water. In the dim light from a string of small bulbs strung from the deck to the mast, she could see he was wearing gray slacks and a striped jacket with a white shirt open at the neck. She sucked in a sharp breath. He was so handsome, he took her breath away. He'd been a hunk in college, but he'd matured into an even better-looking man because of the character in his face. Let alone his gorgeous body. She clenched and unclenched her hands, trying to get a grip on her emotions, trying to damp down the fire that flooded her face. Alex turned and looked at her for a long moment, then frowned.

"Now what's wrong?" Jane said. "Did I take too long?" She pressed her lips together. He might be the best-looking man around, but his manners could use some work. He might be worried sick about Sofia, but so was she, and she didn't scowl or snap at him.

"Nothing," he said. "Let's go."

But something *was* wrong; Alex was too quiet. It must be Sofia's clothes. But what choice did she have? And he had been the one to suggest she wear them.

Once they were back at the dock they walked down narrow streets and became part of the *volta*, the see-and-be-seen evening stroll. They passed lively cafés full of noisy crowds enjoying tiny cups of strong coffee or tall glasses of ouzo.

Jane felt encouraged by Sofia's call to her parents. It was a good sign, a sign that she hadn't been kidnapped. Then there was the infectious sight of so many people having such a good time. Let Alex mope if he wanted to; she wasn't going to join in. What could they do about finding Sofia at nine o'clock at night?

The reality was that Jane was on an island in Greece. She would never be here again. She was wearing a beautiful, outrageous dress that she would never wear again. Wherever Sofia was, Jane had a feeling she would approve of her actions. Hadn't Sofia spent years trying to get Jane to loosen up, to wear fun clothes, and kick up her heels?

She wouldn't approve of Jane lusting after Alex, of course, but women had always lusted after him. Sofia probably wouldn't mind if Jane occasionally did, either, as long as it wasn't a mutual lust. And Jane could assure her of that.

"What do you think she meant, ask the oracle?" Jane said.

"How should I know?" Alex snapped.

"I know you're worried," she said, "but you could at least be civil."

"Civil? How can I be civil when you're wearing her clothes?"

So that *was* it. "You told me to wear them," Jane pointed out. "And I can hardly go out for dinner in my rumpled shorts and shirt."

"I know." He shook his head. "I'm sorry. You're right. I'm worried about Sofia, my shoulders are on fire, and we're lost. You look great, by the way, and I have no idea where we're going."

"You should have told me you were sunburned. I have some lotion. . . ." *Did he just say she looked great, or had she imagined it because that's what she wanted to hear?*

"In your purse, I'm sure you do. Don't worry about it, I'll live."

"Let me see the map," Jane said, her arm brushing against his. "I think we're here." She pointed to a dot on the napkin. "If we make a right turn up here . . ." She walked a few paces ahead of him, stopped at the corner, and beckoned him to follow her. He looked even more grouchy than he had a few minutes ago.

"We don't have to stay too long," she said softly when they arrived at the door of the house. "Just long enough to be polite."

"Polite in Greece means shutting the place down; eating and dancing and drinking until you're falling down drunk or passed out."

"Like last night."

"Yes. Only unlike last night, I'm not going to have a knock-down-drag-out argument with anyone. And

I wish to God I hadn't had one last night. If I'd only gone home when you did . . ."

"Sofia would have been even madder."

"I don't know how she could have been. She threw a vase at me."

She looked at him in the light of a lantern hanging from a doorway. "Lucky for you she has bad aim."

"Yeah, lucky," he said with more than a tinge of irony.

"Jane. Alexander." Their host called to them from the balcony overhanging the street. "Come up."

Fortunately the party wasn't like the one last night, because Jane had no chance of walking away from this one. Instead of being the bridesmaid, she was the center of attention. She didn't know why; maybe it was Sofia's dress, or maybe it was just that she was the only American woman there.

Every man in the place wanted to dance with her, except for Alex, which was just as well, because she was bound to stumble and step on his feet. No, Alex sat at a table on the huge wooden balcony overlooking the town, talking with family members and other guests while Jane started with the slow shuffle of a dance they called the *syrto*, and worked her way up to *tsiphte teli*, a sensuous belly dance the other women delighted in teaching her.

For once, she didn't mind being the center of attention. In fact, the focus on her made her feel downright giddy. She even enjoyed watching Alex watch her. It must have been the retsina, that delicious resin-flavored wine that caused her to forget that she couldn't dance. To forget she wasn't the type to show off in front of an audience. She certainly wasn't the only woman twisting her hips and clapping her hands over her head, but she was the only one Alex was looking at.

She couldn't tell what he was thinking, but at this point she really didn't care. It felt so good, so liberating, to wave her arms around and gyrate her hips to the music. If she looked ridiculous, the others didn't seem to notice. She smiled at Alex, but he didn't smile back. She laughed out loud, and he frowned. She twirled around and got so dizzy, she thought she saw Sofia at the edge of the circle cheering her on—Sofia wearing a long transparent gown and beaming her approval. Jane blinked and Sofia was gone.

When the dance stopped, she was dripping perspiration and a very handsome Greek man, who might have been Kostos's son or his neighbor, took her hand and led her to a table outside in the warm evening air.

Before she could sit down, Alex grabbed her by the arm. "Are you ready to leave?" he asked.

"Now? No, I'm having a good time."

"I noticed. I thought you said we could leave early," he muttered.

"Not yet." That had been someone else; the old Jane. That Jane had been taken over by a wild Gypsy woman. "Why don't you dance?" she asked him. "Look, the men are getting up to do the *syrtaki*."

"Never mind." He put his hands in his pockets and stalked away. What was his problem, anyway?

Kostos sat down next to her and handed her a glass of wine and a plate of *dolmades*. "You are a wonderful dancer, Jane. You have both grace and joy. Are you sure you aren't part Greek?"

She laughed and wiped her forehead with a napkin. "I don't think so. But I love your music and your food and wine."

He lifted his glass. "Let us drink to that, *steen yassou!*" He jumped to his feet and clapped his hands. Everyone stopped dancing. The musicians stopped playing. Alex returned to her side.

"A toast to our American guests," he said. "To their wedding, and may they live happily ever after."

Everyone drank to their happiness, then everyone clapped and cheered.

Jane couldn't read the expression on Alex's face, but he must feel as uncomfortable as she did. She gamely lifted her glass and dutifully sipped her wine.

"Kostos," she said, when the musicians had resumed playing and the attention on her and Alex had drifted away again. "Is there an Oracle of Artemis on the island?"

"Yes, of course. It is a very beautiful spot to visit. Do you have a question for the oracle?"

"Several questions," she said.

"I can answer one of them right now," he said. "You will have a very happy marriage. Alex loves you very much. I see it in his eyes."

Jane choked on her wine and set the glass down.

"I said the same thing to him," Kostos said with a big smile. "And I have a wedding present for you." He pressed his amber beads into her hand.

"Oh, Kostos, thank you, but I can't take your beads from you." *Besides, I'm not getting married.*

He shook his head. "I have others. These are for you. Not that you need them; once you are married, you will have no worries. But try them out."

It would be rude to decline such a gift, so Jane smiled and thanked him again.

"If you have more questions, you must go to the spring tomorrow and consult with the oracle. It is about one-half mile from town, well marked so you cannot miss it. You take honeycakes for the oracle who resides in the gorge behind the spring. You will hear what you must hear. And then you must see all the other beautiful places on our island." He smiled. "You think I am bragging, but we have a saying in Greek: 'If you do not sing the praises of your house, it will fall down on you.' "

"I like that," Jane said. She put her new worry beads in her purse, took out a pad of paper, and handed it to him. "Please make a list of what we should see while we're here."

When he finished, Kostos gave the list to her and then tapped her on the shoulder. "Now you must dance with Alex. He is not happy when you dance with others. I watch him and I know. Now it is his turn."

Jane turned around. Alex was leaning against a

post, a drink in his hand, looking dour. But that had nothing to do with her dancing with others, and dancing with her was guaranteed to make him feel worse. Especially if she stepped on his wedding shoes.

"Perhaps it's time to leave," she said.

"The evening is still young. I will tell the musicians to play something for you and Alex." Kostos got up and spoke a few words to the three musicians, then turned and nodded to her. How could she disappoint such a gracious host?

She forced herself to walk across the floor and face Alex. One look at the expression on his face made her want to turn on her heel and go back to the table. "Kostos is having a song played for us. He wants us to dance," she said.

"Aren't you the girl who doesn't dance?"

"We must be polite guests, Alex."

He shrugged. "All right, if it will make him happy. Then we have to leave."

Not only did Kostos provide a throbbing, lovelorn song for them to dance to, he and his wife joined them on the makeshift dance floor. Their host closed his eyes and held his wife tightly as they danced, as if to say, "See, this is how it's done."

She envied them, a couple enjoying a romantic evening after twenty or thirty years of marriage, under a full moon with wine and food flowing, with music and friends and a warm summer breeze off the sea. Would that be her someday? Not if she gave other men the cold shoulder because of a ridiculous crush on someone who considered her only a good friend.

This time it was Alex who stepped on her feet. "Sorry," he said. "I've had too much to drink—or not enough." His hand, which had been firmly placed on the small of her back, drifted down to the curve of her hip and pulled her close. Now it was her turn to stumble. He steadied her with his hand on her shoulder and pulled her even closer. Whoever's idea this was, it was a bad one.

Alex was so close she could smell the shower soap that lingered on his skin, and she felt that old familiar knot in the pit of her stomach. She could feel the soft cotton of his shirt and even feel the muscles of his chest. Now she was so close she could feel the steady beat of his heart. So close she could feel the throbbing of his organ against her belly.

What *was* wrong with him? Too much to drink? Not enough? The loss of Sofia? Her cheek brushed against the dark stubble of his five o'clock shadow. He hadn't shaved since they started this trip. Was he going native? Or was she? It was scary, disturbing, and downright erotic.

She closed her eyes and let herself drift away on a cloud of desire.

"You lied to me, Jane," he said softly. His lips brushed against her ear.

Her eyes flew open. "What . . . what do you mean?" she asked, her palm damp against his shoulder.

"You said you couldn't dance."

"I said I *didn't* dance. But when in Greece . . ."

"I should have known. All those men in your life, you couldn't get away without dancing."

"Of course not," she said. "There were masked balls and military balls and charity balls. It was never ending."

"All those balls," he said thoughtfully. "It must have been exhausting. How many were there?"

She blinked. "Balls?"

"Men."

She raised her eyebrows. "You make it sound as if it's over."

"All right, how many have there been?"

"I've lost count. Why do you care?" she asked.

"I'm just making conversation," he said.

"Let's just dance."

"You call this dancing?" he asked, and she realized that while they were swaying to the music, their feet hadn't moved for the past five minutes. The musicians continued to play. "I'll show you what dancing is." He spun her around and bent her backward over his arm. The blood all rushed to her head. He pulled her back up and kissed her on the mouth. His lips were warm and set her whole body on fire. She knew the kiss meant nothing to him; it was just part of the dance. Kostos and his wife clapped. Jane wobbled on Sofia's high-heeled sandals. The whole patio was spinning around.

"Let's go," he said abruptly.

They thanked Kostos, and he came out on his balcony to lean over and call "Good night" to them as they started down the street.

"Happy wedding day!" Kostos yelled. "Send us a picture."

They waved back to him.

"You should do that," Jane said.

"That might cause some confusion," Alex said, "since he thinks you and I are . . . Tell you what. You send him a picture of your wedding."

"What wedding?" Jane said as she walked unevenly on the cobblestone street. "I'm not getting married anytime soon."

"You said there was 'someone.' "

"I didn't say I was going to marry him. I haven't decided," Jane said breezily.

"Marriage would put a damper on things, wouldn't it? No more affairs with professors or lunchtime quickies."

"You haven't heard the half of it."

"Go on, I'm listening," he encouraged.

"Not tonight." His attention and his interest in her nonexistent past were flattering, but she was too fuzzy-minded to invent a few more lovers right now.

She was careful not to take Alex's arm; she didn't want to get used to his touch, his smell, and his voice in her ear. He was equally careful not to put his hand under her elbow. They lapsed into silence.

By now they had the dinghy drill down. She unrolled the rope from the post. He started the engine. She got in and they took off. At the yacht he got out first, she climbed the rope ladder, and he tied up.

They went to the lounge and turned on the brass wall lamps.

Jane stood there and looked around. "I keep expecting to see her. I keep thinking she'll turn up when we don't expect her. She'll be fine, she'll have some incredible story to tell, and everything will be fine. Sometimes I feel like she's not far away and that she knows we're here."

Alex nodded silently. Jane wondered what he really thought. For her sake, she hoped Sofia had run away with a lover, but it would be easier on Alex's ego if she just ran away with a friend to teach Alex a lesson.

"Which reminds me," she said, "Kostos told me where the Oracle of Artemis is. We can go tomorrow."

"And do what?"

"I don't know. Look for clues. Look for Sofia. Ask for information. Whatever you do at an oracle." She yawned.

"Go to bed," he said. "I'll sleep here. You take the stateroom."

Jane paused in the doorway and gave him a look of sympathy and understanding. "Don't worry," she said. "We'll find her." Then she was gone—five-feet-eight inches of sunburned skin, blond hair, long legs, and soft lips.

Alex put his head in his hands. Don't worry? Easy

for her to say. He was worried he'd driven Sofia away. Worried that she didn't want to be found by him. He was also worried he might be losing his mind. For the first time in a long time, and just a few days before his wedding, he was lusting after another woman. If it was just a random nude person on the beach or belly dancer on the dance floor, he wouldn't worry.

But it wasn't. It was Jane. He told himself it was the wine and the food and the music and the sea air.

Tomorrow he would abstain from all known aphrodisiacs. But how was he going to abstain from Jane?

Chapter 7

Alex turned over yet again and tried to get comfortable on the white leather cushions of the sofa. The sunburn on his shoulders was keeping him awake. He took off his T-shirt and tossed it on the floor. It didn't help; the sheets felt like sandpaper. He thought of the lotion in Jane's purse and imagined her cool fingers on his skin. He gritted his teeth and told himself to cool down. She was probably asleep by now, anyway.

He sat up and looked at the clock on the wall. Almost two o'clock. Way too late to bother Jane. He desperately needed a little pain relief, though.

Yeah, right. You want relief, but not that kind.

In his boxers he walked forward to the stateroom

and knocked softly on the door. If she didn't answer, he'd just go back to bed.

"Yes?" she said sleepily.

"Can I come in?"

In a few moments Jane opened the door. Her silky hair was tangled like a halo around her face. Her face was creased with lines from the pillow, and she was wearing a pale, silky nightgown with thin straps. Just a shrug of her shoulders or a tug on those straps and the gown would slither off her shoulders and lie in a pool at her feet. In the pale light from her bedside stand, Alex could see the profile of her breasts and the outline of her nipples against the fabric.

"Sorry to bother you," he said, his voice unsteady as his body reacted. Where was his willpower when he needed it most?

"What's wrong? What happened?"

"It's my sunburn. You said you had some cream?"

"Yes, sure. Come in."

He stood in the doorway, wishing he'd just toughed it out. But it was too late now to back out and say he was okay. He'd already behaved like a borderline schizophrenic all evening, sending her messages like stop dancing with other men and dance with me. Come here, go away. Right now he only had one message for her: *Come here, come here, come here. Don't go away.*

Alex watched her get her purse, sit on the edge of her bed, and dump a pile of tubes and bottles on the table. He clenched his jaw and delivered a warning to himself: hands off.

She held a tube up to the light and read the label. "This should work; it's loaded with Vitamin E. Come here, I'll rub it on you."

"I can do it." He couldn't risk feeling her hands on his skin.

"You can't reach your own back, unless you're some kind of contortionist. Sit down."

Alex took a deep breath and willed himself to be strong. You asked for this, he told himself, sitting on the edge of her bed. Now deal with it. He could deal with the cool lotion that smelled like mint and lavender. He could deal with the touch of her fingers, warm and caressing. But he couldn't deal with that shaft of desire that rammed him in the gut like being hit by the boom on a sailboat when you forgot to duck.

He didn't know what to do about it. He knew what he *shouldn't* do: come to her room in the middle of the night and ask her to put her hands on his bare skin. Even worse, he didn't know what to make of her. It was as if a dormant cactus had blossomed into an exotic flower.

It was just Jane, he told himself. However many boyfriends she'd had, to him she was still the Plain Jane he'd known for ten years. Jane, who'd been his friend before he'd met Sofia. The same Jane he'd danced with at the freshman mixer, tossed a Frisbee with in Mexico, shared laughs and coffee with in the student lounge. And yet . . . and yet . . .

He jumped to his feet as if he'd been stung by a bee. "Thanks," he said, and left the room without a backward glance. He could imagine her sitting there wondering what the hell was wrong with him. She must think he was losing his mind, and maybe he was. Tomorrow he'd try to explain.

The thing about Jane was, she would understand. She'd always understood him. He could only hope she didn't understand too well. That would make everything awkward between them.

It must be the clothes, he thought, when he saw her the next morning out on the deck. The white cotton capri pants that hugged her hips, and the pink-and-white striped shirt knotted at her waist, showing a stretch of skin, made her look like a piece of candy. Forbidden candy. Candy that he must not covet, touch, and especially not taste.

"How's your sunburn?" she asked.

"Fine. Thanks." The less said about last night, the better. He took a big gulp of fresh damp, sea air. "Let's get some coffee," he said, and they got into their dinghy and cast off for town.

In a *kafeneion*, sitting outside at a tiny table, they ordered small cups of dark, muddy coffee, *sketo* (no sugar), and some thick, homemade yogurt with dark honey and walnuts sprinkled on top.

"This is delicious," she said, licking her spoon.

"I thought we should discuss our strategy," Alex said, wishing she wouldn't do that with her tongue. Wishing he could concentrate on something besides Jane's mouth and her perfect white teeth and her pink lips and her tongue. It wasn't her fault he wasn't on his honeymoon; it wasn't her fault the air was soft and perfumed with the verbena hanging from pots at the edge of the terrace; it wasn't her fault he wanted to cover her mouth with his and plunge his tongue into her mouth—and this was only breakfast!

He tried again. "Assuming Sofia is on this island, we should make a list of possible scenarios, locations, and so on."

Jane reached into her purse and pulled out a pad of paper and a pen. "First the oracle, right?"

"Right, though what do we think we're going to find there?"

"I don't know. But Sofia said, 'ask the oracle.'"

"So we'll ask her—or it. What exactly *is* an oracle? How do they communicate with us mortals?"

"Since this is the oracle of the virgin moon goddess, maybe she only speaks in the moonlight."

"We can't hang around that long." He drummed his fingers on the tabletop. "For all we know, Sofia may have taken off for another island. We should leave this afternoon. Sooner, if we get the hose." He needed to take action—to do something, go somewhere, anywhere.

"Fine, as long as we have time for the oracle. It's possible she speaks only to those who truly believe."

"That lets me out. Or maybe she speaks only to virgins, which lets you out." Alex paused, to let her deny it, but of course she wouldn't. At one point he might have thought she'd stayed a virgin all these years, but she'd made her status as a guy magnet clear when she'd confided in him yesterday.

"Do you really think there's an oracle who can tell you what you want to know? If there was, wouldn't everybody in the world be lined up to see her or him?" he asked.

"Maybe they are lined up. All I know is what Sofia said."

"But why did she say it? Is it because she's there? Or did somebody tell her what to say, so we'd go off on a wild-goose chase and not find her at all? Did you think of that?"

She sighed. "No. But I'm going."

"I know; I'm going, too." Alex shoved his chair back from the table.

"What about our list?"

"After the oracle, what have we got? A lot of tourist attractions. This is Wednesday; we've only got till Saturday."

"I know," she said soberly. She put her pad back in her purse. "Kostos gave me directions how to get to the oracle. He also gave me a list of other sights to see."

"We have no time for sightseeing," Alex said as they walked up the street. "How about renting mopeds? Have you ridden one?"

"Once on vacation in Bermuda. I went on a cruise with my aunt, and we rode around Hamilton on mopeds. The hard part was they drive on the left side of the road, which was a little scary. This should be a breeze."

"Your aunt rode a moped?" he asked. "That's pretty cool."

Jane laughed. "No, my aunt is eighty-four. It was the social director and I."

"What kind of activities did this social director direct?" Alex asked, stopping suddenly to put one hand on her shoulder and look her in the eye. He had a feeling those social directors hit on every single woman under the age of sixty-five, and Jane was just vulnerable enough to be taken in by some sleaze with a big mouth and fast hands.

"What does that have to do with anything?" she asked, her nose wrinkled up in that way she had when she was puzzled.

"I just wondered. Was there dancing in the evening?"

"Oh, definitely. Dancing in the disco, dancing in the cocktail lounge, dancing at the captain's reception. He was a great dancer. I'm sure that's part of his job description." She paused. "Alex, let's go. What is this about?"

"I was just curious," he said as they continued walking toward the commercial district. "Was he one of the many notches in your belt?"

Jane grinned. "I wouldn't put it that way."

"How would you put it?"

"We had some laughs and some good times. That's what cruises are for."

"I didn't know you were the type for a shipboard romance."

"I wouldn't call it a romance, exactly. You know,

my aunt wasn't shocked. I don't know why you should be, Alex."

"I'm not shocked. I just want to know what happens when the ship docks and you go back to real life?"

"Nothing. It's over."

"So you tossed him away like an old banana peel?" Alex's mind was reeling. Where was the Jane he used to know?

She brushed her hands together. "Just like that," she said.

"Love 'em and leave 'em," he murmured.

She nodded. "I'd hardly settle down with someone who's gone all the time."

"It doesn't sound like you intend to settle down at all. And why should you? You're having way too much fun," he said, angling a glance at her.

"You've got that right," she said with a little smile. "There's a bakery. I've got to buy some honey-cakes for the oracle."

"Cakes for a two-thousand-year-old oracle?" Alex asked incredulously as she ducked into the small shop with the smell of fresh bread wafting out the door. "Okay, okay, whatever you say. Whatever makes her answer questions."

At the bike rental store, he chose two mopeds, or *papaki,* as the owner called them, and paid for a day's rental. When Jane joined him, they wheeled their mopeds out onto the sidewalk. She tried out the levers that controlled the throttle, the brakes, and the clutch. He strapped her purse onto the rack behind the seat. Then he rode his moped out onto the street and waved to her to follow him.

She shot out of the driveway and passed him, a big grin on her face. A car honked at her and somebody yelled, *"Opa"*—"Watch out!" Alex caught up with her and called to her to slow down, but she just shook her head.

He pulled ahead of her and she rode behind him down a city street. Signaling with his arm, he turned onto a partially paved coastal road that had spectacular vistas of the blue-green sea on their right hand. He turned to look at Jane, and she waved to him, then took both hands off the handlebars and raised her arms in the air. She had guts, that girl. He'd give her that.

Then they started climbing.

Jane realized she was falling behind. There hadn't been any hills in Hamilton. Her heart was pounding, her legs were aching. She pushed hard and muscles in her calves screamed out, but she kept pedaling and finally crested the hill. Alex was so far ahead of her, he was only a blur. At the top she had a great view of the sea before she started down the hill. Coasting down the hill felt like flying. The wind tore through her hair and whipped her face. It was wonderful!

She decided to get a moped when she got home. She'd ride it to work. It would save on gas, and with a little pedaling she could even climb the hills of San Francisco.

She slowed down and she soon pulled up alongside of him.

"I forgot how much fun mopeds are!" she shouted over the sound of the motors.

And he'd forgotten how much fun it was to watch Jane having fun.

They turned off the road at a sign that said THE ORACLE OF ARTEMIS and followed a narrow, bumpy road lined with olive trees toward a rocky gorge. There they parked their mopeds and followed the signs that pointed to the oracle.

At the edge of the gorge with a deep spring at the bottom, they sat down on a grassy field under a tree and looked around, uncertain what to do next. There were a few tourists, a handful of teenagers throwing Frisbees, and families having picnics.

Jane glanced at Alex.

"She's not here," he said. Not that he'd really expected Sofia to be there waiting for them. "Come on, let's ask our question and get out of here."

"It's not that easy," Jane said, taking her guidebook from her purse. "Here are the instructions for communing with the oracle. 'The true believer is anointed with oil and led up to the gorge, and with honeycakes in each hand, he is lowered in a coffin-like pit and left there for several days. After a long communion with the oracle, he is lifted out feet first and tells all he has learned.' "

Alex leaned back on his elbows. "That lets me out, because I'm no true believer. But don't let me stop you. Take your honeycakes, and we'll get someone to lower you into the pit. And if you come here, I'll anoint you with oil. I owe you, after last night."

There was a gleam in his eye that caused her to swallow hard and look away. Did he think she'd been trying to seduce him, when she'd only been interested in easing his pain? Not that she didn't want to rip his clothes off and roll around in the grass with him, but she certainly didn't want him to know that.

"You don't owe me anything," she protested a little too strenuously. She didn't want him putting lotion on her back; she didn't want to even think where that might lead. She wasn't made of stone.

He took her travel-size hand lotion out of her purse and shook some in the palm of his hand.

"Turn around," he said.

"What for?" She hesitated. She didn't want to make a big deal of it and make him suspicious. And after all, what could happen out here in public?

"Do you or don't you want to consult with the oracle?" he asked.

"Yes, but—"

Before she could move away, he'd knelt behind her and lifted the hem of her shirt to spread lotion on her back. She took a deep breath and braced herself for the way she knew he could make her feel. As if her vertebra had all dissolved and she was nothing but aroused nerve endings.

"Relax," he said. "Did I tense up on you last night?"

"We're in a public place," she reminded him and herself. Before he'd even started, the skittery feeling raced up and down her spine. It was a warning:

Watch out. Don't let him touch you. You're a weak-ling.

"It was your idea to come here," he reminded her, working the lotion into her skin with his strong fingers. "You're the believer."

It was like the best Shiatsu massage combined with sexual foreplay. She had to press her lips together to keep from moaning. Of course, he was just trying to humor her in her effort to contact the oracle. Anything else was purely the fault of her overactive imagination.

Her head fell forward. She felt as if she were melting like butter in the hot sun.

Many minutes later, after his fingers had left lasting traces on her skin that no shower could ever remove, Jane finally came to her senses. "That's enough," she sighed, inching away from him. *It's not enough. I want more. I don't want you to stop until I'm lying here under the trees and your fingers are everywhere, working their magic. . . .*

He recapped the lotion and handed it to her. "Ready to be lowered in the pit?" he asked briskly. His expression was neutral; anything sexual was clearly all in her head.

"You're not serious enough about this," she said. "You're making a mockery of the oracle, and oracles don't take kindly to being mocked."

"Does it say that in your book? For all we know, oracles have a terrific sense of humor."

She leafed through the pages. "Wait," she said, "there's another way. 'One can lie on the ground under the trees and listen for the oracle's voice in the rustling of the leaves.' "

"Then how does she get her honeycakes?" he asked. "Better get them out, just in case."

Jane gave him a look that was supposed to stop him from making light of the oracle, but he was having way too much fun laughing at her. Well, better that than seducing her. She took the cakes out of the bag and set them on the grass. "All right, there they are," she said.

Alex lay on the grass on his back. "I'm ready," he said. "Although if the oracle speaks in Greek, we won't be able to understand her."

Jane lay down, too, a careful distance from him. She closed her eyes and listened to the rustling of the leaves. She could feel the sun flickering on her face through the branches of the trees. The grass tickled her bare arms. She felt silly lying there, coated with lotion, Alex on one side, two honeycakes on the other. He was probably right to be skeptical.

Where was Sofia? she asked both herself and the oracle. Why had she told them to come here? Or did she mean another Oracle of Artemis, not this one?

The leaves rustled and she thought they said something. She thought they whispered, "Come." She sat up and looked around. *Come? Come where?* Alex was snoring softly. She watched the sunlight make shifting patterns on his face. She wanted to reach over and touch his arm, to run her fingers under his shirt and over his collarbone.

Then she took a deep breath and told herself that if she wanted to keep him as a friend, she had to control herself. She reminded herself that he'd wished she hadn't come along, and right now she wished the same. How much longer could she pretend she was immune to his looks, his personality, his humor and his sharp mind? Let alone his touch. She could handle the rest and still tell herself they were only friends. But when he reached under her shirt— Oh, Lord, that was where she almost lost control and threw herself at him and pinned him to the ground. Wouldn't he have been surprised! Plain, sensible Jane having a meltdown.

And now his vulnerability touched her to the core. He was worried and hurt and confused. He covered it, but she knew it was there. She'd never seen him that way before; he'd always had everything under control. Everything but Sofia, and Sofia's unpredictability had made her even more desirable to him.

Restless, Jane got to her feet. She could wake him to tell him she was going for a walk up to the gorge, but he probably needed his sleep. They needed a break from each other, and if that *was* the oracle speaking to her, it would be foolish to ignore her.

Jane took the marked path that led up to the top of the gorge. She passed a few people along the way, and some tourists speaking German passed her. She took her camera from her purse and snapped some shots of the rocks and the water falling over them into the chasm below.

When she got to the top, she leaned over the railing and looked down. Hit by a dizzy spell, she stepped back. It was cool and misty up there. She was alone. The other tourists had disappeared.

"Sofia," she called softly. "Are you here? Where are you?"

No answer. Just the sound of falling water.

"Artemis," she said, addressing the oracle in a clear voice. "Where is my friend?"

No answer.

Of course not; she'd left the honeycakes back on the grass. But she could try again, in case it wasn't the honeycakes. Maybe the oracle just wanted to be addressed more respectfully.

"O great oracle, hear my plea." Feeling self-conscious and silly, she looked around, but she was still alone.

Jane called a little louder this time. "Please answer my question. Where is Sofia?" Her voice bounced off the rock walls of the gorge. "Sofia, Sofia, Sofia." A wind came up from the gorge below, and Jane shivered.

She turned and hurried back down the path. This was ridiculous. There was no oracle. There may have been one two thousand years ago, but she didn't speak any longer. Maybe she was tired of answering stupid questions over the years, like: How can I find a reliable mechanic to fix my chariot? How many bushels of grain can I steal from my patron before he catches on? Why does my wife always have a headache at night? How can I stop my neighbor's rooster from crowing at five in the morning?

When she reached the bottom, there was a young woman posing in front of the entrance to the gorge. Her companion was taking her picture.

"Would you take our picture?" the woman asked Jane in heavily accented English.

"Of course," she said.

They posed in front of the rocks and smiled at each other. Jane felt a pang of loneliness. They were so obviously in love.

Jane returned to where Alex was still lying on the grass with his eyes closed. She took out her camera and snapped his picture. He blinked, sat up, and looked at her.

"Be careful. I've been known to break cameras, and to burn out good film. What do you want a picture of me for?"

"To put in my scrapbook," she said.

"Along with the other men in your life? At least I should get a page to myself."

"No problem," she said. Little did he know that she had many, many pictures of him—on campus, off campus, at graduation, at parties, in the city, with Sofia and without her. When she got back, she'd have to dispose of them. It was time. It was past time.

If only she could forget about him as easily as she could throw away the pictures. She'd do her best, but it wasn't going to be easy. Sofia assumed the three of them would stay good friends. If she got her wish, and she always did, they'd be bound by old ties, memories, and genuine fondness for each other. But Jane couldn't deal with it anymore. Before this trip she might have. Now she knew she couldn't.

"Where have you been?" he asked.

"I went for a walk up into the gorge."

"Too bad," he said. "You missed the oracle."

"What? She was here? You're not the nonbeliever you pretend to be. How does she look?" she asked.

"Pretty good, for a two-thousand-year-old woman."

"What did she say?"

"She said Beauty is Truth and Truth is Beauty."

Jane smiled. "So she reads Keats. Was that all?"

"Know thyself."

"Uh-huh. What else?"

"Fix your eyes on the greatness of Athens and fall in love with her."

"Athens? Is that where we're supposed to go next?"

"I doubt it. I think she was just spouting the usual quotations from the ages, whatever she thought we pilgrims wanted to hear. Or she might be working for the tourist bureau. With an oracle, you can never tell."

Jane scanned the area. "Where are the honey-cakes?"

He looked around. "I guess she took them. It was her right, after all."

"The whole package of them? Really, what happened to them?" Jane asked, her forehead puckered in a frown.

"Really, I don't know. Maybe some kids stole them while I was asleep. What about you—did you get any message up there?"

"Nothing. I guess you're the one she chose to communicate with, even though you're a cynic and you weren't even anointed."

He shrugged. "There's no accounting for the taste of oracles. Shall we go?"

"Where to?"

He looked at his watch. "We have some time before the hose arrives, so I'd like to see some of the things on Kostos's list. The little Theatre of Dionysis, for example, and the Temple of Zeus. I may not get a chance to see much, later."

"Why not? You'll be on your honeymoon, sailing from island to island. You can stop at deserted beaches, visit all the ruins you want—maybe not those particular ones, but lots of other temples and theaters."

"Sofia doesn't like ruins. Or deserted beaches. She likes parties and crowds. She likes to see and be seen."

"Not all the time. Sofia knows how to have a good time, yes, but she's very interested in culture. This is her culture, after all." Jane racked her brain to think of an example of Sofia's interest in Greek culture. She belonged to the Orthodox Church. She volunteered to sell her mother's baklava for their annual bazaar.

She was always busy, always in motion. She craved excitement, fun, friends, activity. Jane could understand that better now. Wearing Sofia's clothes, dancing and hanging out in cafés, and riding a moped, she was living Sofia's life—and she was liking it.

She was liking it so much, she knew she would have a terrible letdown when she returned to her own life. There was something about these Greek islands—the sun, the polished rocks, the flowers, and the incredible color of the sea—that made everything else seem gray by comparison. It might have had something to do with Alex, too. He made her feel like a fun-loving, sexy, devil-may-care woman having a fling.

When things got back to normal, Jane feared normal wouldn't seem all that much fun. There was no man in the world who looked like Alex, talked like Alex, and looked at her like he did with those dazzling blue eyes.

But she'd just have to deal with it. Even though she would once again be in the background, back in her old, boring clothes, leading her old, boring life. A life she'd thought was just fine, until now. A life that would *be* just fine, once she got used to it again.

"Besides, I'm not sure she'll want to take a honeymoon. Or marry me." He sounded uncustomarily glum.

"Oh, come on, Alex, she was mad, but you know Sofia—she'll get over it. She's probably over it now."

"Then why doesn't she come back? Go home?"

"Maybe she has. Maybe she's back now. We'll call when we get back to the boat. Meanwhile, let's go see the ruins."

Before they got to their mopeds, the couple whose picture Jane had taken stopped and asked if they would like a picture of themselves.

"Thank you," Jane said and handed over her camera. Why not? Although she wasn't sure what kind of memories it would bring back. Would they be bittersweet? Tinged with regret? But she posed with Alex anyway, next to their mopeds. The man who was taking their picture motioned them to get closer together. Alex put his arm around Jane's waist and pulled her next to him. Afterward, the nice couple waved and went on their way. She knew what they must have thought—what everyone thought—that she and Alex were honeymooners, or sweethearts, at least.

She felt cold and alone as she got on her moped. What was she going to do with a picture of her and Alex visiting the oracle, or Alex sleeping on the grass? There was no room in her scrapbook or in her life for memories of this day or yesterday or last night.

She could make room for wedding pictures—yes, those were the kind of pictures she desperately needed. Pictures of Alex and Sofia beaming at each other, beaming at the camera, dancing and eating wedding cake. Seeing those pictures would make it clear once and for all. Finally she could say to herself, "It's over," and mean it.

She could get on with her life. Find someone else to marry. Warren? Maybe. Maybe not.

Jane started her moped and once again thrilled to the power beneath her fingertips. It was only a glorified bicycle, but it made her feel so free. The wind whipped through her hair and whistled past her ears. She followed Alex back to the highway, squeezed the throttle, and felt the engine respond. They turned down a small, paved road to the ruins.

There were only a few people at the ancient theater, walking around it and climbing the crumbling marble steps to the top, where there was a view of the surrounding countryside.

Jane and Alex sat on a stone seat, halfway between the chairs labeled for priests and dignitaries and the seats allotted for the average citizens. In the middle of the stage was a huge throne with carved lion paws for the priest of Dionysis.

"Imagine watching a play here," Jane said.

"You wouldn't be watching a play. Women weren't allowed to go to the theater," Alex said.

"What if they sneaked in?"

"The punishment might be severe."

"I'd take a chance."

"Like you did with Professor Goodrich? Like you did with your boss at the accounting firm? You continue to amaze me, Jane. I thought you were . . . I don't know, different."

"Say it: you thought I was a goody-goody. That's what everyone thought."

"You had me fooled. Now I find out that under

that buttoned-down exterior there was a wanton woman, a wild child." His heated gaze traveled over her crisp shirt, to the gap above her shorts where she'd knotted it over her stomach, to her bare calves and ankles. She felt shaken down to the tips of her toes, and when he finished his long tour, his gaze locked and held hers.

At this point, even she didn't know who she really was. She felt as if she was changing by the minute. It was because of the clothes, the beach, the boat, the moped, and more than anything—Alex.

"You are a CPA, though, right?" he asked, putting one large, warm hand on her knee. "That's kind of a conservative job for someone like you, isn't it?"

"What do you know about CPAs?" she asked, her voice a little breathless as she tore her eyes away and tried to keep the conversation going. Tried not to imagine his hand moving up her leg to her thigh, and then . . . Try as she may, her imagination ran away with her and desire swept through her, wild and hot. She licked her dry lips and fought off the sensations. She told herself it was nothing, just a friendly gesture.

"I know I need one in my new business. You're not looking for a job, are you?"

"You think I'd work for you?" She gave a shaky laugh. She'd work for Alex when hell froze over.

"I'm not used to having my job offers laughed at," he said, taking his hand back. "I'm a great boss. You can have long lunch hours and a bonus at Christmas."

Jane took a deep, steadying breath. This was a subject she could address. "Things will be different when you have your own business. You'll have a budget. You may have some hard times ahead. Instead of giving long lunches and bonuses, you'll be asking your staff to take stock options instead of wages, and put in long workdays."

"I need someone like you to explain that to the employees. I'm no good at math, and terrible about the financials. So what do you say, do you want to think it over?"

"It would be exciting to work for a start-up," she said wistfully. "But I can't afford to give up my job. I have security, and someday I might make partner."

"Security?" he said. "Is that really what you're looking for? That doesn't sound like Jane the risk-taker."

"I only take risks in my personal life," she said. That was a lie. Warren was a very safe bet. She couldn't go wrong with him.

"Let me know if you change your mind." Alex looked down at the stage. "So, what would you rather see, a comedy or a tragedy?"

She smiled at the ease with which he changed the subject. She hoped she hadn't hurt his feelings by turning him down. Of course, he wasn't seriously offering her a job; it was all in fun. She shuddered to think about working next to him all day and watching him go home to Sofia at night. Seeing Sofia waltz in the office in a sleekly tailored suit and sit on the edge of his desk, swinging her beautiful legs and tempting him to take her to lunch. *Sofia, come back. Come back now, before it's too late. While I still have my wits about me.* She shifted back in time to 480 B.C. "Comedy, please."

"How about *Lysistrata,* where the women with-hold their favors until the men stop fighting? It's just as believable today as it was then. That's a good one."

"You amaze me, Alex," she said. "For an architecture major, you know a lot about a lot of things."

"Architecture and Greek theater are all wound up together," he said, waving a hand at the stone pillars. "You have to know the function of the building before you can design it. See the vaulted tunnel and the archway down there? That means it was once used for a stadium. Arches were supposed to be a Roman invention, but this place was built way before the Romans. So where did they get the idea? My feeling is that Alexander brought it back from India."

She nodded, dazzled not only by his knowledge, not only by his good looks, but by his enthusiasm. She knew he was smart, but she had no idea how broad his knowledge was. He wasn't perfect, but right now, she couldn't think of anything wrong with him. Oh, God, she was in even bigger trouble than she'd thought.

"Were you always interested in Greece?" she asked, keeping the conversation impersonal.

"I studied Greek architecture in school," he said. "Then I met Sofia, and I started reading about Greek history and some of the literature."

"I feel like I missed out."

"You were the math whiz; science, too—except for that regrettable event in chemistry lab. Before you go home, you should stop in Athens and see some of the great old stuff: the Acropolis, the Parthenon, the Temple of Athena. 'Fix your eyes on the glories of Athens and fall in love with her,' as the oracle said."

"I don't know if I'll have time."

"No time to fall in love? You've gotta *make* time, Jane. Someday you'll have to quit playing the field and make a commitment."

"I was only talking about skipping Athens. I have to get back to work."

"And to that man in your life. Or should I say the men in your life? Isn't that really why you're rushing back?"

"Not really." She'd thought about Warren very little—he paled in comparison with Alex. She was going to be on the first plane out of there as soon as Alex and Sofia had said their vows. No more parties, no dancing, no cavorting in crystal clear waters. Back to work. Back to normal. Back to Dullsville.

"You have to make time for the Parthenon. It's amazing, what they did in the fifth century B.C. They slanted the columns." He angled his hands on his knees to show her what he meant. "You stand there looking at it and you could swear the columns were completely vertical, but they're not. If they were, they'd seem to be leaning outward."

"So it's an optical illusion," she said.

His eyes lit up. "Yes, exactly. And how did they do it?" He put his hand on her shoulder and looked into her eyes. "You'll like this. They used a sophisticated mathematical formula. And they had skilled stonemasons. If I could build something that would last half that long, I'd die a happy man."

"You will. I'm sure you will," she said.

"Die a happy man?" he asked.

"Why not? And I'm sure you'll build something to last, too." He had to at least have a chance to try. Surely Sofia would see that.

He dropped his hand from her shoulder. "Let's have a look at those columns up there."

She followed his gaze to the stone pillars on the hillside above the theater. Then she consulted her guidebook.

"Vestiges of the Temple of Zeus, erected in the fourth century, B.C."

They walked up a paved path to the top, where there were only a few sun-bleached pillars standing stark-white against the intense blue of the sky. They stood on rough stones with tiny yellow wildflowers sprouting up through the cracks. A few other people wandered around taking pictures and reading guidebooks.

Alex leaned against a pillar. "See what I mean? It's leaning inward." He took her hand and placed it on the stone. "Feel how smooth the marble is. It was the perfect material, decorative and functional at the same time."

They stood there for a long moment, their hands pressed together against the warm, smooth stone, the play of sun and shadow across the stones, and on Alex's face. Jane wondered how many men and women had stood there like this, lost in time, over the years, over the centuries. She felt herself slipping backward in time with Alex at her side. It made her feel slightly, wonderfully delirious.

"Of course, there would be a roof to protect the worshipers from the sun," he said, shading his eyes. "Tell me what you know about Zeus. I feel his presence, don't you?"

She felt a shiver go up her spine. "Of course. This is his temple, after all." She opened her guidebook. "Here it is. 'Zeus, the father of all the gods and the most powerful.' "

"But not the nicest. He did some pretty bad stuff, didn't he?" Alex leaned against the pillar and looked off across the hill. "Poisoned his father, seduced half the goddesses on Mount Olympus and quite a few mortals along the way. Almost everyone was related to him. Like Aphrodite, the goddess of love, and Artemis, of course. And they owed him big-time for fixing the weather, rolling back the seas, making the seasons, whatever."

"You learned all this in architecture class?" she asked.

"I read it somewhere."

Jane held up her book so Alex could see the picture of Zeus with his long beard and his thunderbolt. "And here's Artemis with her bow and arrow.

One of Zeus's mortal daughters was Helen of Troy, the most beautiful woman in the world. Sorry, no pictures of her."

"We have to assume she didn't take after her father in looks or behavior. Wasn't she the face that launched a thousand ships?"

"Uh-huh. The cause of the Trojan War. When her husband turned his back, his enemies stole her away. No one knows if she went willingly or if she was abducted."

"Like Sofia," he said soberly. There was a long silence. "I shouldn't have turned my back. Did Helen's husband go after her?"

"Yes, and he brought her back. It all turned out for the best. They appreciated each other more after she came back. They didn't argue so much, and they had a new slant on things. She agreed to let him start his own business in Troy, and they lived happily ever after."

A slow smile crossed his face. "You're making that up."

"It could be true. Who knows? It was a long time ago." Jane looked around at the broken pillars and the rough stones. "Imagine what it was like," she said dreamily.

"A couple thousand years ago? You'd be wearing one of those white robes with the cords tied around here." He ran his fingers under the swell of her breast.

She gasped and her heart rate shot up. On the outside she was burning up, but on the inside she was freezing. This was just what she was trying to avoid. Or was she? Wasn't it just what she'd been dreaming of for the past ten years? Alex's face was dangerously close to hers. His gaze was warm, intimate, teasing. If she tilted her head and angled her mouth, he'd kiss her.

His fingers lingered, and it felt as if he'd burned a hole through her cotton shirt. Her whole body was on fire. Was it her or was it him? Was it because she was wearing Sofia's sexy clothes? If that was it, she knew what she had to do.

"Alex," she said, taking a step backward, "we'd better leave."

Chapter 8

$\mathcal{A}$lex raised his eyebrows in surprise when Jane suggested they go back to town. After all, he didn't know what he was doing to her equilibrium. Especially if he thought she was now some kind of a swinger, he'd have no idea that his touch was incendiary.

Flying down the hill on her moped, she felt the wind cool her overheated cheeks and blow some sense into her head. He was just caught up in the moment, as was she. When he met her gaze back there at the temple, she'd seen something that scared her; she saw desire flicker in his bluer-than-blue eyes. But now she knew why.

It was simply because she was wearing these sexy clothes. It was so obvious, she should have thought of it before. So she'd stop wearing Sofia's clothes and buy some of her own.

There were a few boutiques that catered to well-heeled tourists, and while Alex went to pick up the new hose, Jane wandered down the narrow little streets and peeked into shops filled with chic, expensive clothes. Window mannequins wore dresses with plunging necklines, skimpy curve-hugging shirts that looked like they could barely fit a full-grown woman, and tight, low-cut pants. These were not the kind of clothes she usually wore, or clothes that she ought to buy at this point.

But she couldn't keep wearing Sofia's clothes. If her sexy clothes weren't having an effect on Alex, they were definitely having an effect on her and causing her to have an identity crisis. If she had her own clothes, she'd start acting like herself again instead of some—what was it he'd called her? A wild child?

She was in Greece. She might never wear these clothes again, but who cared? Here on the islands, at least, she would blend in and not stand out like a wrinkled tourist. Once she was wearing clothes that she'd chosen herself, everything would be back to normal. Maybe this line of reasoning wasn't exactly sound, but it was better than feeling as if she was taking on too much of Sofia's belongings. She took a deep breath and walked into a shop.

A musical chime sounded and an ageless clerk, wearing a chic black dress and lavish gold jewelry, her hair pulled back in an elegant chignon, appeared and offered to help her. She gave Jane's clothes a brief, dismissive glance as if to say, You've come just in time. Put yourself in our hands.

"Resort wear?" the woman asked.

"Yes, I guess so. I really need a little of everything—shorts, pants, shirts, and a dress. But nothing too . . . too bare or daring. I mean . . ." *Nothing too sexy.*

The woman gave a wave of one manicured hand. "You're American. I have many American clients. I know exactly what you need," she said in charmingly accented English. She began taking dresses from a rack and holding them up for Jane to see. Sundresses with tiny straps, halter-top dresses in bright prints, and a dress with wide stripes of every color in the rainbow.

Jane was dazed. Confused. Overwhelmed. But the woman was not confused. She had definite opinions. She had Jane try on the rainbow dress, then she stood back and surveyed her through glasses perched low on her nose.

"No," she said. "It is not right for you. Wait here."

In a minute the woman was back with a bright red crocheted dress.

Jane took a step backward. "I don't wear red."

"You should," the woman said.

When Jane reluctantly tried on the dress and looked at herself in the mirror, she knew the woman was right. Red brought color to her cheeks, made her hair look lighter, even made her skin glow. The dress hugged her body as if it were knitted just for her. But wasn't it a little too . . . you know, sexy?

"Isn't it a little tight? I mean, what do I wear underneath it?" Jane asked, aware that with its bare back, this was another no-bra dress.

"With your body, just a thong," the woman said and held up a small item in red silk.

Jane wavered. This wasn't what she'd had in mind. Yes, the dress was stunning, but when would she ever wear it? And when she heard how much it cost, she shook her head reluctantly. Maybe she didn't need a dress at all. Especially a bright red crocheted dress with a high neckline and a low back that stretched to the base of her spine. She wouldn't need one after this vacation. And she especially shouldn't wear one on this vacation. At least not until Sofia was found.

The woman helped her take off the dress and put it back on the rack. "I'm sorry," she said. "It suits you."

Next Jane tried on a pair of purple-and-turquoise print wide-leg pants. When the clerk gave her a purple sweater to wear with them, Jane started to say "I don't wear purple," but she knew the woman would say—you should.

"For dancing," the clerk said. "Tango, rumba, cha-cha, you know."

Jane almost said she didn't dance, especially not the tango, the cha-cha, or the rumba—but the new Jane *did* dance. The way things were going on this trip, she definitely shouldn't dance anymore, but it was a great outfit. She decided to buy it even though she didn't know exactly where she'd wear it. She was tired of saying no. She was tired of being conservative.

"Now I need something practical," she said, thinking baggy shorts and roomy shirt. She was feeling light-headed for indulging in the dance outfit. "I'm traveling by boat."

"I have many customers who travel by boat. That doesn't mean you can't dress up."

"Other American customers?" Jane asked casually, standing in the dressing room in only her bra and panties. Or rather, Sofia's see-through lace bra and bikini.

"Many. Today there were two. One was looking for pants and a jacket to climb up to the Koreas Cave."

"Where is that?" Jane asked, though she was sure it couldn't be Sofia. She wouldn't hike anywhere, let alone to a cave. Sofia got her exercise at her health club.

"The Koreas Cave is on the island of Kellia. Inside, there are ancient relics, and it is a very beautiful hike. I recommended some shorts, a shirt, and some sturdy boots." The woman held up a pair of sturdy but stylish boots. This was a boutique, after all.

"Was she . . . I'm just wondering if that was my friend who came here. Was she about my height, with long dark hair?"

The woman wrinkled her brow. "Yes, I think so, although many customers have long, dark hair."

"She's very pretty."

"Yes, she was. But also today another very pretty American customer bought a denim skirt, very short, like this." She held up the tiniest skirt Jane had ever seen. It was just the kind that would show off Sofia's legs.

"And to wear with it—this tank top."

Jane rubbed the stretchy fabric between her fingers. "That's all she bought?"

"Oh, no, she had to have a complete wardrobe."

Sofia would need a complete wardrobe, since all she had when she left was the nightgown on her back.

"She bought a chiffon top, stretch pants, a silk embroidered jacket. And some shoes. Then she asked my opinion of where the most romantic place in Greece was."

Jane swallowed hard. If that was Sofia, she would already have chosen the places to go on her honeymoon. So why . . .

"I suggested the Castle of Marianti. And I recommended she purchase something romantic to wear there—a long dress."

"Where is the castle?" Jane asked.

"On the island of Marmara, one of the loveliest in all of Greece. The castle is in a thirteenth-century village. At night they close the gates and pull up the drawbridge, so no one can leave or enter until morning. This adds to the atmosphere, no? The castle has been converted to a beautiful hotel."

"Did my friend say she was going to go there definitely?"

"I only saw her write down the information on a small card. Are you, too, looking for the most romantic spot in all of Greece?" the clerk asked with a knowing smile.

"No. Yes. That depends."

"Then you must not miss the castle."

"I won't," Jane murmured. *Especially if Sofia is there.* "I'm curious. How did she pay for all those clothes?" Sofia had left without her purse.

The woman blinked as if that was an impertinent question, and she was deliberating about whether to answer it or not. "With euros," she said at last.

"I see," Jane said. But she didn't see. If it was Sofia, who'd given her the money? Who was she traveling with? And more important, what would Alex say when he heard about this? But this might not be Sofia at all. It probably wasn't. "Did she buy the dress or not?" Jane asked.

"Yes, we had it altered. She's coming back this afternoon to pick it up."

Jane dropped the pants she was thinking of buying. "What time?" she asked, her skin prickling with sudden awareness.

The woman shrugged. "Anytime. It is ready now." She reached behind a curtain and brought it out for Jane to see. It was peach silk with a tight bodice and full-flowing skirt, just the kind of dress

that would show off Sofia's olive skin and her cur-
vaceous figure.

"Perhaps I'll wait for her," Jane said, her heart
pounding with anxiety. "It could be my friend."

If it was, what would she say when Sofia breezed
into the store to pick up her dress?

"Hi, Sofia. What are you doing here?"

"Jane! What are you doing here, in my clothes?"

"I'm looking for you. We've come to find you."

"Now you've found me, you can go home."

"What about your wedding?"

*"Oh, that. It's not until Saturday. I'll be back in
time."*

"But what are you doing?"

*"Taking a break, that's all. All that wedding stuff
got to me. Alex was right. It had turned into a
circus."*

What could Jane say to that? She'd feel foolish
for having worried and for having come after Sofia
at all.

Or maybe Sofia would come into the store, stop,
and burst into grateful tears at the sight of her best
friend.

"Jane, at last, you've come to rescue me!"

"Yes, we're here. What happened?"

*"I was kidnapped by a crazy fisherman. I've been
sharing the hold of his boat with a crate of slimy jel-
lyfish, and I smell awful. I just slipped out of the
ropes I was tied up with and I was going to call you,
but I didn't have any money for a phone card.
Where's Alex?"*

"He's at the boat. We'll take you home now."

"Thank God. And thank you, Jane, for being so determined. I knew you'd come for me. I can't count on Alex, but you, you're the best friend a girl ever had."

"Credit or cash?" The woman's voice interrupted Jane's reverie.

"Credit card," Jane said, fishing it out of her purse. "I'll take the khaki pants, also. And perhaps I should try on a pair of boots." Just in case. If that really was Sofia who was going to hike the gorge, Jane would have to hike it in order to find her. And if she was going to stay at a castle . . . "And the red dress. That, too."

The woman smiled as if she knew Jane couldn't resist. "You'll be the . . . how do you say? The talk of the town. The belle of the ball. I'll throw in the thong. You won't be sorry."

But Jane *was* sorry when she saw the sum of her purchases. She'd be even sorrier a month from now when her credit card bill came, and she was back in foggy San Francisco, with a closet full of clothes suitable only for dancing on the Greek Islands or visiting old castles.

"If you don't mind, I'll change into the short skirt and the tank top, then I'll wait and see if it's my friend who bought the dress."

The woman waved a hand at the dressing room. When she came out wearing her new clothes, with Sofia's clothes in her shopping bag, Jane felt much better. She took a small upholstered chair in the corner where she could watch the passersby, and read European fashion magazines while she waited. Some deeply tanned German tourists wearing shorts came in and the woman switched to speaking German as she showed them the latest in resort clothes.

Getting anxious, Jane put the magazines down and kept her eyes on the people strolling by on the street. Many women stopped to look in the window, but none of them was Sofia. A few came in and looked around. It was almost six o'clock, the busiest time of day for cafés and shops, and Alex would be wondering where she was. But she didn't dare leave the shop in case Sofia came in. Yet the shop was open until eight, and she couldn't wait that long. Besides, it was a long shot that Sofia had actually bought the dress.

Finally Jane stood and walked slowly out the door. She couldn't keep Alex waiting any longer. At that moment a tall, dark, dashing-looking Greek man brushed past her and entered the shop. She waited outside, and in a minute he came back out carrying a shopping bag.

Jane watched him walk briskly down the street, then went back inside.

"Was that by any chance—" she said.

"Yes, that man came for your friend's dress."

"Thank you!" Jane ran out of the shop, her purse over her shoulder, her own shopping bag in her hand, and rushed down the street in the direction the man had taken. But he was gone. Disappeared in the crowd. From a distance he looked like the same man she'd seen Sofia leaving with the night of the party. Of course, the country was full of men who looked like that. And at the time she'd been sure it was Alex. Now she wasn't sure about anything.

Except it was clear Sofia had been on this island and maybe still was here. The scrap of her torn nightgown was evidence of that, along with the dress shop clerk's description. It was all so maddening, frustrating, and depressing. What was she going to tell Alex? She had learned nothing of substance. And she'd lost her one link to Sofia.

Alex was leaning against a post on the dock, next to the dinghy.

"You're here," Jane said.

"What did you think, I'd leave without you?"

"You did before."

"Where the hell have you been?"

"Shopping. I told you."

He looked her over, his eyes traveling slowly over her miniskirt and tank top until she was radiating heat from every pore. He snagged the waistband of her short skirt and her skin sizzled where his finger met her tender flesh. "This new?"

She nodded.

"Nice," he said, his gaze dropping. "Nice legs." Then he let go and rocked back on his heels. "I picked up the hose but it's too dark to fix it tonight," he said shortly. "We'll have to wait till tomorrow and get under way in the morning."

"Where are we going?" she asked, her voice a little breathless.

"To find *Sofia*."

"I know that." So he was irritated. Well, so was she. She'd had a chance to find Sofia and she'd blown it.

"I have some ideas," she said. "Can we sit down and talk? I'm hungry and thirsty. But first I want to walk through the marina. I thought I saw a man who looked like the man Sofia might have left with."

He stared at her. "What? When? Where?"

"In the boutique a few minutes ago. He was picking up some clothes for a woman I thought might be Sofia."

"What are you talking about?" Alex demanded, glowering at her. "You *might* have seen a man who *might* have looked like the man who *might* have gone off with Sofia? You're not making sense."

"We can't afford to overlook anything. We have to follow up on every clue."

"What's the clue?" His voice rose.

"First, let's just see if there's a boat from Mios here."

"We already did that."

"Yes, but maybe we missed it. Sofia *was* here, we know that. And she came by boat."

They walked up and down the piers where yachts and fishing boats shared space. Fishermen were unloading their catches, throwing fish from their boats into bins on the docks. But no fishing boats were from Mios.

The decks of the yachts were full of well-heeled tourists enjoying cocktail hour. But no yachts were from Mios, except theirs. Jane longed to be aboard the *Aphrodite* right now sipping something cool, dressed in comfortable stretch pants and a roomy T-shirt. But the clothes in her shopping bag, while flattering and the latest style, were not designed for comfort. What madness had come over her in that dress shop?

She wasn't here to sip cocktails, though in her shopping bag she had all the clothes for that kind of life. There was no way she could relax until they found Sofia and got her safely married.

Jane's purse felt heavier than ever. One shoulder sagged. For once she regretted carrying all the tubes and cans and kits she kept there for emergencies. And the handles of her heavy shopping bag were wearing ridges in the palm of her hand. As if he knew, Alex took the bag out of her hand, and she sent him a grateful look.

"Okay, I give up," she said when they came to the end of the docks. "She's not here." But how could she be sure Sofia wasn't slipping into her designer clothes right now on board a fishing boat? Improbable? Yes. Impossible? No.

They were now at the end of the docks, where there were only fishermen and dockworkers. They stopped at the first café they came to. Though it was too early for dinner, there was a smell of oregano and the yeasty scent of fresh bread in the air. Before they even looked at a menu, a waiter brought them a plate of thickly sliced warm bread and two glasses of wine.

At the next table were a group of blue-shirted workers talking loudly, and at the bar fishermen playing a game of dice, slapping their palms on the counter and laughing. Jane broke off a piece of bread and ate it hungrily.

"This is the real Greece," Alex said looking around the room with satisfaction. "Not a tourist in sight." He lifted his glass of wine and surveyed its clear red color with approval. "Now, what is it you were trying to tell me? Why were we looking at the boats again?"

"It's probably silly, but . . . when I was at the store, the saleslady told me there had been another American customer in today. Two, in fact."

"Was one of them Sofia?" he asked, leaning toward her.

"I don't know. So I waited. That's why I was so late. Oh, my God, Alex, there he is." Jane stood up and pointed to a tall man in a hat and jacket who was just leaving the restaurant. "He's the one who took Sofia!"

Alex almost knocked over his chair in his hurry to get out the door. Jane saw him catch up with the man on the sidewalk and put his hand on the man's shoulder. The man turned, and suddenly Jane wasn't sure—of anything. He could have been anyone. Alex said something to him. Jane grabbed her shopping bag and started for the door, but before she got there, the man punched Alex on the chin. Alex staggered backward, then fell to the ground. A few men turned to look at Jane when she ran past their table, but after she left, they went back to talking, laughing, and throwing dice.

Chapter 9

Alex had hit his head as he fell and he felt as if he'd also been run over by a steamroller. Every bone, every muscle screamed out in pain. He pulled himself up so he could sit instead of lie on the sidewalk, and rest his aching head on his knees. He was trying to catch his breath and figure out what had happened. Or rather why. And by whom?

He tasted blood on his lip. When Jane appeared, she mercifully didn't ask him any questions, she just propped his head up with her cool hands. At least he thought it was Jane. His vision was so blurry he couldn't be sure. It smelled like Jane, with that fresh flower smell, and it felt like Jane, with those soft hands that soothed and excited him at the same time. Right now all he wanted was to lie down and close his eyes.

But Jane wouldn't let him. She lifted one eyelid with her finger and peered into his eye. Her face was creased with worry lines, and her brown eyes were full of tears that threatened to spill down her cheeks.

"What's wrong?" he asked, fearing she'd been attacked, too. He tried to force his eyes to open wider than slits.

"That man hit you. But why?"

"How should I know? I've never seen him before in my life."

"How do you feel?"

"How do you think I feel? Like hell. It's my head." He groaned.

She ran her hands through his hair until she found a lump on the back of his skull. He winced.

"You can't stay here, someone will trip on you," she said.

Crowds of noisy workers jammed the sidewalk, walking around him and Jane as if they were panhandlers or drunks who'd passed out. No one gave them a second glance, or if they did, it was one of disdain.

Jane stood and held out her hands to pull him up. "You're strong for somebody your size," he muttered.

"Thanks," she said.

Her arms were around him now, with her shopping bag over one shoulder, her purse over the other, and he was leaning against her. They staggered together down narrow walkways, past fleets of boats, to their dinghy. Alex stumbled getting into the boat, and Jane was there to steady him with her hands. She untied the ropes and he started the engine.

"I'll drive us back," Jane said.

He didn't think she could do it, but he was too tired to argue. He sat in the bow and put his head in his hands—partly because his head was pounding, and partly so he wouldn't have to watch Jane crash into another boat in the crowded harbor.

He didn't look up until they'd come alongside the *Aphrodite,* then he stood and tied the dinghy to the yacht. His legs felt like rubber and his fingers like stumps of wood. As soon as he made it up the four rungs of the ladder, he was going to break into the liquor cabinet Nikos had stocked for their honeymoon.

Jane was quiet as she followed him down the steps to the lounge, and he was grateful. Sofia would have been chattering nonstop. Every small sound was like an anvil in his head, amplified a hundred times. She watched him open a bottle of Scotch and fill two glasses. He handed her one, sank onto the leather cushions, and propped his legs on the coffee table. He exhaled loudly and took a large gulp of Scotch. "Arrrgh!" He sat up straight as the whiskey hit his split lip.

Jane looked at him with an anxious frown. "What happened back there?" she asked, swirling the Scotch around in her glass. "Before he hit you."

"I asked the guy who he was and if he knew anything about Sofia. He said something in Greek, and then bang, I was on the sidewalk. What do you make of that?"

"Either he does know something about her or he doesn't."

"Brilliant," Alex said morosely. "Or you could say either he understood me or he didn't."

"Are you sure you should be drinking?" she asked. "You might have a concussion. How do you feel?"

"I don't have a concussion, and I feel fine for somebody who has a cracked skull and a split lip and was knocked down by a guy he's never seen before. What did you ask me, back there on the sidewalk?"

"I said, 'Who was he?' "

"What do you mean, 'Who was he?' You said he was the guy who abducted Sofia."

She squirmed uncomfortably. "I thought he was. I know he was the same man who came to the boutique to pick up her clothes."

"What clothes?"

"Sofia's clothes. Or at least they could be Sofia's. I told you all this before." She set her glass down and stood. "You're having trouble remembering, aren't you? That's a sure sign of a concussion." She crossed the room, leaned over to peer into his eyes, and cupped his chin in her hand. "I think something's wrong. You don't look normal."

"I don't feel normal. I feel like I was run over by a five-ton truck. My head feels like a punching bag."

"Let me check that lump on your head again." She ran her hand through his hair once again, gently massaging his scalp with her fingertips.

His scalp tingled and he felt the room tilt to one side. "Uh-oh, there must be a tidal wave," he said, trying to stand. "We're listing."

"We're not listing," she said, pushing him gently back down on the cushions. "You obviously have an inner-ear problem."

He obviously had a problem, all right, but it wasn't his inner ear. His problem was Jane, whose face was inches from his, so close he could feel her warm breath on his lips and smell the faint scent of her skin. So close her silky blond hair brushed against his cheek, and her hand in his hair was making him forget both the pain and the woman he was supposed to marry in a few days.

What was his problem? Sofia ran away and suddenly he had the hots for Jane? What kind of a two-timing player was he? Too bad he didn't have a concussion, then he'd have something to blame it on. Or maybe he did have one—what did he know about concussions? Maybe he was seriously brain damaged.

That's what was wrong with him. He lusted for Jane, but it wasn't his fault because he was out of his head.

Yeah, right. There wasn't a court in the world that wouldn't hand down a guilty verdict. Guilty of lust and disloyalty. *Guilty, guilty, guilty.* The words echoed around his brain.

But your honor, he'd protest. *I couldn't help it. It was Jane's fault. It was her mouth, her eyes, her legs, her skin . . .*

"It's my mouth," he mumbled. "My lips are numb."

Jane framed his face with her cool hands and brushed his lips with her fingers. His heart rammed against his chest. He gripped the edge of the cushion in an effort to stay grounded. It didn't work; he was spiraling out of control.

"Feel anything?" she asked lightly, her lips a breath away.

Nothing but rockets going off inside his head. Alex shook his head slowly and prayed he wouldn't go to hell for lying.

She kissed him then, just lightly at the corners of his mouth. She meant it as comfort, but that was all it took. The drumbeats in his head got louder and louder until he went over the edge and down into the whirlpool.

He pulled her down on top of him, and she fit the way he knew she would, every one of her curves matching one of his hollows. Her breasts were pressed against his chest.

Her eyelids fluttered, her breathing came in bursts, but she didn't pull away. "Alex?" she said, her voice a little hoarse. "Are you all right?"

"Not sure," he muttered. "Could you try that again? Just to see if I have any feeling left."

"You mean like this?" She kissed him on the mouth then, her lips warm and sure this time.

"Yeah, that's it," he said, his voice rough as sandpaper. "A little harder. Just to see . . . what the problem is." As if she hadn't noticed exactly what his problem was: he was throbbing, hot, hard, and heavy. She'd have to be made of stone not to notice. And Jane was not made of stone. Jane was made of silk and satin and sugar and spice. And he wanted her, all of her, now.

She kissed him again, but not hard enough. She was probably afraid of hurting his mouth. He was aching, yet he was feeling no pain. He wanted to devour her, to turn her inside out, to be part of her.

Was he delirious? Was he raving? Or had that fall finally knocked some sense into him, and he was finally, at long last, himself?

He took over then, returning her kisses, faster and harder until they were both panting, kissing open-mouthed and frantic to go deeper, wilder, and longer. He'd forgotten about his lip, he'd forgotten everything but how much he wanted her.

Jane pulled away to catch her breath and looked down at him, her dark eyes full of questions he couldn't answer.

His only answer was to tug at her shirt, pull it off over her head, and reach for the front hook of her bra. Then it was his turn to ask the unspoken questions— How far will this go? Do you want what I want? Do we stop now, or . . . ?

Her answer was to unhook the bra herself and

free her breasts. Alex shuddered deeply and pro-
foundly. He felt as if he'd been given the ultimate
gift, one he didn't deserve. Gone were his guilt, his
worries, his headache, and his fears. Inside his
chest there wasn't just a drum, but a whole percus-
sion section beating a wild, passionate rhythm that
wouldn't stop.

He brushed Jane's deep pink nipples with his lips
and realized this was what he needed. His mouth
wasn't numb at all. It was unbelievably sensitive.
Desire raged through him like a wildfire, and he
groaned deep in his throat.

Jane's hands trembled as she tossed her bra to
the floor. When he put his mouth on her nipples,
her whole body shook with fever. In all of her
wildest dreams, it had never been like this. In all
her modest sexual experiences, it had never, *ever*
been like this.

The little voice in the back of her mind that said
this was wrong was barely a whisper now, one she
could tune out with very little effort. Which was
good, because in another second she'd be incapable
of making any effort at all. She was doing what he
wanted, what she wanted, what she'd always
wanted. She'd face the consequences later. But
right now, there was no right and wrong; there was
only Jane and Alex, and nothing that felt so right
could possibly be wrong.

Alex rolled her over, and she shivered all over.
Hot then cold, from one extreme to the other. Was
she sick? If she was, she didn't want to get well.

He braced his arms on either side of her bare shoulders. "This is it," he said. "The point of no return. Are you with me, Jane, or—?" He broke off, unable to finish his sentence.

She couldn't speak, either. She'd been waiting all her adult life for this moment, and there was no way she was going to say no. Not with the way he was looking at her, his eyes hot and hungry. She nodded.

He smiled slowly until the smile reached his incredible Aegean blue eyes, and the laugh lines at the corners deepened and he looked as if he'd just won the lottery. How could she have ever dreamed up anything like this? A yacht in the Aegean, curtains fluttering in the sea-scented breeze, her whole body burning with sexual awareness, aching for release, and the one man she'd ever loved asked if she was with him. She smiled back and tears of joy prickled at the backs of her eyelids.

The breeze cooled her overheated breasts, until he started a tour of her body with his mouth. There was no sea air that could compete with the heat he caused as he worked his way from the tender place behind her ear, to the hollow of her throat, to the underside of her breasts, then down her belly, where he peeled off the new skirt and the bikini panties. He kissed concentric circles around her navel. She gave a ragged sigh, wanting more, *needing* more.

She told him she had to have more. He gave her more. With his hands and his mouth, he explored her heated core. He muttered something, but she didn't understand it. She grabbed him by the shoulders. The sweep of his tongue at her most sensitive nub made her laugh, and then she cried out. She told him to hurry, but she wanted him to slow down. She wanted it to last forever, and yet she wanted it now.

He spread her thighs with his warm hands, then he reached for that slick spot and stroked.

"Yes," she cried. "Yes, yes, yes."

He smothered her cries with a scorching kiss that reached down into her soul. And he kept his hand on the spot where she wanted it, stroking, deeper, longer, faster until she couldn't wait another minute. She shattered into a thousand pieces, and her cries split the air and rivaled those of the gulls on the beach.

"Oh, God, Alex," she said when the world came back into focus. He was on his side, his head propped in his hand, watching her with a smile on his face that made her toes curl and her whole body hum with satisfaction. "Don't look at me like that," she said, her face flushed and her hair hanging in damp tendrils.

"How should I look at you? You're beautiful and you're amazing," he said. "And I never knew."

She flushed all over from the compliment and ran her gaze down his body, admiring his amazing and obvious erection. Just her heated gaze seemed to make him bigger and pulse with need and want.

First she reached out to gently touch his swollen lip. He sucked in a sharp breath. Then she ran her fingers around his chin and down his chest, reveling in her power, her newfound sexuality. Sure, she'd had sex before, but this was a whole different thing. It was making her so giddy, she giggled. She, who hadn't giggled since she was a teen, had done so twice today.

She gave a huge sigh of pleasure and trailed kisses down his chest and belly until she came to his magnificent erection. Then she took him into her mouth and slid her lips back and forth.

Alex let out an oath and tried to sit up. "Jesus, Jane, you don't know what you're doing," he said in a harsh voice. "Are you prepared to face the consequences?"

Before she could answer he had her on her back, her damp skin stuck to the leather couch while he straddled her. She arched against him, ready, waiting, wanting nothing so much as for him to fill that aching void within her. It was what she'd always wanted and needed.

He came into her then, filling her as she knew he would, taking her with slow, easy strokes at first, until the rhythm built and built until there was nowhere to go but over the top.

Thunder roared in her ears, and lights flashed all around the cabin.

Alex shouted her name, then he collapsed on top of her. She welcomed the weight that crushed him to her. When he rolled over and held her by the shoulders, she buried her head between his chin and his shoulder. She clung to him, tears running down her face, unwilling to let go. Unwilling to face reality. Unwilling to end it. Because it had to end.

The realization of what she'd done, of what *they'd* done, hit Jane with the force of a hurricane. She pulled away from Alex and got to her feet, shivering wildly, her skin breaking out in goose bumps everywhere. She grabbed her clothes while he lay there watching her, and ran to the stateroom without a backward glance. Words were not necessary. If the guilt hadn't hit him yet, it would.

A minute later he was standing in the doorway of the stateroom, his pants riding low on his hips, his chest still bare. He rubbed his chin thoughtfully, watching her dress silently. She didn't bother with underwear, she just yanked her shirt over her head and pulled on a pair of drawstring pants she found at the bottom of Sofia's suitcase.

"What's this about?" he asked. "Your running away like that."

"As if you don't know," she said bitterly. "This is about you and me and Sofia."

"How do you feel?"

"Sick. Awful. How do you think I feel, after I've had sex with my best friend's fiancé? How do *you* feel?"

"Pretty damn good," Alex said, not even bothering to conceal his smile.

She shook her head vehemently. "You do not. You're mad at Sofia, you're angry and hurt and now you're guilty, so . . ."

He grabbed her by the shoulders. "Don't tell me

how I feel or why I did what I did," Alex said, his smile gone. "There's something between you and me. There always was, and there always will be. Don't deny it." His blue eyes burned hot and steady. She couldn't take the heat and she wouldn't admit he was right, so she looked away.

"It doesn't matter," she said. "We had no right—"

"What about Sofia? Did she have the right to run away with some other guy? Does she have the right to make her parents worry, to make us comb the Aegean looking for her?"

She shook him off. "She's your fiancée, she's my best friend," she said, her voice rising.

"Jane," he said quietly, "I know who she is. I know who you are, too. Maybe what we did was wrong—"

"Maybe? *Maybe?*"

"Are you saying you're sorry it happened?" he asked, his voice sober, his eyes deep and dark.

"No. Yes. I don't know. All I know is that we have to forget it happened. And never let it happen again."

"I'm not going to forget," Alex said. There was no way he could do that. He'd been stupid in the past. He'd thought if there was something between them, he would have noticed it long ago. He *had* noticed but he'd dismissed it, because of Sofia. When Sofia was around, no one noticed Jane—not even him. But that was when he was young and immature.

What would happen when Sofia reappeared? Would Jane fade into the background?

Not after today. Not in his mind. He was a different person from the guy who fell for Sofia ten years ago. A lifetime ago.

His whole body was thrumming with contentment, satisfaction, and total sexual fulfillment. Jane had been his friend; she was now his lover, and so much more.

But how did he fit into her plans? Was he just another man on her long list of conquests? All she could talk about was her guilt, but was that just an excuse to let him down easily?

What would he do about Sofia? What would happen when he saw her? Why didn't he feel as guilty as Jane did? Was it because he had no morals, no loyalty, and no scruples? Was this just about sex? The best sex he'd ever had?

The pain in his head came back with a vengeance. Alex tasted blood on his lip. He'd survive this accident, but would he survive what had followed? That was *no* accident. That was meant to happen.

"I'm going to the galley and make something for us to eat. I can't think on an empty stomach," Jane said.

"What do you want to think about?"

Alex didn't want to think. He just wanted to sit down and watch Jane get dressed or cook or whatever it was she was doing. She fascinated him, intrigued him, and turned him on with the most ordinary movements. He couldn't explain it, didn't even want to try. All he wanted was to bask in the afterglow for a few minutes, and to share it with Jane.

"I need to think about what happened to you," she said as he followed her to the galley. "Before," she added pointedly.

"Oh, that." For a moment he'd almost forgotten about his alleged concussion.

Jane cracked eggs into a bowl while he sat and watched, memorizing her every movement as if he might not see her again.

"Yes, that. I don't know why the guy would hit you, unless he has Sofia and doesn't want you to find her," she said, as if they hadn't been making love just minutes ago.

Did it really mean that little to her? Was that how she managed to go through all those men in her life? By putting them aside to crack eggs?

"Or maybe he's just what he seems," Alex said, trying to match her nonchalance. "An ordinary fisherman who doesn't like being accosted by strangers. Maybe he'd had a bad day. Maybe he blames me and all Americans for the bad catch this season. We could go on and on about this, but nothing makes any sense—so let's talk about something else." *Like you and me. Like what we're going to do about what happened.*

"But I'm telling you that was the guy from the dress shop." Jane beat the eggs ferociously while she proceeded to tell him about the shop and the clothes, all over again. Her words blurred together in his head. It all added up to a big nothing, as far as he was concerned. When she started describing the clothes, he exhaled and impatiently told her to get to the point. She stopped abruptly and glared at him.

"The clothes are the point," she said. "They're clues to where Sofia is going. They're clues to whether this really was Sofia or not."

"If you say so. I don't see how women can get so excited about what they wear. What difference does it make? Take the nudist beach."

A flush crept up her cheeks. He didn't know anyone who was approaching thirty and who blushed anymore. Especially after tossing her clothes off and making passionate love a few minutes before. Instead of shutting up about it because it embarrassed her, it only made him want to elaborate, just to make his point.

"As you saw from the people at the beach, if you're not wearing clothes, you have no hang-ups about class or status or anything. It levels the playing field and saves everybody a lot of money. People are accepted for what they are, not what they wear. They let it all hang out."

He grinned at her, hoping to elicit a smile. He didn't.

"Metaphorically speaking," he added. "Isn't that a better system?"

"I don't know." She sighed. "I'm only telling you so you can have a say in where we go next."

"A say?" He choked on the bourbon he'd brought in with him. "I may have been brain damaged back there, but I have more than a say."

Jane didn't seem to notice his reaction. She persisted in acting as if she hadn't made love with him only minutes before. Did it really mean nothing to her?

"I vote for the castle, because Sofia is more the castle type," she said. "Then, if she's not there, we go to the cave."

"We'll talk about it in the morning." Alex wasn't in the mood to argue with her. He was reaching the point of oversaturation. Too many words, too few strokes.

"You're not going to put me off so easily," she said. "You can't go to bed yet. You need some food. I'll have this omelet ready in a minute. Just sit tight."

Like he could do anything else? He was in a half-waking state, satiated, shaky, and overstimulated.

In the back of her mind, Jane knew the Leonakises would be happy to know they were getting some use out of the food they'd stocked on the yacht. She turned out two perfect omelets onto two plates, then took the seat across from Alex at the small table. He looked around at the built-in refrigerator, four-burner stove, and small freezer, as if he were trying to figure out where this food had come from. She was afraid he really had been brain damaged. When he took a bite of omelet and chewed slowly, she relaxed a little.

"Look what you have to look forward to when you're married. Greek food every night," she said with forced good cheer, trying to act as if this were a normal dinner.

What had happened to her moral code? She'd just performed the ultimate sin—screwing her best friend's fiancé—and she was going to rot in hell.

"How do you figure? Sofia can't cook."

"Maybe not now, because she has no reason to. But she has all the recipes, and sooner or later she'll get homesick for her mother's cooking."

"You mean her mother's cook's cooking," Alex said.

Jane studied his face, watching while his lip swelled more by the minute. She should never have kissed him that way; she'd made it worse. She'd made *everything* worse. But she couldn't turn her back on him, either. She loved him. She always would.

"It's your lip," she said. "Does it still hurt?"

"You know what to do to make it feel better."

"Please, Alex." She jumped up to clear the table. "It was my fault that you got hit." She stood at the sink, her back to him. She didn't trust herself to look him in the eye. "It was my fault for trying to make you feel better. I take full responsibility for what happened here tonight. We have to agree that we'll go to our graves with this secret. It shouldn't . . . it won't make any difference. It was a mistake, that's all."

"Hey," he said, getting up and putting his hands on her hips. His breath was warm on the back of her neck, and the warmth of his hands made her want nothing more than to grab his hands and hold on. "I'm not sorry. How can I be? And you're not responsible for it. I am." He let out a long breath, and she wanted to turn and put her arms around him.

She straightened her shoulders. "We have to call Nikos and Apollonia."

"I know. We can't put it off any longer."

"Oh, God." She buried her face in her hands. "What will we say? You won't mention how you got hit, will you?" *Or what we just did here.*

"There's no point. What about the scene at the dress shop?"

She shook her head, and they sat down again and stared off into space together, trying to summon the courage to call. Then the phone rang. Jane jumped out of her seat to reach the cell phone anchored to the wall. "It's them. It's got to be them." She picked up the phone.

"Nikos," she said, her heart hammering, "have you had any word?"

"Sofia called us," he said.

"What . . . what did she say?" She looked at Alex and nodded.

Alex stood and leaned against her, his shoulder pressing against Jane's arm as he tried to listen in.

"She said not to worry about her. She's fine," Nikos said.

"But . . . but where is she? When is she coming back?"

"I don't know. It was a bad connection. She said something about a cave, whatever that meant. What about you? Have you had any luck?"

Jane turned to Alex. *The cave,* she mouthed. He nodded and took the phone from her hand.

"Nikos, it's Alex. We have some idea of where she is. Or at least where she was. We're taking off from Andros tomorrow. How did she sound? . . . That's good. How are you and Apollonia? . . . Of course you're worried, but you know she's alive and well. . . . She said that? If she's able to phone you and tell you she's going to a cave, then she's okay, more than okay. . . . Oh, that doesn't mean anything, just wedding jitters. Everyone gets them. . . . For Jane? I'll tell her. Okay, we'll call you tomorrow."

He hung up and sat down at the table, his face propped in his hands. The color was drained from his face, making his eyes look darker and bigger, his cheekbones standing out. His broad shoulders sagged and he looked so bereft, Jane wanted to put her arms around him. But that would just lead to more complications.

Jane went to the stove to make coffee. She was waiting for him to tell her what they'd said, but Alex didn't speak for a long moment.

Finally he looked up. "That smells good," he said with a half-smile that quickly faded.

She heaped a few spoonfuls of powdered creamer in his cup and filled it with coffee.

"Nikos said the connection was bad, but he heard her say that she was fine and that she didn't want anyone to go looking for her. She'd be back when she was ready to come back."

"She doesn't mean that," Jane said quickly.

"How do you know?"

"I know her. She's doing this to punish you. It's so obvious. She wants you to come and get her."

"That's not all she wants. She wants me to forget about working for myself. She wants me to stay with the company."

"I'm sure once you explain it to her—"

"I have explained it to her. She's made it clear; if I want her back, I have to forget my plans."

"You can't do that," Jane said. "There's got to be a way to compromise."

He shook his head.

If Sofia were there, Jane would have taken her by the shoulders and shaken her. Didn't she realize how much Alex loved her? And how much his career meant to him? Wasn't she willing to make a sacrifice for him?

Jane knew the answers. They were no, no, and no.

Alex got up from the table and put his coffee cup in the sink. "Anyway, we know where to go tomorrow. I'm going to turn in."

"You take the stateroom," she said. "You need a good night's sleep."

"I'm fine in the lounge." He braced his hand against the counter. "The message for you was that some man called you and wants you to call him. I didn't catch his name."

"I know who it is." She didn't want to call Warren. He'd ask her if she'd thought about his proposal, and she was in no state to think about it.

"You said there was someone special."

"Did I?" she said absently.

"You've forgotten already? What about him, does he know about your past?"

"What—" She almost said, What past? But she caught herself just in time. "What business is it of yours?" she said.

"How can you ask, after what happened between us? You are my business, whether you like it or not." His blue eyes blazed. "And I'm yours. If you're worried about my telling him about anything, including what happened here, you don't need to."

"There's no chance of you telling him anything. When we get back, you'll be in Seattle, I'll be in San Francisco. Everything that happened here will be long in the past. We're not going to see each other."

"Ever?" he asked incredulously.

"What's the point?" Obviously he thought he could handle it. For her, it would be impossible. Seeing him with Sofia would be excruciatingly painful. He wouldn't understand that. This thing that happened between her and Alex was about sex and lust and guilt and retribution. It was a way of getting back at Sofia for hurting him. She understood that, even if he didn't.

"It's not that far," he insisted. "We'll come and see you. Sofia will insist, and as you know . . ."

"Whatever Sofia wants . . ."

"Sofia gets."

His smiled didn't look happy. "Good night, Jane."

All Jane wanted to do was to follow him back to

the lounge and fall asleep in his arms. To soothe that swollen lip, to make him feel better about Sofia and his job and his life. But that was Sofia's job. When they found her, she'd do what she had to do, including accepting Alex's decision to leave the company.

The door closed behind him, and Jane cleared the table and filled the sink with hot water and soap. She stood for a long time staring at the dishes, already planning her excuses.

"Sorry, Sofia, I'm busy this weekend. Sorry, Sofia, I'd love to get together, but I have the flu. Sorry, Sofia, I can't come up for the baby's christening, I'm having a triple bypass."

Hot tears stung her eyes as she thought of what she'd have to endure, all because she'd given in to her impulses.

Maybe they should just go back to Mios and wait for Sofia to come home. Obviously she was okay. Why should they go off to some cave looking for her? Jane hated to think of Alex giving in to her, but maybe she'd do the same thing under those circumstances. He loved Sofia and he didn't want to live without her. Jane knew she couldn't marry anyone until she felt that way about him. She'd have to tell Warren. Maybe this was a good time to call him.

She washed and dried the dishes, rubbing them so hard she was afraid she'd erase the blue anchors on the white plates. When she put them back in the cupboard, she admired the matching anchors etched on the glasses. Everything on the boat was first-class. By marrying Sofia, Alex's life would always be first class. But that wasn't what attracted him to Sofia; he was much too honest to marry for money. She remembered the first day he'd seen Sofia—he looked as if he'd been struck by lightning. Sofia had that effect on people.

Jane went to the stateroom and unpacked her new clothes. She laid them on the white quilt with the eagle appliqued in red and the border of red stars, and felt a pang of buyer's remorse. On top of all that guilt. Where on earth was she ever going to wear clothes like these? She didn't need them to find Sofia. She didn't need them back home. She never went to clubs, discos, or parties. And she never went to balls, either.

She ran her fingers over the purple sweater and heard the woman say, "It's your color." Well, she'd bought them and she'd keep them. It wasn't likely she'd be doing the cha-cha or the tango, but if they went to the castle to find Sofia-who-didn't-want-to-be-found, she'd at least fit in. If they hiked up to a cave to find her, she had the capri pants, the thick-soled rope sandals, and the white shirt that would reflect the sun.

She didn't want to wear one of Sofia's slinky trousseau gowns to bed. Those were the gowns Alex would peel off of her before they made passionate love in this very bed.

She went through Sofia's suitcase and found a long, ribbed cotton T-shirt that was stretchy, clung to her body, and hit her mid-thigh. It was better than the negligee and besides, who was going to see her in it?

She had a little silent conversation with Sofia, during which Sofia assured her she was welcome to anything in the suitcase.

"You don't think it's too tight?" Jane asked.

"Who's going to see you? Anyway, it's about time you wore something that showed off your body," Sofia said. *"You have nothing to be ashamed of. I've been meaning to tell you you've turned into a knockout. What are you worried about?"*

What was she worried about? *Oh, Sofia, if you only knew.* But she would never know.

In the middle of her reverie, Alex knocked on her door.

"Jane?"

When she opened the door, he rocked back on his bare heels. She should have thrown on the terry-cloth robe from the bathroom, but it was too late now.

He stood there in his boxers, staring at her, his chest and his legs bare. No matter how awful he looked and felt, he took her breath away. But his eyes were bloodshot. He looked as if he'd just woken up or hadn't slept at all. His face was pale. She balled her hands into fists to keep from reaching out to him.

"What's wrong? Do you need a pain pill?" she asked.

"If you have one. Of course you do."

She went to her purse, shook out two orange

pills, and put them in his hand. A spark of electricity leaped from her hand to his. She jumped. The air crackled.

Walking across the carpet must have caused the spark. Shivers ran up and down her skin. It was nothing, she told herself. When the air was dry, the sparks flew. "Static charge," she explained. "It happens all the time."

"I guess I missed that lecture. So it even happens with bare feet?" he asked, his eyes boring holes in hers.

"It's unusual, yes, but it happens." Her voice was calm, while inside she was shaking. "I'll get you some water." She went to the head and came back with a glass of water, careful not to brush against his hand. She was still trembling from the last encounter.

He tossed the pills down and chased them with the water. "Thanks." He left and she breathed a sigh of relief.

"Wait," she said and opened the door. "Why don't you sleep here? You'll be more comfortable."

"I'm fine out there."

"You don't look fine."

"You sure do. What is that thing?" He raked her over with his sharp blue gaze.

"This?" She fingered the edge of the T-shirt that brushed her thighs. "It's a . . . shirt."

"Are you going somewhere?"

"No, of course not. I suppose I could wear it out, but—"

"I wouldn't advise it," he said dryly.

"I won't. I'm going to bed."

He nodded, then again his hooded gaze meandered over the T-shirt that covered her from her throat to her thighs. A shudder went through her whole body, and her nipples tightened.

When he finally left, Jane collapsed on the bed and hung her head over the edge, the blood rushing to her head. Maybe this would help clear her brain of runaway lust.

A few minutes later Alex stuck his head in the door without knocking.

"Who's Warren?"

Chapter 10

Jane rolled over on the bed and sat up so suddenly, her head felt like a bobblehead. She pushed her hair out of her face.

"Warren? He's a friend. Why?"

"He called a few minutes ago. Must be a good friend, to track you down out here."

"Why didn't you tell me?"

"I am telling you," Alex said irritably. "It was a bad connection, so he wants you to call him. You might have better luck with this if you go out on deck." He handed her the cell phone.

She was in no condition to have a conversation with Warren. She didn't know what to say to him. But she didn't want to hurt his feelings by not calling, either. Maybe she'd luck out and have trouble getting through. She went to her purse to find her international calling card. When she looked up, Alex was still standing in the doorway.

"Change your mind? Want to sleep here?" she asked.

He shook his head.

"Then what do you want?" she asked.

"You don't want to know," he said ominously.

No, she didn't want to know why he was standing there looking at her with that faraway look on his face. If he was hurting, if he was having trouble thinking, why didn't he go back to bed and stop staring at her? She was already self-conscious enough in this T-shirt.

He stood aside while she brushed by him in the narrow doorway and she caught a whiff of coffee on his breath and soap on his skin. She almost got by, but before she did, his hand snaked out and grabbed her around the waist.

"Alex," she whispered as he pulled her tight against him. "Don't."

He dropped his arms and immediately she was sorry. She was cold and alone. She didn't have to be; she could wrap her arms around him and pull him into the stateroom and into bed with her. She could sleep in his arms all night long. And in the morning, what then? She'd just feel worse.

She had to stop now, while she still could. She grabbed the worry beads Kostos had given her and marched up the steps. Alex followed her to the deck.

She took a plaid blanket and wrapped it around

her shoulders, then sat in a deck chair and propped her feet against the railing. She had the phone in one hand and the worry beads in the other, waiting for Alex to go below. The waves lapped against the hull and the bouzouki music wafted over the water from the land. Alex stood at the railing, illuminated by the bright moon, facing the brightly lit tavernas on shore. The water in the harbor shimmered with the reflections of the open-air seaside restaurants and bars.

Was Alex thinking he should be on shore looking for Sofia? No doubt he was thinking how different it would be when he was dancing with Sofia in one of those tavernas on his honeymoon. She hated for him to be out here watching and not doing, thinking of what he was missing. She hoped he wasn't picturing Sofia out there somewhere in her peach dress, dancing with that tall fisherman. Jane could picture it only too well, but that was because she had such an active imagination. It allowed her to picture a lot of things that weren't true, like all those men in her past.

She got up and stood next to Alex at the railing and clicked her beads.

"Worried?" he asked with a glance at her hand. "You shouldn't be. She'll soon be on her way back home. And you know what will happen when she gets there: Nikos and Apollonia will welcome her with open arms, no matter what anguish she's caused them."

"You're probably right." There was a long silence.

Jane fingered the buttons on the cell phone. She didn't want Alex to hear any of her conversation, however bland and boring. Knowing him, he'd have something to say about it.

"Shouldn't you be in bed?" she asked him.

"I should. So should you." He paused to let the meaning of his words sink in. She wrapped her arms around her waist and squeezed her eyes shut tight.

"Go ahead," he said. "Make your call. Don't worry, I won't listen." He inhaled loudly. "I think the air out here is doing me some good. Clearing my head."

She walked across the deck as far from Alex as possible, leaned against the far railing, and punched in the access code, the country code, and Warren's number.

"What's going on?" Warren asked. "Where are you?"

"I'm out on the Leonakises' boat. It's a beautiful evening. Maybe you can hear the music from shore." She held the phone up.

"Who was that who answered the phone?"

"That was Alex, Sofia's fiancé." Jane was very conscious of Alex, even though he was ten feet away with his face half in shadow, his bare shoulder half turned toward her.

"Is it a big boat?" Warren asked.

It was too small. Way too small for two people who shouldn't be doing what they were doing. "It's very nice, very luxurious," she said.

"How's the wedding going? Sofia's mother sounded rattled."

"Did she?" Jane wondered how much Apollonia had told Warren about what had happened. Hopefully nothing. "Well, it's quite a production. Everything has to be done by the book, and it's a big book. How's everything back there?" She hoped he'd say fine and hang up, but he didn't. He talked about his patients. He was very popular with the kids whose teeth he straightened. Another plus—besides earning a good living, he was good with kids. But right now Jane was not in the mood to hear about overbites and malocclusions and problems with lost or broken retainers or the cute things the kids said. Warren had told her often what a good listener she was, but right now she was only half listening and half daydreaming. She shifted from one foot to the other, sat in a deck chair, and crossed and uncrossed her legs. The music, the lights, the sound of the waves, and the knowledge that Alex was leaning against the brass railing, made it hard to pay attention.

And right now she wanted someone to listen to *her*. If only Sofia were here. Sofia always had good advice when it came to men. What would she say if she was just Jane's best friend and not Alex's fiancée?

She'd say she understood. Alex was an attractive man and hey, Sofia was off doing her own thing, so go for it, Jane. Tell him how you feel. Tell him you've always loved him. Take advantage of the situation. You don't have much more time; what have you got to lose?

What *did* she have to lose by telling him how she felt about him, even assuming Sofia was out of the picture, which she wasn't? Only his friendship. Only her self-respect.

Jane could just imagine the look on his face if she told him she'd been in love with him since that day in chemistry class, when he'd grabbed the beaker out of her hands and shielded her from the fumes billowing from it. Then he'd taken the blame for the explosion that blew him across the room. She'd thought he'd felt something for her, then, too.

If she told him that, first his jaw would drop. When he recovered, he'd be kind and sympathetic. She didn't want his sympathy. She wanted to forget him. If she'd known how long this trip would last, how they'd be thrown together, that they'd make love in the honeymoon suite, she never would have come. She would have stayed behind to comfort the Leonakises, the way Alex wanted her to.

She told herself to shape up. She'd had ample time to get over him. More than ample.

"I have to go now, Warren. It's late and I'm keeping the others awake."

"Give my best to Sofia," Warren said. "And come back soon. I miss you."

Jane mumbled something and hung up.

She should leave the deck, go down to the stateroom, and go to bed. The boat was rocking gently, but it didn't make her sleepy. She was wide awake and restless. She couldn't take her eyes off of Alex, his half-naked body outlined by the moonlight. It was almost worse than seeing him totally naked downstairs, or at the beach in the sunlight. Why didn't he go down and go to bed? He was the one who'd been injured.

"How's Warren?" Alex asked.

"Fine."

"You didn't tell him why we're out here in the middle of the Aegean."

"I didn't want to go into the whole thing with Sofia. It's so hard to explain."

"And so hard to understand," he said. "He wouldn't be jealous, would he?"

"Of you? Of course not. He knows we're old friends."

"He knows about me?"

"He knows Sofia, and he knows about the wedding, so of course he knows about you."

"Are you going to tell him what happened here?"

"Of course not." Her face flamed, but he wouldn't notice in the dark. "I'm not going to tell Sofia, either."

It bothered Alex to think this Warren wasn't jealous of him. Didn't the man realize how sexy Jane was? And how dangerous it was to let her loose on a boat in the Aegean with a man who wasn't married—yet?

Normally it might work—two people thrown together in an awkward situation, two people of the opposite sex, with normal sexual drives, on a small boat together. But these were not normal conditions. He and Jane had a past.

He could only hope that tomorrow he'd be back to normal; rational and focused on finding his bride. Tonight there was nothing he could do but stand here at the railing and listen to the waves hitting the shore and look at Jane in the shadows, and try not to think of how she looked when she climaxed and how she sounded and how she felt when she collapsed in his arms.

He knew one thing: if Jane was *his* girlfriend he wouldn't want her out on a yacht with another man, even if that man was due to get married in three days. Not that he wouldn't trust her. He just wouldn't trust any guy around her.

"Why haven't I met your boyfriend yet?" he asked.

"Duh—you live in Seattle and he lives in San Francisco. Also, he works long hours."

"Maybe you don't want me to meet him. You're either ashamed of me, or of him. Or you're afraid I'll tell all your secrets, is that it? Don't worry, your past is safe with me."

Jane stood, and he thought she would make some retort and go down to bed, but instead she walked over to the railing where he stood.

"I hope I can count on your discretion," she said, bracing her arms on the top railing, and brushing his arm with hers. "And I don't just mean what happened here. I'm talking about my past. I've told you some things I haven't told anyone else."

He leaned toward her so he could see her face in

the moonlight. "You haven't told me what you and the social director did after the midnight buffet."

She smiled. Anything to avoid talking about the two of them. "You mean after we'd had drinks at the piano bar and they'd played my favorite song?"

"Which is?"

" 'For the Longest Time.' "

"That Billy Joel song?"

"Yes."

"Did you go to the concert he did on campus?" he asked.

"Of course. I had a huge crush on him. I have all of his records."

"Do you still?"

"Have the records or the crush?"

"Either."

"Yes, I do," she said.

"Go on," Alex said.

"About Billy Joel?"

"About the social director. What happened next?"

"You want to know what happened after we closed down the casino and the disco? You mean back in my cabin?"

"That's exactly what I mean." Even in the semi-darkness, he could see her eyes sparkle and the smile that played on her lips. "That must have been quite a night," he said dourly.

"It was. I'll never forget it."

He closed the gap between them. "Well?"

"All I can say is that he couldn't go to work the next day."

"What about you?"

"The next day I got up to play bridge with my aunt and we won the game."

"I was hoping to hear some details."

Jane grinned. "She opened with two hearts and I doubled."

"That's not what I mean," he said.

"I know what you mean, but Alex, some things are sacred."

"A one-night stand with a social director is sacred?" he asked, incredulous.

"Did I say it was only one night?"

"I guess not."

"That's enough," she said with a sigh. "Don't worry. I usually don't kiss and tell. It's just that tonight has been . . ."

"Yeah, I know what you mean." With one finger he traced the outline of her cheek, then he kissed her beneath her ear. "It has been."

"I've talked too much," she said, feeling her blood heat up again and race through her veins. "I forgot what a good listener you are."

"That's all?" he asked. "That's the best you can do for my ego?"

He couldn't be fishing. Not Alex. He was full of confidence. Still, there was something almost wistful in his tone.

"That's not all, and you know it," she said. "Your ego doesn't need any stroking."

Maybe his ego didn't need any stroking, but another part of him was in major need. He said good night and watched her walk away in that shirt that was more provocative than no clothes at all, the way it hugged her butt when she walked. All he could think of was her body underneath it.

It was bad enough before he'd made love to her; then he had only his fantasies. Now he had reality to contend with. The very real memories of making love to her in the stateroom. The music, the air, the smell of her skin, the taste of her lips. Memories he wouldn't be able to put aside the way she seemed to do.

Thinking of Jane in her cabin on her cruise ship with a stranger made him feel as if his head were going to explode. He dragged himself down the stairs to the torture chamber that was the lounge, and tried to sleep on the cushions that by dawn felt like marble slabs.

The next day everything was worse but his head. His impatience to find Sofia, his anger at her, the pressure she put on him to stay at her father's company, and the way he felt about Jane, all combined to make him snap at her when she asked him how he was feeling.

"Fine, I'm just fine. Can we forget about what happened last night? I mean . . . I don't mean . . . I mean when I got punched. So I fell and hit my head. I'm not an invalid."

"Sorry," she said. "Can I make you some coffee?"

"No coffee. I'm already strung out."

"I noticed."

"We have to get going. We've already wasted too

much time sightseeing and socializing. If we hadn't gone to that dive—"

"I thought you didn't want to talk about it."

"That's right." He jabbed the key in the ignition, started the engine, and drowned out Jane's voice. He knew what she'd said . . . "But where are we going?" And he had no answer. He just knew they couldn't stay there any longer.

In a few minutes they'd docked at the pier and tied up. They got out while the boat was serviced. Jane took the opportunity to take a straw basket from the galley and go shopping for food. When she got back, Alex was watching the operator fill their fuel tank.

A workman in blue overalls stopped and spoke to her. "You are from Mios?" he asked with a glance at the hull of the boat.

"Yes, why?" she said.

"Another boat from Mios was here this morning. A fishing boat."

Alex whirled around. "Was there a woman on board?" he asked.

He nodded. "A beautiful woman."

Alex clenched his jaw. "Where did they go from here?"

"They asked about the route to the island of Kellia. I told him there is no good fishing there. He laughed and said he is not fishing today. Women don't like fishing."

Jane took Alex's arm and pulled him aside. "Kellia Island has that cave the woman in the shop told me about. She said that Sofia, if it is Sofia, was buying clothes to hike to the Koreas Cave. And then her parents said she was going to a cave."

"They also said she told us to ask the oracle, which led to nothing," he reminded her. "And Sofia doesn't hike. Even if she did, why would she hike to a cave?"

"It's a beautiful area and supposedly there are ancient relics inside."

"Sofia doesn't like ancient relics, unless she can wear them around her neck," he said.

"I know—but how many beautiful women are sailing around in fishing boats from Mios that are not being used for fishing? Do you have a better idea?"

He shook his head. "Let's go."

They didn't talk about Sofia or anything until they were out on the water sitting at the controls. Alex's face was shaded by a cap with a logo written in Greek on the brim. He was wearing wraparound sunglasses and he looked like he was exactly where he belonged, on a yacht sailing through the Greek Islands. No one would guess he was beside himself with worry about his fiancée. Maybe he was feeling reassured by the phone call from the Leonakises last night, knowing that Sofia was all right.

Jane wished she had a picture of him just the way he looked at that moment—sexy and romantic, every woman's fantasy. Though she'd have to tear it up and throw it away; it was bad enough to have the image engraved on her brain.

Jane fastened a large-brimmed straw hat of Sofia's under her chin and unfolded the map. The sun was dazzling, and the water was so clear she could see the fish swimming along the bottom. If they were there under different circumstances, she'd think she was in heaven. Warm sun, clear skies, smooth sailing, and Alex next to her in a wrinkled polo shirt, shorts and flip-flops, the hat and the sunglasses, his bad mood of this morning apparently gone.

She reached into her shopping basket, pulled out two *tiropita*—flaky turnovers filled with feta cheese—and handed him one.

When he'd finished eating it, he leaned back in the captain's chair and rested his hands on the steering wheel. "I've been thinking of changing my plans and continuing to work for Nikos. That's what Nikos wants; that's what Sofia wants. If she gets word I've changed my mind, she'll come back."

Jane's heart sank. "Oh, no, you can't do that."

"Why not?"

"I thought you hated it."

He shook his head. "I never said that. I'd rather work for myself, but if it means losing Sofia . . ."

Jane's heart plummeted. That had nothing to do with his goal of finding Sofia, though. She was just worried about him giving up his goal.

"But it's your dream. You'd give up your dream?" She knew the answer to that. Yes, he would. He loved Sofia that much. Her heart felt like it was being squeezed by her ribs.

"I thought you'd be on her side," he said with a glance in her direction.

"I'm not on anyone's side," she said. "I love you both." He didn't say anything. "Why don't you think it over?"

"Why don't you go back on deck and get some sun?" he suggested.

She got the message: *I don't want to hear any more of your ideas. I've made up my mind. It wasn't an easy decision, but I made it. Now go away and leave me alone. I don't want to think about last night and every time I see you, I'm reminded of what we did.*

So she took her basket of food to the galley and put everything away, then she went to the state-room and changed into Sofia's white strapless bikini and slathered herself with sunscreen. She remembered when Sofia bought the suit and how sensational she looked in it. The stretch fabric conformed to Jane's body, and knowing Sofia, Jane was sure she would want her to wear it—no matter what Jane had done. Sofia was the most generous person in the world. Anybody who'd betray her had to be a total creep. And Jane didn't have to look in the mirror to know who that creep was. She also didn't have to look in the mirror to know that no one filled out a bikini like Sofia did. But Jane was just grateful to have a suit to wear. She looked in the mirror and mouthed *I'm sorry, Sofia. Thank you, Sofia.*

Up on deck, with her guidebook in hand, Jane stretched out on a deck chair where she couldn't see Alex and hopefully he couldn't see her.

If he was alone for a while, maybe he'd think it over and change his mind. He had to; it was emotional blackmail. *Change your mind and I'll come home. Otherwise . . .* What could Sofia do? Sail around on a fishing boat forever? Give Alex up? She would never do that. No, he couldn't give in.

The small green islands they passed, the blue sea so calm it was like glass, and the cloudless sky were all so beautiful it almost hurt her eyes to look at them. Was Sofia enjoying these same sights aboard a fishing boat? If so, were they just a few miles ahead of them or nowhere around at all?

Jane opened her book and read about the island they were going to, and the village on the lower slopes of the mountain where they would start their hike to reach the cave. She also read about the castle on Marmara and imagined Sofia leaning out of a tower, her long hair cascading over her shoulder. Who could resist her? Who was she traveling with?

With the guidebook in her lap, Jane pressed her fingers against her temples and forced herself to concentrate. "Where are you, Sofia?" she said. "Give me a sign." The wind riffled the pages of the book, and when Jane looked down it was open to the page that described the cave where Zeus was born. She closed the book. "Yes, I know. That's where we're going."

Alex knew he should call the Leonakises now, before he changed his mind. He had to get Sofia back in time for the wedding. He had to get her back because he loved her. He had to get her back before he lost his mind and did something really stupid, like giving in to his lust for Jane again.

Just when he had himself convinced that he had his body under control, Jane appeared in a white bikini, cut high on the hips with no straps on the top and no visible means of holding it in place. It was more provocative than her wearing nothing at the nudist beach. He was hit with a violent reaction in his groin and an immediate need to escape.

"Good," he said, jumping to his feet. "You can take over for me. I'm going to get a beer. Can I bring you something?"

"Some mineral water and the food from my basket. We can have a picnic up here."

She looked so enthusiastic, so cute with her sunburned nose, so sexy in that suit, he felt all his best intentions fade as fast as his dream of his own business. Of course he wasn't going to touch her, kiss her, or peel that suit off of her. He didn't need to do any of those things to be disloyal to Sofia. Just thinking about them was bad enough. To get over these urges and forget what they'd already done, he'd tease Jane, laugh at her, and above all, keep it light.

When he came back up on deck after spraying his head with a stream of cold water for a long, long time, she was gazing out to sea with the binoculars.

"Dolphins," she said. "I love them. Here, take a look."

When she handed him the binoculars, her fingers brushed his. Electricity arced through the air and traveled up his arm, and there was no good excuse except for the way her bikini revealed that her nipples were erect under the white fabric. Then there was his fear that the bandeau top would slip out of place, and he'd be subjected to yet another view of her bare breasts. That was enough to send his blood pressure up above 280.

He kept the binoculars fastened to his eyes, though he didn't see any dolphins. That way he wouldn't have to look at her and wonder what would happen if he told her he would never forget what had happened last night if he lived to be one hundred. Even if he married Sofia and they had ten children. He could never think of Jane as just a friend again, no matter how hard he tried. And worst of all, he'd do it all again if he could. Right now, at this very moment, he was having a hard time keeping his hands off of her.

Her chocolate brown eyes would widen, she'd blush, and maybe, if he was lucky, she'd just laugh it off. She had Warren and God only knew how many other men on the string. If she'd had as many men in her life as she said she had, Alex would just be another notch in her belt. She couldn't possibly feel the guilt he was feeling, because she wasn't getting married on Saturday. Saturday—tomorrow! They didn't have a moment to waste.

Jane was rustling around in the food basket. He put down the binoculars and took a bunch of grapes out of a paper sack. He'd intended to go back on deck with them but he was so comfortable just sitting there with her next to him, so relaxed in the silence between them, that he stayed there. Stayed and watched the sun glistening on the water, felt the warmth of the sun beat down on his shoulders.

From behind his sunglasses, he sneaked glances at Jane, watching her steer the boat and eat at the same time. Watching the *tzatziki* sauce from her chicken souvlaki dribble down her chin, he wondered if he should wipe it off with his finger. Or his mouth.

He had an unreasonable desire to take the pita bread out of her hands and kiss her pink lips again, just to see what she'd do about it this time. He was afraid she'd either slap him or kiss him back, and he didn't know which would be worse. Either way, he'd be in bigger trouble than he was now.

So he just sat there next to her, sharing a souvlaki and cucumber salad without talking. He thought of asking her how she felt about him, how she was dealing with what had happened between them, but deep down, he didn't want to know. She loved them both. Who did she love best? Sofia, of course.

He finished his food, drained his bottle of beer, and picked up the binoculars. "That must be it—Kellia. I see the mountains and a flat plateau."

"What about a cave?"

"We're a little far away for that."

"What about Sofia?"

He shook his head. She was joking. It wasn't possible to see her, and yet . . . and yet . . . he thought he did see her. Wearing knee-length shorts and stout boots, her hair tied back in a bandanna. She was bounding up the trail and she was holding hands with a tall man.

It couldn't be! Sofia didn't hike, she didn't wear hiking boots, and she never bounded anywhere, especially not with a strange man. What was wrong with him? Was this a dream or a nightmare or just wishful thinking? He put the binoculars in his lap and tilted his head back.

"What's wrong?" Jane asked, turning to face him. "You're having a relapse, aren't you?" She touched his mouth with her fingers, and a shudder went through his body and he gripped the edge of the captain's chair. She was only checking to see if his lip was swollen from last night; it meant nothing. *Forget it; she isn't going to kiss you.* But that didn't stop him from remembering how it felt to have her soft lips on his. She was so close, and yet so far.

"The swelling has gone down," she reported.

"Thanks for checking," he said dryly. Maybe the swelling of his mouth had gone down, but everything else was way, way up.

Chapter 11

The island of Kellia was smaller than Andros and not as popular with tourists. But it was beautiful in its own way, with the stark rocky mountains and the plateau in the distance. Along the harbor, bright red and white boats knocked against each other as fishermen repaired their nets. Alex didn't see any boats from Mios, and no one who resembled the man who'd punched him. And no women. No surprise there; women on fishing boats were supposed to be bad luck. But any man who had a chance to sail with Sofia would certainly be willing to overlook that superstition.

They tied up right at the dock. He'd changed into hiking shoes he found in a built-in locker below, probably belonging to Sofia's brother George, then he hung a water bottle from his belt and waited for Jane on the pier. When she came above deck, he held out his hand to steady her as she stepped over a stretch of water between the boat deck and the pier.

"Are you sure I shouldn't bring my purse?" She let go of his hand immediately, as if she was afraid she'd catch something from him. He didn't understand her. Sometimes she recoiled at his touch, other times she welcomed it—like when she touched his mouth, causing him a near meltdown. This was a hard time for both of them, thrown together in this mission impossible.

"No purse. We're going hiking," he said. "That thing weighs about fifty pounds. In a few miles you'll be listing to one side and asking me to carry it for you."

"No way," she said. "If real men don't get the jitters, I'm sure they don't carry purses. I wouldn't subject you to that."

"We're roughing it today. That means getting along without your sewing kit, your antiseptic lotion, and your medicine chest."

"Don't knock my medicine chest. You've benefited from it as much as I have."

"I'm hoping I won't have to benefit from it anymore."

"What do you think's going to happen when we get to the cave?" she asked, suddenly filled with doubts. "I mean, what if she isn't there?"

"Don't get your hopes up," he warned. "She may be nowhere near here at all."

"But we've come all this way."

"And we're going to see it through. At the very least, we'll have a look at a bunch of stalactites hanging from the ceiling and stalagmites jutting up from the floor."

"But what's going to happen?"

"We'll look around," he said shortly. "If Sofia's here, we'll take her home." He tried to picture Sofia in the cave, but he couldn't. She didn't like to walk much, let alone hike. So what the hell were they doing here? "First I'm going to walk around the dock and ask some questions."

"Okay, and I'll hit the shops along the waterfront. If Sofia came to this island, that's where she'd go first. And people tend to remember her."

Alex grimaced at the thought of Sofia strolling through the shops, as if she didn't have a care in the world, while they searched high and low for her. "I'll meet you back here in thirty minutes."

But thirty minutes later, he'd found out absolutely nothing. Nobody spoke English and nobody knew anything. Frustrated, he went back to the boat. Jane had had no luck, either.

"We'll go to the cave anyway. We're here. We're ready. I don't see us waiting around. Let's go."

Then he saw the donkeys along the harbor, laden with baskets of oranges, stepping around Gypsies selling strings of garlic. Gypsies who reminded him of Sofia, with their olive skin, their dark eyes and their red cheeks. Suddenly he could picture Sofia astride a donkey, looking like an advertisement for the department of tourism, her bracelets jangling, her drawstring blouse hanging over one shoulder.

She wouldn't walk so why should we? If she wanted to get somewhere, she'd hire a donkey. Let's see if we can rent donkeys.

He stopped and bought a sack of oranges, then he asked one of the vendors about getting donkeys to take them to the cave. The man didn't speak much English, but when Alex drew a picture of a cave on a scrap of paper and pantomimed riding a donkey, the man smiled broadly and mentioned a sum of money that seemed reasonable. Alex pointed to Jane and the man nodded.

While they waited for their donkeys to be fitted with saddles, Alex wondered again what the hell they were doing there. The chances of Sofia actually being on this island, actually riding a donkey to a cave, were minuscule. Why didn't they just go back to Mios and wait for her to come home? He'd send her the message that he'd do whatever she wanted—and if that didn't bring her back, nothing would.

So why hadn't he done it before? Why hadn't he called the Leonakises and told them what to tell her? Maybe he'd thought she'd give in first. He should know better; she wouldn't. She'd hold out until she got what she wanted. She always did; she always would. Was this something he could live with for the rest of his life? It was a hell of a time to ask himself that question, but better late than never.

A few minutes later they'd mounted their donkeys and were on their way. No more time to think about the rest of his life. For this he was grateful.

Alex didn't realize they'd hired a guide along with the donkeys, but he soon realized that they needed one. There were no signs pointing "To the cave." There were no other donkeys or hikers headed that way. They rode along the trail, passing graceful pink-and-white houses that marched up the steep hillside. Little children came running out to call "hello" and wave excitedly. There couldn't be many tourists on this path. That was good, in terms of seeing the real Greek countryside, but in terms of finding Sofia, it was bad.

They rode single file on the narrow path, with Jane between the guide and Alex.

"How do they know we're American?" She swiveled her head toward him and waved to the children. "It can't be my clothes; I bought them yesterday."

"Maybe it's your hair," he said noting the blond strands that escaped from her hat, more blond now from the sun than when he first saw her on the ferry. "Ever ridden a donkey before?" he asked as he watched her lurch back and forth, her back and shoulders taut and stiff.

"No, why? Does it show, my lack of experience?"

"Just relax and go with the flow."

"Like you have experience donkey riding?"

"It's like a horse," he said. "If you don't loosen up, you'll be stiff tonight. I'm surprised none of your boyfriends has taken you riding."

"Too slow, I guess," she said as the donkeys ambled up the trail and she rocked back and forth in her saddle. "My boyfriends are into speed. Motorcycles, fast cars . . ."

"Planes?"

"Definitely. One had a Lear jet. We flew everywhere in it. Acapulco, Cancun, Key West."

"What about Warren?"

"He doesn't have a plane."

"Fast car?"

"Not really."

"What does he have?"

"A good job."

"As . . . ?"

"A Navy SEAL."

He whistled through his teeth. "Isn't that dangerous?"

"It must be. He's not allowed to talk about what he does. It's top secret."

"I'm impressed."

"I thought you would be."

"Sofia never mentioned it."

"I told her not to."

"He must be gone a lot, on assignment. Sneaking around in some dangerous outpost, diving down and setting off explosives under enemy ships."

"I can't say."

"Because you're sworn to secrecy?"

"If he told me, he'd have to kill me."

"Hmmm."

They rode in silence for a long time. Compared

to a Navy SEAL, an architect must seem pretty boring. On the other hand, when the Navy SEAL was gone on these secret missions, Jane would be alone much of the time.

Unanswered questions buzzed around Alex's brain. Did she mind being alone? What did she do with her time? She couldn't be going out with other men, could she? What kind of arrangement did they have? Was she really serious about this guy?

He watched her getting more comfortable in the saddle, her shoulders sloping and her butt moving with the animal. They were climbing now: the trail was rocky and the donkeys stumbled from time to time. Jane was looking at the sky. She raised her hand and pointed to a large bird circling overhead, then shouted something he couldn't understand.

The guide turned and smiled at them. Alex wondered where in hell this cave was. Did their guide really know, or did he just take their money and was taking them nowhere?

There were grassy fields filled with sheep on both sides of the trail, and workers who stopped repairing their fences to stare and wave at the strange trio. Were they the only tourists who'd ever come this way? Was there really a cave somewhere?

Five or six out-of-work windmills stood forlornly on the hills, their cylindrical shapes stark white against the sky. The whole scene was so elemental Alex felt as if they were not only the first tourists to come this way, but the first Greeks who'd discovered the cave.

He rocked back and forth in his saddle, lulled into a pleasant stupor by the motion, by the afternoon sun, and the sight of Jane riding in front of him. When their guide yelled and waved his arm, he sat up straight and looked around. They'd come to the ridge of the mountain. They stopped their donkeys and got off. Jane let out a long sigh, and he knew her legs had to be as stiff as his.

Their guide motioned toward a huge rocky outcropping some fifty yards away.

"Is that it?" Alex asked.

The guide spoke a torrent of Greek words, none of which he understood.

"I think I'd rather walk the rest of the way," Jane said, swiveling her hips around and rotating her shoulders.

"Sore?" he asked. "You need a massage."

"Sign me up, but I don't see a day spa around here," she said.

"I don't see Sofia around here, either."

"Maybe she's in the cave," Jane suggested hopefully.

"Yeah, right. She's probably wandering in the grotto, picking up relics and admiring the stalagmites."

"I'm sorry," she said with a tired sigh. "This was a dumb idea."

"We're almost there," he said. "Dumb idea or not, we're going to see it."

They walked slowly, clutching the reins in their hands, following the guide, who was old and spry and apparently had no stiffness from a two-hour donkey ride.

When they reached the yawning opening to the cave, Jane stood at the entrance for a long moment. The guide staked the donkeys and then entered the cave, but Jane didn't follow him.

"What's the matter? You wanted to come here, remember?" Alex said, putting his hand on her shoulder.

"I know. But . . . do we have to go in? Couldn't we just stand out here and call her name?"

"And miss the stalactites?" he joked. "What's the matter? Did you forget your claustrophobia pills?"

"How did you know?"

"You've got that look on your face." He tilted her chin with his thumb and looked in her eyes. Big mistake. Why had he never noticed they were like brown velvet? He'd noticed how full her lips were; he'd kissed them and he knew how they tasted. But he hadn't had enough of them or enough of her, and he never would.

He needed to pound it into his thick head that what had happened between them on this trip was over, and should be forgotten as soon as possible. Jane's gaze wavered, and her lower lip trembled. Was it fear from claustrophobia or fear of getting more involved with him?

He dropped his hand. "Stay here if you want. I'm going in."

"I'm coming, too," she said.

Jane had no wish to be left behind. Whether it

was a nudist beach or a prehistoric cave, she was not waiting outside. She wanted to be there when they found Sofia. She ducked and entered the cool interior of the cave. Cupping her hands around her mouth, she shouted Sofia's name. Her voice echoed eerily around the flaked dry stone walls—"Sofia, Sofia, Sofia"—but there was no answer.

Well, now that they were here, she wasn't going to leave until she'd seen some stalactites at least. As long as she could keep the opening of the cave in her vision, she'd be okay. Just as long as they didn't go off down some narrow passageway. The guide shined his flashlight above them, where strange, eerie shapes hung down.

"Now aren't you glad you came?" Alex put his hand against the wall and gazed at the cavern above them.

"Are you?"

"This is fantastic. Besides the stalactites, there are drawings on the walls. See how primitive they are? These caves were places of worship in Neolithic times, and then during the war, they were hideouts for the Resistance fighters. Fascinating."

Jane stumbled over a wine bottle. "Someone's been here more recently," she said, picking up the bottle and placing it to one side of the path. She brushed her foot across a pile of ashes. "Look, they had a fire." She tried to imagine Sofia huddled around a fire, drinking wine.

Alex ran his fingers over a design on the wall.

"This looks like some kind of calendar," he said, "where they counted off the days."

"How many days could you stay in a cave like this?" she asked with a little shiver.

"Depends on what was out there waiting for you," he said. "Other tribes, enemies of one kind or another."

"Wild animals," she suggested. "Like those." She pointed to wall pictures of bearlike creatures and bison with horns.

The guide motioned for them to follow him down a passageway, exactly the kind of place she didn't want to go.

"You go ahead," she told Alex.

"Come on, I'll hold your hand." He took her hand and squeezed it. It defied all logic, but she felt the warmth from his hand all the way to her heart. If she had any sense, she'd go back outside and wait for him there. It was cold in the cave, and she was afraid she'd get stuck where she couldn't get out. The walls of the passageway were narrow and so dry they looked as if they might crack and split into a thousand pieces of stone, burying them forever. She gripped Alex's hand tighter and kept walking, following behind the guide, stopping to step over loose rocks and fantastic stalagmites, and to look at drawings of animals and fish on the walls.

She tried to concentrate on the freedom fighters and the religious orders who'd been there long ago, so she wouldn't think about the walls closing in on her. Or a rock slide suddenly blocking the entrance. If it did, how long would they last without air?

Again, she thought about Sofia. She must have been the boutique customer who was headed for the lap of luxury at that castle, the most romantic place in Greece, dressed in a gorgeous silk dress, being treated like the princess she was.

That was where she and Alex should be right now. Sailing to the island of Marmara, checking the register at the Castle hotel to see if Sofia was there. Finding Sofia in the turret where she was leaning out of the window with her hair hanging down like Rapunzel, just waiting to be rescued by her prince. Alex would sweep her away in his arms, and they'd sail back to Mios in time for the wedding.

Jane pulled her hand from Alex's. The wedding— she had to keep it in mind. It was so easy to forget about it, here in no-man's-land. It was easy to pretend Sofia had dropped off the face of the earth, and Jane had taken her place. They were on the honeymoon boat, she'd worn Sofia's honeymoon clothes, she was eating the food that had been stocked for Sofia and Alex—and worst of all, she and Alex had made love.

Even still, right outside the cave, when he had looked at her, she saw raw, naked desire in his eyes, and she'd almost dissolved right there on the spot.

It was only her willpower that got her through these moments, only her common sense that kept her from fantasizing that he loved her and not Sofia.

Did Sofia know how lucky she was to have Alex? Apparently not, or she wouldn't have left. No, Sofia didn't believe she was lucky, she believed she deserved the best. And Alex was the best.

What was Jane going to do to forget how she felt about him? Stop acting like this was a vacation or a honeymoon, for one thing. It was a rescue mission. *But what if Sofia doesn't want to be rescued?* a little voice in the back of her head asked. *Too bad. We're going to rescue her anyway.* Sofia didn't always know what was best for her. *And you do?* the voice asked. Jane didn't have an answer for that.

Then the flashlight failed. Just like that, they were plunged into total darkness. The entrance was nowhere to be seen. A bat flew past her face, and she screamed.

Alex grabbed her hand. "Calm down, you're okay."

"We have to get out of here!"

She heard a scratch, smelled sulfur, and in a moment there was a small circle of light. Their guide had lit a candle.

"At least one of us was prepared," Jane said. This time she held on to Alex's hand and didn't let go. She was too scared, and she needed the warmth and comfort of his touch. After they got out of the cave, she'd hop on her donkey, even though her thighs were screaming for relief, and ride back to town.

As soon as they found Sofia, everything would be back to normal. Sofia would take her place as the sun in the heavens, and Jane would revert to being one of the planets that revolved around her. Alex would make things right with his bride-to-be and go back to treating Jane like the good friend she was.

She stumbled over some loose rocks, and she gripped Alex's hand tighter. Finally she saw the opening. She ran ahead, and in a moment she was outside in the hot afternoon sunshine.

Jane breathed a sigh of relief and narrowed her eyes against the blinding brilliance of the sun. Then she stretched her arms out to catch the rays. She'd never appreciated the fresh air and the sun so much.

Alex came out, followed by the guide, both blinking in the bright light.

This time she was behind Alex on the way down the mountain. Her butt was so sore, she wanted to cry or get off and walk. But she'd never keep up if she started walking, so she bit her lip and winced every time her bottom hit the saddle. Alex looked as if he were out joyriding, turning his head from side to side to admire the blankets of wildflowers on the hills and the rocky outcroppings along the way.

Jane was only dimly aware of the picturesque scenery and of the dark-eyed children who came out to wave to them and shout, *"Yassou!"* She strained her eyes, hoping to see the roofs of the houses in the town below, feeling every step her donkey took reverberate through her back, her posterior, and her legs.

"Where's your camera?" Alex asked, turning to look at her. "Don't tell me you left it in your purse."

"Yes, unfortunately. I'd love to have a photo of these kids. And you on a donkey," she added, smiling despite her pain. It was a funny sight, the big man on a small donkey. His feet almost reached the ground.

"How do you feel about them?" he asked.

"I'd rather have a moped."

"I meant kids," he said, waving at a new group who'd appeared to stand and stare at them.

"I like them," she said.

"Plan to have some of your own, or would that put a damper on your career?"

"It probably would," she said. But the problem wasn't so much her career; it was that in her dreams, the kids all had deep-set blue eyes and devastating smiles and small clefts in their chins. "I'd want to quit my job."

It was a strange conversation to have on the back of a donkey on a trail on an obscure Greek island, but at least it distracted her from the pain. Maybe that was his plan. He could be very perceptive. Maybe too perceptive. Maybe he'd guessed how she'd always felt about him. The thought of it made her cheeks burn.

When the trail widened, she moved up alongside him so she didn't have to shout.

"My mother worked," she continued. "I think I told you this once a long time ago. Like you, I had no dad around. I was a latchkey kid. Not that it bothered me." She didn't want him to feel sorry for her; she didn't want anyone to feel sorry for her.

"Same here," he said. "I liked the freedom. Nobody knew where I went after school."

"Where did you go?"

"Construction sites. I snuck into the Hard Hats Only area. I loved to watch the buildings going up. I wanted to wear a hard hat and sit a few hundred feet up in the air on a girder. It didn't occur to me until much later that I could design one of those buildings, although I used to build them with my Legos at home. What about you? What did you want to be when you were a kid?"

"It wasn't what I wanted, but what I was good at."

"Math and science."

"Yes."

"But what did you love?"

"Birds, I guess. I had this big book and I'd try to identify the birds in it. Did you see that bird back there on the mountain? I think it was a Griffin vulture."

"Wait till the gang hears this." He grinned.

"Don't laugh. They'll be impressed," she said.

"I'm sure they will."

"Anyway, when I was a kid, I had a hummingbird feeder outside the window, and I watched them come and go. They're so tiny and so beautiful. I wanted a real birdhouse, but we lived in an apartment, and there was no place to put one."

Alex was about to ask if she had room for one now, when he realized he had no idea where she lived now or with whom. "What about Warren, does he like birds?"

She leveled a glance at him as if she was going to say again, "What business is it of yours?" But she merely said, "He loves birds. He has two finches. They're so cute. When he goes out of town, I take care of them for him."

They were above the town now, looking down at the red roofs and terraced gardens, the restaurants and shops that lined the port.

"Look, down there," Jane said excitedly. "A sign that says Cavo d'Oro. *That* has to be the cave Sofia was talking about!"

Chapter 12

Jane didn't realize how bad the pain was until she got off her donkey. Her back ached. Her legs were so sore, she could hardly walk. If she never got on a donkey again, it would be too soon. She limped down the street with Alex, who didn't seem to notice or be the least affected himself. If it weren't for the sign they'd seen for the Cavo d'Oro, she would have sat down on the sidewalk and cried.

But in a few minutes they discovered the Cavo d'Oro was a taverna and not a hotel. They stopped in front of the wide green awning that sheltered the outdoor customers and looked at each other. Were they wrong in thinking it had to be a hotel on Andros? Was there a hotel of the same name somewhere around here? Could Sofia be right here, under this awning?

The restaurant was full of people, both inside and outside, sipping ouzo and drinking coffee and eating pastries dipped in honey. After a turn around the place, with no sign of Sofia, they sat down at a table. The waiter soon brought glasses of retsina and a plate of *keftades, dolmades,* and *oftes patates.*

"This is wonderful," Jane said, biting into a crisp, hot potato. "I don't think we had lunch."

"We are going to have dinner, though," Alex said. "Since we're docked here, we can go back to the boat, shower and change, and go find a fish taverna. You can't leave Greece without trying octopus, red mullet, or fried calamari."

It sounded divine to Jane. It also sounded suspiciously like something people did on their honeymoon. Go to the boat. *Make love.* Shower, change, eat at some colorful taverna on the water. Back at the boat, gaze at the lights reflected in the water. *Make love.* Fall asleep as the boat rocked gently. *Make love again. No, stop! Get a grip, Jane. That's not what he meant.*

"What about Sofia?" she asked, setting her fork down abruptly.

"What about her?" Alex asked, his muscles tensed. "If she doesn't want to be found, she won't be. What are we supposed to do, hole up on board, live off hardtack and water, and wait for her to send us another clue? I've had enough." He drained his wineglass and put some money on the table. "Come on, let's go."

It was hard for Jane to decide which was more painful—walking or sitting. Her thighs, her calves, and especially her butt, were stiff and throbbing. Alex gave her a quick glance as she stepped, stiff-legged, down onto the boat deck from the dock.

"Sore?" he asked.

"Post-donkey-ride-syndrome, that's all," she said, her jaw clenched, her tone resolutely cheerful. "I'll be all right after a hot shower."

"A shower will help, but you need more than that. Fortunately, I've had a lot of experience with your syndrome," he said. "I know something that will make you feel a lot better."

"Is it something that's in my purse?"

"It's something right here." He flexed his fingers. "Lucky for you, I've been trained in massage therapy."

"Hah. I'd like to see your credentials," she said lightly, trying not to think about how his hands would feel on her bare skin.

"You've seen them," he muttered. "For your information, I was trained by an old Japanese master therapist who taught me everything I know before he went to his Nirvana. Go take your shower and call me when you're done."

The hot water beating on her aching muscles felt good, but he was right, she needed more than that. She blocked out all the words of caution in her head, all the little warnings that banged against her subconscious, trying to get in. Because she *wanted* to feel those hands on her back, on her legs, and on her bottom. She wanted him to touch her, all over. But she had to be strong this time; grit her teeth and bear it. All she had to do was say no.

She tied the robe around her waist and went to the lounge. Alex was looking at a map, trying to figure out how to get to Marmara, no doubt.

"I'm done," she said briskly. Maybe he'd forgotten; maybe he'd go in and take his shower now. That would be best for both of them.

He lowered the map a fraction so that only his eyes were visible, and he gave her a long, slow look. Every inch of her skin felt a burst of heat like a blast furnace. All the breath was sucked from her lungs. She couldn't risk anything more intimate.

"I feel fine now," she said. "There's no need for a massage."

"Sure?" he asked, getting to his feet and letting the map fall to the floor. He was standing so close to her, she could smell the wine on his breath. If she had been thinking, she wasn't any longer. Alex traced the outline of the deep V of her robe with his finger, and she felt her knees go weak. She tried to say something, but her lips wouldn't move. She tried to back up, but her legs wouldn't move. The look in his eyes held her like a magnet. She couldn't look away.

"Well, maybe just a little lotion on my back." Was that her voice that said that? Was she deaf to the warning bells?

"Whatever you say," he said, turning her around by the shoulders. "We'll go to the stateroom. A massage table is best, but we'll have to make do with what we have."

Jane walked one step ahead of Alex, dragging her feet. She wasn't afraid he'd take advantage of her; she knew he'd only do what she allowed him to do. But she feared how Alex could make her feel; feared she'd never get over it.

In the stateroom he pulled the curtain closed and switched on the brass wall lamp. "Lie down," he said.

Obediently she lay down and buried her face in the cool quilt, her thick terry robe tightly wrapped around her. If she kept it there, nothing could happen, right?

"Show me where it hurts." He sat on the edge of the bed.

She raised her arm and pointed to her back, her butt, and her legs.

"I'll get some lotion." He went to the bathroom, and a minute later he was rubbing an icy gel that smelled of verbena and lemon onto the backs of her legs. The sensations raced up her legs and pooled in the deepest part of her. She opened her mouth to protest, but no sound came out. When he lifted the edge of her robe and his hands traveled up her thighs to her bottom, she tensed.

"Relax," he said.

"Are you sure you know what you're doing?" she asked in a muffled voice. This was her last chance. After this she was putty in his hands.

"Money-back guarantee if you're not one hundred percent satisfied when I'm done."

Satisfied? She'd be a speechless, breathless, quivering mass of jelly. "I'm feeling better. Maybe I don't really need this." But her voice sounded uncertain and weak in her ears.

"I saw you limping this afternoon, and I can feel that your muscles are tied up in knots. Do you want to be crippled tomorrow?"

"No, of course not, but—"

"Okay, then." The next thing she knew, he'd loosened her robe and slid it down her shoulders. Her bare breasts were pressed into the smooth quilt. His hands started long, gliding strokes on her shoulder blades. She took a deep breath and relaxed with a shudder. How could this kind of massage be dangerous? How could anything that felt this good be bad? As long as she stayed on her stomach, and his hands stayed—

He tugged at her robe and removed it completely. She tensed. She should have protested, but how could she when his hands were moving slowly, smoothly, sensuously down, down, rubbing aromatic gel into her skin, surrounding her with the citrus scent?

"Don't worry," he said. "I have everything under control."

She had nothing under control. Especially when his hands reached the curve of her hip and he began to knead the contours of her bottom. She moaned; she groaned. It was where she was the sorest, but Alex's magic hands were making her forget her pain, forget everything but him.

He straddled her, with his knees pressed into the bed on either side of her hips. She could hear him breathing hard, feel him breathing with her, together, in and out, fast at first, then slowly, deeply. It was so intimate and so incredibly sensuous, she knew it had to be forbidden. She felt as if she'd been disconnected from her body and was looking down at herself from above.

"You're really good at this," she murmured. So good at it, she wanted to roll over and feel those beautiful hands on her aching breasts. She knew how his fingers would feel as they circled the swell of her breasts, coming closer and closer until they skimmed her nipples, then stroked, tugged, sucked. She felt his erection through his shorts, and she groaned. Just thinking about turning over to expose her body was wrong. As much as her whole being clamored for it, she would not give in.

But oh, how she wanted to look up into his eyes. To see what was there—desire, passion, lust? To make sure she wouldn't give in, she gripped the edges of the quilt and held them tightly in her fists.

Alex didn't say anything. His hands did the talking, sending the message his eyes had sent earlier. He thought she was desirable. He thought she was sexy. He wanted her.

Was he going to do anything about it this time? A one-time lapse might be understandable, but a repeat? Never.

Did he know how she really felt about him? She hoped not. She hoped he thought this was business as usual for her, that this was no big deal.

With Alex's hands on her back, her legs, moving dangerously close to the juncture of her thighs, where she throbbed and ached, her control was ebbing away. She was all body, no brain. All feelings, no rational thought. All sensations, all primal urges—nothing else.

She moaned and sighed and made breathless sounds of pleasure as his fingers worked their magic on her knotted muscles, but it was as if the sounds came from someone else.

He was working on her feet now, spreading cool citrus gel between her toes and into the arch of her foot. Her heart caught in her throat. Was there no place he could touch that wouldn't send her over the edge? It was worse than the first time—or better. So much better, her body said *more*. She had never known she could feel this way; never dreamed her body would respond like this. . . .

He started briskly tapping her muscles with the edge of his palms, starting with her calves and gradually moving up to her shoulders. Then, he stopped.

She held her breath.

He got off the bed.

"That better?" he asked.

Better? She was shocked by the suddenness of it. She was cold, alone, overstimulated, and her body was crying out for a release that wasn't going to come. Not now, not ever again.

When she didn't answer, he said something about a shower and left the room.

Alex stood in the compact shower stall and turned on the cold water full force. It stung like needles on his sore muscles and sunburned skin. He didn't care, as long as it forced him to face reality. Jane was a friend. A good friend whom he was in danger of losing, if he kept this up.

Fortunately, she didn't know what she'd done to him the first time around. This time he'd left her just in time. Another minute, another second, and he would have gone over the edge and exploded.

This was all his fault. What did he think would happen if he had her naked body beneath him on a bed? It was no use pretending he could resist her. With the curtains drawn and the soft light shining on her soft skin, and the sounds she made in the back of her throat, he didn't trust his self-control to hold up under the onslaught. Jane, he thought, her name echoing around in his brain—Jane, Jane, Jane. There was something between them he could no longer deny. Had she always been this hot? How had he never noticed it? Had he been blind?

All those years she'd been in the background. Lately, she hadn't been around at all. He'd thought about her. He'd asked Sofia how she was doing, but Sofia was vague. He'd suggested they get together, but Jane was always busy. Finally he got the message. If Jane didn't have time to see him, if their friendship meant so little to her, why should he care? If she'd forgotten him, he'd do the same.

But he hadn't. Now he knew he'd never forget her. But he'd try to forget what had happened here; he had to.

If Jane knew how close he'd come to turning her over and making love to her again, she'd be on the next ferry back to Mios. He didn't want that. He wanted her around. He wanted to look at her in her white bikini that stretched when she moved, that showed off her tight little butt and her small, perfect breasts. He would look, but he wouldn't touch. Never again.

Even though he hated to think of her making love to others, he found himself hanging on every word when she told him about her past. What had happened to the Jane he thought he knew?

If he were truthful, he wanted her to say that none of those men compared to him. He wanted to make her forget them, pinning her to the floor or the table or the bed and making her cry out with pleasure as he gave her everything he had. But that wasn't going to happen—not in this lifetime.

He thought she might want what he wanted; he saw hints of it in her eyes and he heard it in her voice. He felt it under his fingertips in every pore of her body.

They had to get back to Mios before something else happened they'd both regret.

He got out of the shower, his erection gone, his willpower back in place. Then he caught a glimpse of her in the stateroom, wearing long, tight printed pants that flared at the ankle and a purple sweater that outlined her breasts.

Before she saw what just the sight of her could do to him, what was blatantly obvious under his towel, he ducked into the lounge and closed the door behind him. So much for his good intentions. He went through his suitcase and pulled out a pair of charcoal pants and a gray shirt—both wrinkled. It didn't matter. No one would notice what he was wearing once they got a look at Jane in that purple sweater.

Then he made the phone call he'd been putting off; the one that would seal his fate for many years to come. After that, he went up on deck.

Jane was leaning against the railing, watching the people strolling along the docks and listening to the bouzouki music coming from the cafés and tavernas. Her body was outlined against the bright lights on the dock. The mast lights were designed only to warn other boats they were there; they shed no light on the deck.

"You look great." His voice sounded like sandpaper. "How do you feel?"

She turned to face him. "Good. Fine, thanks to that massage."

He wasn't sure what that meant. He couldn't see her expression in the shadows, and the tone of her voice gave nothing away. Did she accept it at face value—just an attempt to soothe her aching muscles? Was he the only one who was aroused to the point of desperation? Was he the only one who had to bolt out of the room for fear of doing something he'd regret?

"I called the Leonakises," he said.

She walked over to him and stopped abruptly, a foot away. "What happened? You look sick. Is it bad news?"

"Good news, actually," he said. "They've heard from Sofia."

"Is she coming back?"

"I . . . not yet. But I told them to tell her that I'd changed my mind; that I'd do what she wanted. I didn't make it too specific, so Nikos wouldn't know what I was talking about, but Sofia will get the message."

"Then she'll come back." Jane sounded relieved.

Of course she was relieved; so was he. Now they could go back to the villa on Mios, and everything would be back to normal.

"Do they know who she's with?" Jane asked.

"They know she's with somebody, but they don't know who. They said she sounded like she was okay, so they're not as worried."

"Are you?"

He hesitated. He *was* worried. He was worried he'd made the wrong decision. He was worried that even if he made the sacrifice, she wouldn't come back anyway. He was worried about the way he felt about Jane. He was worried about whether he knew what he was doing.

"No," he said firmly. He was no longer very worried about Sofia. If he was right, she'd get the message and decide to come back.

"Good. What should we do next?" she asked.

"Eat dinner."

"I mean after that."

Make love under the stars out here on the deck. It would be so perfect, give us something to remember. Just one more time.

Was he crazy? Something to remember? As it was, how was he ever going to forget?

"I suppose we could head back to Mios," he suggested.

"That seems premature," she said. "I won't feel right until we actually see her and make sure she's okay."

Relieved, Alex took Jane's hand to help her up onto the dock. Then they walked along the pier hand in hand—he didn't want to break the connection. It wasn't just physical, it was much more than that. Besides, holding hands couldn't lead to anything unless they wanted it to, which they didn't.

They walked down the narrow, twisting streets, passing tavernas that stretched out to the sidewalk. They passed restaurants where a headwaiter wearing a tuxedo stood outside and called to them, offering discounts and free drinks. They passed forlorn, empty cafés and full, noisy cafés. By unspoken agreement, they kept walking, reading menus posted outside, and laughing at the English translations of the classic Greek dishes: Stuffed Vine Lives, String Deans, Staffed Tomatoes, and Lamp Chops.

He didn't know what they were looking for, but he knew they'd know it when they found it.

It was there, around the next corner. Brightly lit, full of Greeks, with rustic copper pots hanging from the ceiling, a menu written only in Greek, and heavenly smells coming from the kitchen.

They sat at a table in a dark corner, the candle in the center of the table making Jane's skin glow. He couldn't tear his eyes from her face, and he wasn't sure what they ordered, but the waiter smiled approvingly and even made a few suggestions. He brought a bottle of chilled local house wine, poured some in each of their glasses, then disappeared.

"I know you're disappointed I gave in about the job," Alex said. "You think I shouldn't have caved."

"I didn't say that."

"You didn't need to. It's written all over your face." He reached across the table and traced the curve of her cheek. She pressed her lips together, as if to keep from saying something she'd regret, or because she didn't want to hurt his feelings by voicing her opinion.

"Alex, what you do or don't do is your business. And Sofia's. If this is what you want, you have to do it."

"You know it's not what I want. But maybe I was being selfish before. I was only thinking about myself, when my decision affected not only Sofia, but Nikos and the whole family. That's a hard one for me to grasp—how important family is."

"You're right. You're part of a big family now. I envy you that."

"You do?" She'd seen the family in action; all their quirks and eccentricities and their ethnocentrism. She'd known them even longer than he had. And she still envied him?

She nodded. "When I was growing up, it was just me and my mom. When I met Sofia, I couldn't believe how big her family was, how important they were to her and she was to them. I wanted what she had—aunts, uncles, cousins—the whole works. I guess I've always been a little jealous, and I'm not proud of that. Especially when the family has been so good to me."

She sighed. "So I do understand why you changed your mind. I just wish you could still do what you want to do. Maybe later?"

Later? Later, he'd be so immersed in the family business that he'd never be able to get out. He covered her hand with his. "Sure."

She squeezed his hand reassuringly, and he felt her warmth and sympathy, and saw it in her soft brown eyes.

She pulled her hand away, sipped her wine, then set her glass down and looked at him, her expression serious.

"Alex," she said. "I have a confession to make."

Chapter 13

"What is it?" He looked alarmed. "Are you going to tell me you had affairs with the whole football team, too?"

Jane shook her head, having second thoughts. Now was not the time to tell him about her feelings for him. If she wanted to confess anything, she ought to tell him she'd been lying about the men in her past. But what was the harm of a few white lies? It was fun to come up with new imaginary men.

After he got married, he'd never give her situation another thought. If he found out she'd been lying, he and Sofia would just have a laugh about it. He'd confess he'd been fooled.

Or had he? Sometimes she wondered if he saw right through her and was just humoring her.

"The whole team? Of course not."

"What then, just the quarterback?" He frowned at her across the table.

She smiled at the image of her and those big, dumb football players. "I've never been interested in athletes," she said. "I prefer brain over brawn."

"So your Navy SEAL is not just a tough guy?"

"Oh, no. He's very smart. He belongs to Mensa."

"Really?"

He looked skeptical. Maybe she'd stretched the truth too far this time.

"Let's talk about something else," she said, hoping he'd forget she was going to make a confession.

"Like your job? I'm afraid I'm going to have to retract my job offer, unless you want to come to work for Leonakis Construction Company."

"I'll pass," she said.

"Why? We have a great future—bigger buildings, taller garages, and monster shopping centers." There was more than a hint of bitterness in his voice.

"Alex . . . when we get back to the States, things will be different."

"No kidding."

"I mean—"

"I know what you mean. I was hoping we could stay friends. Maybe that's not going to work."

"It's not," she said firmly.

"I'm sorry. I'm to blame for that."

"We're both to blame."

He shrugged. "Let me know if you change your

mind. You'd like Washington. There are a lot of birds there."

"I didn't know you noticed."

"I will when I go back. I have a cabin at Long Beach."

"I know. Sofia told me."

"Did she also tell you there's nothing to do there?"

She should lie; should tell him Sofia had said nothing of the kind. Tell him that Sofia loved the pounding surf and the dunes and the many gray, foggy days when there was "nothing" to do.

"Will you stay up there or will you move to the San Francisco office?" she asked instead.

"I don't know what Nikos has in mind."

Or what Sofia has in mind, Jane thought.

It was a relief when the waiter brought the traditional *horiatiki* Greek salads with tiny tomatoes, crisp lettuce, savory olives, and slices of creamy white feta cheese on top. Alex had made up his mind; what good did it do to try to convince him he was making a mistake? Maybe he wasn't—it was his life.

"What would you do if you were me?" he asked, setting his fork down.

"I don't know. I've never been in love." She crossed her fingers in her lap and hoped she wouldn't be struck by lightning.

"All those men, and you never loved one of them?" he asked. "That's hard to believe. You seem so . . . so . . ."

"Naive? Gullible?"

"No, you seem like you've got a lot of love to give."

The look in his eyes stopped her cold. What did he mean by that? She picked up her wineglass, but her hand was shaking so much, she set it down again.

"Well," she said. "Maybe I'm saving it for Mr. Right."

"How are you going to recognize Mr. Right when he comes along?" He reached across the table and toyed absently with her fingers, no doubt unaware of how it made those butterflies flutter in her stomach. The contrast between her small fingers and his large hand had her mesmerized.

"You tell me," she said. "I've heard bells will ring, alarms will go off, and fireworks will light the sky."

He grinned. "Sounds like that explosion in chemistry class."

No wonder she'd fallen for him that day. Yes, she'd recognized Mr. Right right away. Unfortunately, there was nothing worse than a one-sided affair.

She pulled her hand away, and they went on to less personal topics while they ate crisp fried calamari and bowls of succulent mussels in white wine sauce. Her whole body was still tingling from that incredible massage he'd given her. She'd wanted to offer him one in return. She had no skill, but maybe she could make up for it with enthusiasm. And—maybe that was just about the worst idea she'd ever had.

They walked slowly back to the boat. The sidewalks were crowded. Women walked arm in arm. Men stood in small groups, laughing and talking and casting glances at the dark-eyed women, who pretended not to notice. Couples strolled hand in hand. She and Alex didn't belong in any of the categories. They were there not by choice; they'd been thrown together by necessity.

It should have been Alex and Sofia strolling and holding hands. It *would* be Alex and Sofia, in another week. They'd be sailing together, eating together, dancing together, and sleeping together. Jane stumbled on a loose cobblestone, and Alex grabbed her arm to steady her.

They passed shops and bars and restaurants filled with customers eating or dancing. Through the open windows, they heard live music and saw young men wearing black trousers and red sashes performing folk dances for tourists who'd come for the Greek Night extravaganza.

The sights and sounds registered, but Jane was thinking of Alex, hoping he'd be able to stay in Seattle if that's what he wanted. She pictured the cottage by the sea with the plovers, the gulls, and the sandpipers nesting on the shore.

When they reached the dock where the *Aphrodite* was docked, a man appeared out of the shadows. "Mr. Woods?" he asked, in heavily accented English. Jane tensed. She prayed this would not be another attack.

"Yeah, that's me."

"I have a message from Miss Leonakis."

"Where is she?" Alex demanded.

"She is gone." The man waved an arm toward the sea. "She will meet you at the Castle of Marianti."

"What? When?"

"When you arrive tomorrow. She will wait for you there."

"So that *was* her at the dress shop," Jane murmured. She had just chosen the wrong customer to follow. Unless Sofia had deliberately led them astray? Or maybe *she* had seized on the idea of the cave to prolong this trip. And now they'd find Sofia waiting at the castle, just as she'd intended.

"Where did you see her? How is she traveling?" Alex asked the man.

He shrugged, as if he didn't understand or he didn't know the answers. Then he turned and walked away.

"Wait," Alex said, but the guy had disappeared into the crowds on the dock. Alex looked at Jane. So many questions hung in the air, and so few answers. "Who the hell was that?" Alex asked blankly.

Jane shook her head and they climbed aboard the boat. "I have no idea."

"I'm going to look up the island on the chart," he said. "We'll head there tomorrow."

"But what if—"

"What if she isn't there? I won't be surprised. Will you?"

Jane shook her head, her face pale in the bright moonlight. "Good night."

Alex sat on the couch in the lounge, his feet propped up on the coffee table, his head resting on a leather cushion, his eyes closed. He wanted to talk, but Jane had cut him off with a blunt, "Good night."

He wanted to tell her how confused he was. After ten years of being in and out of love with Sofia, but always knowing he'd end up with her, he suddenly knew nothing at all.

His brain wasn't functioning, and his whole body was sore from the damn donkey ride. He'd never admit that to Jane, though, or she might want to give *him* a massage. Yeah, that would be too bad. He groaned out loud at the thought of her hands on his muscles, easing the pain and wreaking havoc wherever they went.

He reached for the phone. If he couldn't talk to Jane, he'd call his best friend.

"Doug, it's Alex."

"Where are you?"

"On board the Leonakises' boat, docked at an island. Can you hear the bouzouki music?" Alex held the phone up to the open window.

"I hear it. You wouldn't be calling me to say you're on your honeymoon and there's bouzouki music playing, and you've been out dancing and partying and drinking ouzo, and the beautiful Sofia is waiting for you in some sexy nightgown, would you? You couldn't be so cruel as to call and rub it in, when your best friend is stuck in an office in rainy Seattle. No kind of friend would do that."

"Oh, no, of course not."

"Make my day, Alex—tell me the islands are jam-packed with loud, obnoxious American tourists and the boat sprang a leak and you're bailing like crazy."

"Well . . ." Where to begin, with all the things that had gone wrong?

"Hey," Doug said, "I didn't want to call you and interrupt anything, but I've got good news." Alex's heart sank. "We got the office space we wanted, and I hired the best office manager I've ever seen away from Allen."

Alex cleared his throat. "Look, Doug, I've been thinking things over, and I'm not sure this is going to work. I'm afraid I won't be able to leave the construction company after all."

"You're kidding! What's wrong? This is Sofia's idea, isn't it? What did she say?"

Alex knew Doug would say that. He knew what all his friends thought of Sofia, though they never said anything. They thought she was rich and spoiled. They didn't know how generous she could be, how spontaneous and fun loving, how warm and kind. But it didn't matter what they thought; it was what he thought that was important.

What had she said, when he told her he wanted to leave her father's company? She'd said he was selfish, self-centered, and ungrateful. She'd said he didn't love her. And then she said he'd be sorry. That certainly wasn't for Doug to hear. It was bad enough that Jane had heard it. "She reminded me of what I owe Nikos."

"Of course you owe him, but you've paid him off with all the hard work you've done for him. You ran the office up here like nobody else could. He can't expect you to stay forever, can he?"

"He probably can." At least Sofia did.

"Can't he get someone else to take your place?" Doug asked.

"But I'm family. They put their trust in family. That's not a bad thing." Alex knew he sounded defensive.

"I get that. But isn't this more about the money? You knew you wouldn't make as much starting out as you could at the construction company."

"I don't care about the money," Alex said.

"I know *you* don't."

"Look, Sofia has been raised with certain expectations."

"I know, I know. Look, why don't you let me talk to her? Maybe I can explain it in a way you can't, since I'm not emotionally involved. Put her on."

"She's not here. The wedding isn't until Saturday."

"I thought you were anchored on some island. You're drinking ouzo and listening to music . . . by yourself?"

Alex paused for a moment. "I'm with a friend."

"Man or woman?"

"Does it matter?" Alex said, irritated at the implication.

"I think it does. In fact, I don't think men and women can be friends. So it must be a guy."

"It's a girl. I've been friends with Jane for ten

years, and that's proof that it's possible. There's not . . . there's nothing going on between us." God, he hoped he wouldn't be struck down here and now for lying.

"I've never heard you mention a Jane."

"I haven't seen her for a while."

"You're telling me that a few days before your wedding, you're on a yacht in the moonlight, with music in the background, sailing around the Aegean with a female you claim is only a friend?"

"How do you know there's moonlight?"

"I read travel brochures. I'm a man of the world."

"If you know so much, you know that men and women can be friends."

"Sure, if there's thirty years' difference in age or she's . . . How old is this Jane, by the way?"

"Twenty-eight," he admitted.

"Height?"

"Five-something."

"Weight?"

"Come on, Doug. I know what you're getting at. It doesn't matter."

"I think it does. I don't think you can be friends unless there's something wrong with her. Or you. What is it? Does she eat her peas with a knife? Does she talk too much?"

"She gets seasick and she's claustrophobic in dark caves. Forget about Jane. I'm sorry I brought her up."

"Tell me, how does she feel about you?"

"I don't know." Alex swatted at a mosquito and wished he'd never called Doug.

"Why don't you ask her?"

"I don't have to ask her. She feels just the way I feel about her: she thinks of me as a friend."

"Bullshit. If I was Sofia, I'd be worried. Where did you say she was?"

"I didn't say, because I don't know."

Doug whistled through his teeth. "I smell trouble in paradise."

"I'm sorry I called you," Alex groused. He didn't need anyone telling him he was in trouble; he already knew that. "Goodbye."

"Wait, don't make any hasty decisions. Before you left, you were determined to go through with our deal. You knew Sofia wasn't happy about it, but you said you'd deal with her."

Alex shrugged. "I tried."

"Try harder. Look, I'm not going to cancel anything. I'm putting everything on hold until you come back, or you come to your senses—whichever comes first."

"Goodbye, Doug."

"Say hello to Jane for me."

Alex hung up. He should have known Doug wouldn't understand. Who would believe a man could travel with a friend and keep her at arm's distance, no matter how much he wanted to ravish her? And he hadn't—no wonder Doug was suspicious. Doug wouldn't understand how he could go to a nudist beach with Jane, dance with Jane, make love to Jane, eat and drink with Jane, give Jane an erotic massage, and still remain friends with Jane.

Hell, he couldn't understand it himself. Maybe because . . . it wasn't possible.

After another sleepless night tossing and turning on the couch, he went up on deck at dawn. Jane was standing at the railing, watching the sun rise over the water in a red sky. Her hair was tied back in a scraggly ponytail. She was wearing a loose T-shirt and boxer shorts, she had no makeup on, and she'd never looked more beautiful to him. His mouth went dry. He balled his hands into fists. He wanted her more than ever.

It occurred to him with a terrible suddenness that he was in even bigger trouble than he'd imagined.

"You're up early," he said, managing a casual tone.

She nodded.

"Good night's sleep?" he asked.

She shook her head.

"Me, either." He stood by her, his arm next to hers. "If we don't find her today, we're heading back without her. It's Friday. Tomorrow is our wedding day."

"She'll be there," Jane said. "I know she will."

"I hope you're right." He glanced at the sky. "What's that they say? 'Red sky at night . . .' "

" 'Sailors' delight,' " she said. " 'Red sky at morning, sailors take warning.' "

"Consider yourself warned."

She nodded and went below to change clothes.

After they'd taken on fuel, more fresh water, and fresh food, Alex asked, "What's your view? Can a man and a woman be just friends?"

They were in the wheelhouse. He was at the controls, and Jane was leaning against the bulkhead, peeling an orange with intense concentration as he navigated out of the harbor into the open sea. She was wearing short shorts and a bright scarf tied halter-style around her neck and waist, and he realized she still wasn't wearing a bra. While thinking about her breasts under the scrap of fabric, he suddenly realized he was steering the boat in the wrong direction.

He overcorrected, and Jane stumbled forward. When Alex caught her, he caught a whiff of that verbena scent that reminded him of last night, and the way she smelled and the way she felt under his hands.

He grabbed the wheel and forced his gaze to the sea.

Jane braced herself again and leveled her gaze at him. "Why do you ask? Haven't we already had this discussion?"

"I talked to my business partner last night, and he didn't think it was possible."

"Why not?"

"He thinks it's only possible if one party is old and the other is young, or if there's some other obstacle."

"Like one of them is involved with someone else, making that person unavailable?" Jane suggested lightly.

"That would work." Or should work, if the person had any scruples. He was beginning to wonder about his commitment to Sofia, about hers to him.

About love and about loyalty. Serious doubts about their future entered his mind for the first time. After all these years, was it possible that he and Sofia were *not* meant for each other?

"Was this a theoretical discussion?" Jane asked.

"We were talking about you and me."

"He doesn't even know me."

"But he knows me," Alex said.

"Did you convince him?"

"He's a stubborn guy. And he has a vested interest in my leaving the company. He refused to listen to my arguments for friendship between men and women, or my arguments for staying with Leonakis. He doesn't understand. You do, don't you?"

"Understand why you chose to work for Nikos? Of course. But I wish you didn't."

"I don't think you answered my question," he said, steering the boat into deep water. "About men and women being friends."

"You know the answer," she said.

He didn't know the answer, but he didn't press her any further.

He pointed to the chart on the wall. "Looks like we're going through a narrow channel on our way to Marmara."

"Is that a problem?"

"Not if we stay within the markers. And we've got GPS." He pointed to the Global Positioning Satellite box with a display on the front that was mounted on the dashboard. "So you can go back on deck if you want, catch some sun."

"It's clouding up. I think I'll stay here." She shivered and sat in a swivel chair next to him as if she were his copilot. He handed her a waterproof poncho from the storage chest, just in case. It wasn't completely altruistic on his part; he wasn't going to be able to navigate anywhere with her wearing only a scarf.

The contrast between what Jane had been and what she'd become made it impossible for him to think of anything other than how she'd turned out. Had Greece done it to her? Was it something he'd done? He could have sworn she was her same shy, awkward person when he ran into her on the ferry.

But now she was a different person. A sexy, confident woman, while underneath she was still smart, still a little shy, and so very sweet.

Was that it? Or was he was a different person from the guy who'd gotten onto a ferry at Piraeus? He sure felt different: he'd had a taste of life with Jane. Of course, it wasn't real life. They were sailing from island to island, going from emotional highs to lows, from ecstasy to despair. Where was it all leading? To Sofia, of course. But in the meantime . . .

He watched Jane pull the poncho over her head—good. But there were still her legs—long and smooth and bare. He'd never noticed them before this boat trip. Maybe he'd never seen them before. But now he constantly fantasized about having them wrapped around him.

Jane reached for the binoculars and scanned the

sea. "Can that be a squall up ahead?" She handed them to him. "Dark skies, gray sea."

"Looks like it's right over the channel. Damn."

"I thought it would be warm and sunny here all the time."

"Haven't you heard about the *Meltemi,* the ferocious wind that kicks up this time of year? Then there was that red sky this morning," he said. "You remember how rough it was on the ferry—uh-oh. Maybe you'd better grab a couple of those seasick pills."

Jane dashed downstairs, pulled a pair of long pants over her shorts, and gulped down two pills. She could not get sick again. She had to stay at the wheel with Alex, in case she needed to read the GPS or look for the channel buoys. He sounded calm and assured, but she'd seen the line in his forehead deepen, and she suspected that a storm, especially in a channel, could be dangerous.

When she returned to the wheelhouse, the winds were slapping the waves against the hull.

"I'm pointing her into the wind so we don't get tossed off course," Alex said.

She could see he was struggling to keep the wheel steady. Rain was coming down now, splashing against the windshield and the side windows, and the sky was charcoal gray, making it hard to see.

Jane's stomach rebelled. The pills hadn't taken effect yet, but she couldn't wimp out on Alex. She willed herself to be strong.

When they reached the channel, there were

numerous fishing boats and cabin cruisers heading through the deep, narrow passage, to avoid the rocks in the shallow waters to the sides.

"Too bad about all this traffic," he said.

"What's the worst thing that could happen?" Jane asked, stuffing her hands in the pockets of her pants.

"That you'll throw up on my shoes again," he teased. "Seriously? I guess if we can't see the buoys, we could hit the shoals and rip a hole in the hull and sink."

"The Leonakises wouldn't like that," Jane said. "Especially if they have to call off the wedding because the groom and bridesmaid are missing."

"Can you see anything, like the markers?"

She peered out the side window, straining her eyes, but the sea and the sky were both metal gray. The waves were crashing against the hull. "No." Looking down made her stomach roll and pitch. It was like the ferry, but even worse.

Alex noticed. "Jane," he said, reaching for her arm, "sit down. Never mind the buoys. I'll look for them."

She nodded, sat, and closed her eyes. She wanted to jump overboard despite the giant waves; she'd take her chances there any day over getting sick again. She gripped the edge of her seat.

"Another bad thing," Alex said, "would be crashing into one of these fishing boats."

Jane opened her eyes and looked out the window. Little boats were bobbing up and down in the waves.

They seemed to be moving erratically, though she could see blurry figures and faces in their wheelhouses. She imagined they were just as nervous as Alex was, and maybe just as seasick as she was.

She focused on a small boat to their right. She thought she could see a man and a woman inside the tiny cabin, but that was impossible. Women were bad luck on fishing boats. Unless . . . No, it couldn't be Sofia. It was hard to see anything through the driving rain, let alone faces.

But what if it *was* her and the mysterious stranger she was traveling with? It was possible; they were headed for the same island. They might have left at the same time, though she and Alex had searched the harbor for a fishing boat from Mios.

"See that boat over there?" she asked.

"I see it," he said as they were hit by a vicious blast of rain. "What about it?" He sounded worried, and sweat was trickling down his face. This was not the time to tell him her far-fetched idea that Sofia and her companion were alongside of them.

"Never mind." It probably wasn't them. And if it was, what could they do about it? She didn't know which was worse: to be seasick or crazy.

Alex's gaze was locked on the sea, and his face was pale under his tan as they plowed ahead.

After an eternity, the rain seemed to slow down. The waves were smaller, the sky light gray instead of black.

Jane stood and looked around. The fishing boat she'd thought held Sofia was gone.

"Looks like we made it," Alex said. "I'm not sure how, but we did." He let go of the wheel for a moment and stood up. Then he hauled her into his arms, and she pressed her face against his chest.

"I was scared," she said, her voice muffled against his shirt that smelled familiar, like American laundry soap.

"So was I," he admitted.

"Where do you think we are?" she asked, reluctantly stepping back out of his arms.

He looked at his GPS and jabbed a finger at the chart. "Here. We ought to be at Marmara in another hour or two. I hope it's going to be worth it."

Jane couldn't help asking, "And if she isn't there?"

Alex shrugged. "Then we go back."

"Empty-handed?"

"Do you have a better idea?"

Suddenly Jane noticed the sun shining up ahead. "Look, we're heading for clear weather. It's an omen, don't you think?" she asked hopefully.

"Maybe." The look on his face told her he wasn't counting on it. "But I'm telling you right now, I've had it with these half-baked messages. If she's there, she's coming back with us. Otherwise . . ."

Jane knew what he meant: all bets were off. She sent a silent message to her best friend—*Sofia, if you love Alex, you'd better show. He's making a huge sacrifice for you because he loves you. And you love him—don't you?*

Chapter 14

The skies were clear by the time they reached
Marmara and the tiny port city of Pyriri. The sun
shone so brightly on the limestone cliffs that Jane
put on her sunglasses to shield her eyes from the
glare. The blue Aegean sparkled, as did the pebbly
beaches. She thought it was the most beautiful
island they'd seen yet, with the white houses ringing
the horseshoe-shaped bay. Hillside houses looked
like fortresses, and the castle they were headed for
was barely visible out on a narrow stone causeway.

Jane's heart raced at the thought of what this
island had in store for her . . . for him . . . for them.
It was the end of their trip. A trip she hadn't wished
for, but what a trip. Instead of curing her of her
obsession for Alex, it had made it worse.

She went down to the stateroom to pack a few things in a carry-on bag she'd found in a storage drawer. She didn't realize how nervous she was until she heard the phone ring while she was packing her makeup kit. Her liquid foundation slipped out of her hands and splattered on the tiled bathroom floor.

Jane ran to the lounge. It was most likely the Leonakises, and she didn't know what to say to them. Would it reassure them to think they were close to finding Sofia? Or would it make it worse if they didn't find her?

Her mind spun in circles until she finally grabbed the phone and said hello.

"Jane?"

Jane's knees gave out on her and she sank down in a canvas chair. "Sofia, where *are* you?"

"Sailing around, just like you are."

"I thought you were at the castle! We're coming to get you."

"Get me? You don't have to get me."

"What happened to you? Are you all right?"

"Of course I'm all right. How are you?"

"I'm fine, but we've been worried about you! We've been all over the place looking for you. The beach, the oracle, the cave . . ."

"A cave? Why would I go to a cave? They're damp and clammy—ugh. I left a note. Didn't you find it?"

"You said, 'I'm leaving. Don't try to find me.' It wasn't very reassuring. Your parents are frantic."

"I called them and told them I was all right," Sofia said dismissively.

"They're still worried."

"I know, but that's them. I'll have to call them again. What about Alex?"

"He's here. He's worried, too. We'll be docking in a few minutes at Marmara. I'll bring the phone up so you can talk to him."

"No, no, not yet. I have to talk to him in person."

"Did you get his message?" Jane asked.

"About changing his mind? Yes, but . . . we have to talk."

"Of course you have to talk. When will we see you? Where will we see you?"

"At the castle, just like I planned. It's the most romantic place. You're going to love it."

Would she love a place where Sofia and Alex would reconcile in some romantic castle turret, or would she succumb to a fatal attack of jealousy? "By the way, you're with someone, aren't you? Who is it?"

"The man I told you about. Or I tried to tell you, when you said you weren't good at keeping secrets. You know, the only person who really cares about me."

"What are you talking about?" Jane demanded, her hand gripping the receiver so tightly her knuckles were white. "Alex is the one who cares about you. He's the one you're going to marry tomorrow."

"Oh, Jane, I don't know."

"You *have* to know! You've been in love with Alex for ten years. How can you not know?"

Sofia sighed. "I know. We'll straighten it all out when I see you tonight."

"Tonight? What about today?"

"I can't, I'm tied up today. Take the day off; do something fun. You deserve it after what I've made you go through. Get Alex to take you windsurfing. See you at the castle."

Sofia hung up.

For a long moment Jane just sat there. Then she walked slowly up the steps to the wheelhouse.

"What's wrong?" Alex said. "You look like you've seen a ghost."

"Sofia just called."

He stared at her. "Why didn't you tell me?"

"I am telling you," Jane said irritably. "Do you think it was easy to talk to her, especially when she didn't answer any of my questions, especially when she . . . she . . ."

"Didn't want to talk to me? She didn't, did she?"

Jane looked down. "She was busy."

"Busy?" he shouted. "Does she know we've been busy scouring the Aegean for her?"

"I told her. She said she didn't ask us to look for her."

Alex's jaw tightened. "She has a point there. Is she still mad at me? Didn't she get my message?"

"She got your message, and no, I don't think she's mad at you."

"Is she planning on getting married tomorrow?"

"Well, of course."

"Then why wouldn't she talk to me?"

"She said it had to be in person."

"Fine. We'll dock the boat and go meet her. Where, at this castle?"

"Yes, but not until tonight."

Alex scowled but didn't say anything. He concentrated on bringing the boat into the harbor, and together they tied it up. Then Jane went downstairs, cleaned up her spilled makeup, grabbed her overnight bag, and met Alex on the pier, where he was pacing back and forth.

"I need a drink," he said as they walked rapidly past other docked cabin cruisers and fishing boats. Out of habit, Jane looked at the boats, looking for one that had "Mios" painted on the hull. Alex just stared straight ahead, walking purposefully until he stopped at the first café they came to and sat outside at a tiny marble-topped table.

Alex ordered a glass of retsina and black coffee. Jane ordered a frappé, a plate of pita bread with olives, tomatoes and radishes and ratatouille.

He raised his eyebrows in surprise, but she was more surprised he didn't order any food. It had been hours since they'd eaten. Obviously the news about Sofia had taken his appetite away, while it had only increased hers. She glanced at the shops that lined the port and at a string of horses and carriages waiting on the cobblestone street.

"I remember reading about his place," she said. "There're no cars here. That's why it's so quiet and charming."

"How did she sound?" Alex asked.

Jane wasn't surprised he'd changed the subject. In his mind there was only one subject: Sofia.

"A little off-kilter. I think she's embarrassed she's caused so much trouble."

"But not sorry," he said.

"Well . . ." Jane studied his face to see if he looked hurt. He pressed his lips together and looked more angry than anything else.

"Who is she with?" he said.

"I don't know. Whoever it is, she knew him before. She said she tried to tell me about him, but I wouldn't listen."

"But you saw him with her that night, when you thought it was me, didn't you?"

"I guess I did, but they were so far away and moving so fast, I couldn't tell what he looked like. Obviously, since I thought it was you."

"That night at the party, she was dancing with a Greek guy when I left to go get you," he said, rubbing his forehead as if he was trying to remember—or more likely, to forget. "So for the past three, four days she's been sailing around with him, whoever he is. Some local guy. Are we supposed to believe they're just friends?"

"Like you and me? It's possible," Jane said cautiously.

Alex snorted. "No, it isn't." After this trip he had serious doubts. Doubts about Sofia, doubts about Jane, and—especially—doubts about himself. Absently he reached for an olive on Jane's plate and ate it.

As he watched her eat her vegetables, suddenly he was ravenous. Somehow seeming to know, Jane slid her plate in front of him and handed him a fork. She read him better than anyone he'd ever known. Maybe because she'd known him so long, or maybe because she was just more perceptive than most people he knew.

Whatever it was, his stomach, which had been churning with anger and jealousy over the news about Sofia, was back to normal. Was it possible he felt relief, knowing Sofia had someone else? He shook his head. He and Jane ate off the same plate in companionable silence. He had a dozen questions, but Jane probably didn't know the answers. She'd already told him everything she knew. Or had she? He finished the last bite of ratatouille and set his fork down.

"Is there something you're not telling me? Because I can take it. Whatever it is, I'm going to find out sooner or later."

She shook her head. Her brown eyes were full of sympathy, but at least it wasn't pity. He couldn't take it if it was.

"Never mind," he said. "I shouldn't have asked you. This is between Sofia and me." But even as he said the words, he knew whatever happened between him and Sofia affected what happened between him and Jane.

"No, there is something," she said, leaning forward across the small table, so close, he could see a smattering of freckles across her nose. They made her look young and vulnerable, but he knew she was stronger and tougher than she looked. How had he never noticed those before? Were they a result from yesterday's sunshine? "Sofia suggested we go windsurfing."

He laughed out loud, surprised but not amused. "I don't believe it. She runs away, we chase her all over hell and back, and when we finally find her, she tells us to go windsurfing."

Jane gave him a wan smile. "That's Sofia for you."

"Whatever we do, let's catch a horse-drawn carriage and check into this castle first."

He and Jane climbed up into the carriage behind a little old driver dressed in baggy black pants, a white shirt, and a tie hanging askew. The rhythmic sounds of the horses' hooves on the cobblestones calmed Alex's restless nerves. The whole island, devoid of traffic, had a timeless feel.

"Whatever Sofia has done to us, wherever she's led us, I don't regret coming here," he said as they passed a Byzantine church on a hillside carpeted with wildflowers.

Jane nodded, but she didn't even look at the church or the birds swooping overhead. There was something wrong, something missing.

"What's wrong?" he said. "Where's the Jane who oohs and aaahs over every cypress tree, every hibiscus and every robin? Where's the Jane who stood there in the storm and didn't even get sick?" He studied her profile, her firm jaw and her soft cheek.

He wanted to put his arm around her, tell her everything was going to be fine—but he kept his hands on the worn leather seat of the carriage.

"What is it? Is it Sofia?" he asked. "You can't let her get to you. I learned that a long time ago. You said it yourself, 'That's Sofia for you.' This is vintage Sofia. Impulsive, crazy, and unexpected. If it doesn't bother me, then it shouldn't bother you. Whatever she does, or doesn't do, has nothing to do with you."

"I know, I know. I just . . . Anyway, you're taking it well," she said.

"What choice do I have? She ran away, and either she's coming back or she isn't. Either we're getting married, or we're not."

"I didn't realize you were such a fatalist," Jane said with a wry smile.

"I am where Sofia is concerned. Tell me, what more can I do? I've come after her, I've offered to give up what I want to do by staying with the company. What more could she want?"

"Nothing. You're right, you can't do any more. She's crazy if she doesn't come back."

Alex didn't dispute that. Sofia had always had a crazy streak. It fascinated him, but it also drove him around the bend. He'd always bounced back before, but this time he didn't know if he would—or even if he wanted to. In the past he'd rationalized that Sofia was worth whatever trouble she caused him. This time she'd gone too far, and he was not in the mood to rationalize any longer. Yes, she was exciting, unpredictable, and a little wild. But was that really what he wanted at this point in his life?

The carriage turned onto a narrow stone causeway with the sea lapping at the stones on both sides, and they drove in silence for two or three miles until they reached the vaulted stone gates where the road narrowed into a small lane, and the carriage had to stop and turn back.

Along with other pedestrians in shorts and big hats and cameras hanging around their necks, they walked single file along the narrow streets of the village that surrounded the castle on the hill. Alex grabbed Jane's bag and waved aside her protest that she could handle it; it was a good, long uphill walk on rough cobblestones to the castle looming above them.

Had Sofia come this way yet, or would she only arrive tonight, as she'd said? He couldn't imagine her hiking up there, no matter how charming the castle was. But maybe he'd underestimated her. Maybe he'd never known her at all.

It was a scary thought. If he didn't know her, who did he know? He wished he'd had a chance to talk to her—yet he couldn't imagine what he'd say.

Was it because he was so angry that he felt like he would choke, or because his feelings were so mixed . . . or was it something else? All he knew, with sudden certainty, was that he couldn't marry her tomorrow. It would be wrong.

Maybe she knew that. Maybe that's why she'd left.

He was definitely not the man she'd met ten years ago. Hell, he wasn't even the man who'd arrived five days ago. And she? Was she the same dramatic, willful, demanding Sofia she'd always been? Or had the pressure of the wedding pushed her into being someone else?

Whoever she was, he couldn't marry her. Not now. Not after what he'd been through these past days.

He stopped and shifted the two bags he was carrying, and Jane reached for hers. "I've got it," he said. After a few more switchbacks in the path, they saw the castle itself around the next bend—gray stone with two towers, domes and turrets, escutcheons and icons.

"Wow," he said. "Glad I wasn't here in the fourteenth century and I had to attack this castle. They'd be throwing hot tar down on us from the top of those walls."

The front desk was situated in an immense reception hall, with a huge marble throne in an alcove in the center of the wall. Sunlight poured into the room from twelve Gothic windows.

Jane approached the clerk and asked if there was a reservation for Woods and Atwood. She held her breath while the woman checked. It seemed incongruous to have a computer in this medieval setting, and reading the brochure on the desk, Jane saw there was also a workout room, a sauna, and even a Ping-Pong table on the terrace.

The clerk took so long finding their reservation,

Jane started to worry. Maybe Sofia hadn't made them a reservation—she hadn't thought to ask her. If Sofia hadn't, they'd have to go back outside the old city and look for something else. Or stay on the boat. But now that she was here in the castle, she wanted to stay here—even if it meant running into Sofia and the mystery man every time she walked out into the hall or to the lounge.

A few nervous minutes later the clerk smiled at them and handed them the keys to a room. Before Jane could tell her they each wanted a room, Alex spoke up.

"Do you have a Ms. Leonakis staying here?" he asked.

The clerk checked her register. "Yes," she said. "You are the friends she mentioned. Room 302 at the other end of the castle. I don't believe they're here yet, but if you want to check, take a turn at the vestibule and continue down the hall. You're fortunate she reserved a room for you. We are fully booked tonight."

Jane exchanged a quick glance with Alex. They'd both heard the word *they're*. And the place was fully booked, so the most she could hope for now was a separate bed. Otherwise . . .

"Shall we see if she's there?" She wasn't ready to see Sofia, but maybe Alex was.

"Sure," he said. His light tone didn't fool her; he was just as on edge as she was.

They knocked on the door of Room 302. A maid

in a white apron with a stack of towels in her hand answered. She waved her hands and said something in Greek.

"Sorry," Jane said, and turned to leave. As she did, she caught a glimpse of a double bed, the sheets rumpled and the faint scent of Sofia's perfume in the air.

"Let's go," Alex said brusquely.

Jane shot him a look, but he'd already headed back down the hall. Was he relieved not to have to confront her already? Or was he infuriated and wounded to see that Sofia was really, truly involved with the mystery man, whoever he was?

Their room turned out to be a suite, with a living room decorated in thick woven wall hangings called *flokatis,* a kitchenette, and a solid-marble bathroom. The bedroom boasted a medieval carved-stone fireplace and a king-size four-poster bed.

Determined not to think about the sleeping arrangements, Jane went out the double doors to the terrace and looked at the crystal-clear Aegean as it crashed on the rocks below. The air was fresh and cool and smelled of the sea.

"That's the kind of sound I like to fall asleep to," Alex said from behind her. "It reminds me of my cabin at the beach."

"Mmmm," she said, not turning to look at him. Did he picture himself in this bed, or his bed at the beach. . . . And alone, or with Sofia?

"Since we don't know when Her Highness will

show up, let's get out and look around." Alex put his hand on her shoulder and a brief smile softened his sarcasm.

He looked more like himself; easygoing, untemperamental. Which was how he'd handled Sofia all these years. Maybe she had jumped to too many conclusions too soon.

"I noticed some hiking paths leading up the hill from the hotel," he continued.

"Let's go," she said. It wouldn't take long before he and Sofia would come to their senses and realize that no matter what had happened in these past few days, they couldn't live without each other. Tomorrow, they'd all be on their way back. After a fling with Sofia, the mysterious stranger would be back tending his nets and looking elsewhere for a girlfriend.

They spent the afternoon wandering the hills above the castle and the town. They stepped over craggy rocks along corkscrew paths, and stopped to look down at the charming village with its crooked streets, horse-drawn carriages, and curio shops. Occasionally they stepped off the path to let donkeys with bells around their necks pass by. They sat and rested on a grassy knoll with a spectacular view of the sea below.

"If I were Sofia, I'd be tempted to stay right here in Greece," Jane said with a sigh of pleasure. "The sea, the scenery, the food . . . not that she would, of course. But with that vacation house on Mios, you'll be able to come often."

"What vacation house?" Alex said quietly, his

voice reflecting no surprise or shock, nothing. Maybe he was numb to it all. Or maybe he was keeping his emotions to himself, as he usually did.

"I . . . I . . . You mean you really don't know that the Leonakises are giving you a house for a wedding present? I feel terrible." Jane buried her face against her knees. "Why can't I keep my mouth shut?"

"It doesn't matter," he said. "I would have found out soon enough."

"There's nothing wrong with it, is there? You'll act surprised when you find out, won't you?" she asked anxiously.

"Don't worry, I'll act surprised, all right." He stood up and helped her to her feet. "Let's go back."

She knew what he was thinking: maybe Sofia's there. As they retraced their steps, she couldn't help dragging her feet. Couldn't help wishing for just a few more hours before it was over; couldn't help wishing that this trip would never end. They'd sail the boat on and on into the sunset and just keep going. Just the two of them. The knowledge that it was only going to happen in her dreams made her steps heavy, her heart even heavier.

When they got back it was dusk, and the clerk told them Sofia had not returned. A shadow fell over Alex's face as he glanced at his watch.

"How about a game of Ping-Pong?" Jane said, with all the enthusiasm she could muster. "You used to be pretty good at it."

"Pretty good?" His tone matched hers. His desire

to make the time go quickly clearly matched hers, too. "I beat you a few more times than you care to remember."

The terrace was deserted, and they found the paddles and balls in a cupboard. Alex flipped a switch on the wall and an overhead light came on, illuminating the green wooden table with the white stripes around the edges and down the middle.

"Play much lately?" he asked, hitting a practice ball to her.

"Not since college," she said, hitting it back at him. "I won a few games."

"So did I."

"Not against me." She'd been on the women's intramural team.

"You haven't lost your touch," he said. "I was there in the gym the day you won the tournament."

"You were? I don't remember seeing you."

"I was in the bleachers."

She slammed a ball past him.

"Okay, hotshot," he said. "No more Mr. Nice Guy. I'll bet you anything you want that I can beat you."

"Like what?" she asked.

"The king-size bed. Whoever loses sleeps on the floor."

"It's not going to be me," she scoffed. "You haven't got a chance."

Alex laughed and served.

Jane gripped her paddle tightly, and it all came

back to her—how to spin the ball, and how to smash it where he couldn't hit it.

She got the first point. He got the second. They went back and forth. After playing a score of tie points, Jane finally won.

"Hooray!" She pumped one fist in the air.

He went to shake her hand. "You're serious? You haven't played since college?"

"I have no one to play with."

"What about Warren?"

"Uh, he's gone a lot."

"Oh, right, on those secret assignments defending our country. I bet the social director was one hell of a player."

"I'm sure he was, but we never played on the ship."

"Too many other things to do, right?" he said with a knowing smile. He was leaning against the table, still holding on to her hand. Something flickered in his eyes—an awareness that had nothing to do with Ping-Pong—and kept her there, her gaze locked onto his until she felt tears sting the backs of her eyes.

It was ridiculous. She wasn't sad. She wasn't the least bit unhappy. She'd had a fabulous few days, a bonus vacation, really. She blinked rapidly and tried to smile, but her lips trembled. "So, another game?" she challenged so he wouldn't notice.

As they changed sides, Alex patted her on the butt with his paddle.

Again, the game was close. But she was trying too hard, and he was getting better at it. When Alex hit an ace, she scrambled for it and missed. She ducked under the table to retrieve the ball.

Suddenly the atmosphere was charged with electrons. She could feel it even under the table.

"Sofia," Alex said. "It's good to see you."

Jane raised her head so suddenly, she banged it against the table. And everything went black.

Chapter 15

Alex felt a calm come over him. After imagining all the terrible things that could have happened to Sofia, imagining what he'd say to her and what she'd say to him when he finally got her back, she was standing there looking as beautiful as ever in a low-cut, bright turquoise dress that made her skin glow and her hair look like spun brown sugar. She'd never looked better, never looked more fulfilled.

He walked forward, held her by the shoulders, and kissed her. Her lips were cool, and he felt nothing.

What was wrong with him? She was safe. She was back. The chase was over. He should be overjoyed, they should be dancing around the room, laughing hysterically and hugging each other, celebrating their reunion—if . . . IF there was anything to celebrate. But he was numb. It must be the shock.

She backed away and didn't meet his gaze. If it was anybody else, he would have thought she was nervous, but Sofia was never nervous. She might be excited, agitated, emotional, but she was always full of self-confidence.

"Can we talk?" she asked.

"I think we'd better." He felt amazingly calm, though he knew *Can we talk* was always a bad sign. It meant Watch out, I've got something to say you won't want to hear.

"Where's Jane?" she asked.

"Here I am," she said in a small voice from under the table.

"Are you okay?" Alex asked, pulling her to her feet. Her eyes were anxious, her hand was cold, and he wished to hell he hadn't dragged her along on this ill-fated journey. She'd already suffered through enough of his and Sofia's arguments, separations, and reconciliations. This had to be the final one. He realized that though he'd found their relationship exhilarating and exciting in the past, he couldn't go through any more ups and downs. The uncertainty had driven him crazy, and he couldn't take any more. He had to tell Sofia and tell her now.

If Jane hadn't come along on this trip, he didn't know how he would have managed without her ridiculous purse, her bright ideas, and her faith that he was doing the right thing. Not to mention those cool hands on his back, and his hands on her back, the sight of her blushing body at the nudist beach and then . . . Enough! But the memories just wouldn't quit.

Right now Jane's big brown eyes were huge with worry and apprehension. Her gaze traveled from him to Sofia. She bit her lip, then she went over and hugged her friend. "I'll be in the room," she said, setting her paddle on the table.

"No, stay," Sofia said. "You've been in on this since the beginning."

"I can't." Jane's voice sounded as if she were strangling. And she was gone.

There was a long silence. Alex stared at Sofia, trying to decipher the look on her beautiful, familiar face. What did he see there—pride, sorrow, determination? All those things and something else, too.

Sofia cleared her throat. "I . . . I owe you an explanation," she said.

"I'd say so," he said, sitting on the edge of the Ping-Pong table and tapping the paddle against his knee.

"I don't know where to start," she said, running one hand through her long, lustrous hair.

"At the beginning," he suggested.

"Yes, well—you were late getting to the island."

"I had things to do."

"That's the point," she said. "They were things that had nothing to do with me."

"They had to do with our future," he pointed out.

"Your future, not mine," she said.

"I thought they were one and the same."

"So did I, Alex, until you persisted in this idea of starting up your own business."

"I was willing to give that up." As soon as he spoke the words, he realized he'd said *was,* not *am.* He was no longer willing to give it up.

"I knew your heart wasn't in it."

He had to give her credit for her perception. She was standing there so calm and so cool, while he was worrying about letting her down easily. "What more did you want?" he asked. "Just out of curiosity."

"I wanted someone who put me first. I want someone who's there for me when I need him." Now she was the one who'd switched from past to present tense. "Not someone who was late to his own wedding. You'd left me alone."

"Your whole family was there with you. I've never seen anyone who was less alone."

"I was alone because you weren't there. Five days before the wedding, and you still hadn't arrived. I had to keep on explaining why you weren't there. I started to worry. I started to think maybe it wasn't going to work out after all. Maybe it was irrational, but that's how I felt." Her dark eyes filled with tears.

"So when I got there, you ran away," Alex said. He was trying to understand her, trying to understand her loneliness and her fears. But a growing realization was creeping up on him like an invisible incoming tide, slowly, steadily, until it almost swamped him.

Maybe, just maybe, he'd never really understood her at all. How could that be? He'd known her all these years; they'd gone through so much together. And now it was over. The words hadn't been spoken yet, but he knew it, and she knew it, too.

"I had to get away—I was feeling so stressed. You have no idea how hard it is to plan a wedding. It has to be perfect. There's so much pressure. I was on the verge of cracking. Then you didn't come and you didn't come, and when you did come, you sprang this bad news on me that you were going to leave my father in the lurch."

"Wait a minute, Sofia. I would never have left your father in the lurch. I love him, and I owe him a lot. Before I left, I would have trained someone to take my place. And I didn't spring it on you—I told you months ago what I was planning."

"That didn't make it any easier."

Alex sighed. "So you had to get away. I understand that; lots of people get jitters. But did you have to go so far?"

"I didn't mean to. But one thing led to another. . . ." She drifted off and a light blush appeared on her cheeks.

"Who were you with?" Alex knew what she was going to say, but he had to hear her say it, no matter how hard it was for both of them.

"He's a local fisherman from Mios. His name is Yorgos and I've known him for years. He used to hang around the village and take me out for a sail sometimes. When you didn't show up, I had to turn to someone—someone who understood me, someone besides my family, someone who sympathized with me. He was there. He was always there. He was at the party that night. I danced with him.

"That night, he showed up under my window right after you and I had that fight. I thought we'd go out for a sail on his boat, that's all. But I got kind of carried away, and the more I thought about it, the more I decided to teach you a lesson."

"You did that, all right," Alex said. A lesson she hadn't intended, but one he'd needed to learn. "What about your parents—did they have to learn a lesson, too?"

"Of course not. I called them as soon as I could, and I left a note. There was no need for anyone to worry. I was perfectly safe."

"Are you still safe?"

She smiled dreamily. "Yes." Then her smile faded. "I can't marry you, Alex. And I'm sure you don't want to marry me, after all this."

He nodded. She was right; he didn't. And it was better for Sofia to make the break and to say the words, better for her to think it was her decision and not his. Yet there was a hollow feeling in his chest. It was part relief, but it was a sense of loss, too. He'd loved Sofia for so long, he didn't know how it would feel if he didn't love her.

"So," she said brightly. "We're heading back

tomorrow. I suppose you and Jane are, too. She and I have to have a long talk."

"Shall I get her now?" he asked.

"Not now, Yorgos is waiting for me. If we leave in the morning and head straight back, we should be there by dinnertime. I'll phone my parents and tell them."

"You'll tell them to call off the wedding?" Alex couldn't believe she'd do that, after all the plans, all the money they'd spent. But if that's what she wanted, he was sure her parents would go along with it. Especially when they knew it was her decision.

"Yes. You must be relieved, Alex. Now you can do whatever you want to do, without my nagging you." She gave a little smile. Before he could assure her he was going to work out the business situation in a way that would be agreeable to Nikos, she kissed him on the cheek.

He expected to feel sad, let down, disappointed, or even angry. But he felt none of those. He felt as if a huge load had been lifted from his shoulders.

"I'll see you later," Sofia said, then she turned and her skirt swirled around her beautiful legs and she was gone. Just like that.

Alex stood for many minutes staring off in the distance, then he ran up the stairs to their suite, taking the steps two at a time. Jane yanked the door open the minute he knocked.

"What happened?" she asked. "You look so strange."

"I feel strange. It's over," he said, stepping into the room.

"What? You don't mean that."

"Yes, I do. Sofia has made up her mind."

"She's just upset."

Alex shook his head. "Why should she be upset? She's been out sailing around with Yorgos for days while we were looking high and low for her, while her parents were worried sick about her."

"Who's Yorgos?"

"Some fisherman. Apparently they've been friends for years."

Jane hesitated. "Do you want to be alone?"

"I want to be with you. It must be time for dinner; let's go eat."

"I'll change clothes," she said and went to the bedroom.

Jane came back into the room wearing a bright red dress that made him stagger backward. How had he ever thought she was plain? She was truly beautiful. Had she changed so much, or had he? All he knew was she was stunning.

"Nice dress," he said in the understatement of the year.

"Thank you."

"You won't need your purse," he said.

"Are you sure?" she asked, swinging it back and forth.

Sure? After today, how could he ever be sure of anything? "Trust me," he said, and took it back to the bedroom.

They walked out of the hotel in the dusk, down the crooked cobbled streets of the medieval town, and out through the massive stone gate they'd entered a few hours and a whole lifetime ago. He didn't say anything, and mercifully Jane didn't ask any questions, though she must have wanted to.

They stopped at a tiny crêperie on a side street and looked at the menu.

"Hungry?" Alex asked.

Jane nodded. The smells wafting from the crêpe machine behind the counter made her stomach rumble. They both ordered zucchini-and-cheese crêpes and a carafe of the local white wine. Then Alex leaned back in his chair and observed Jane. The red dress made her cheeks look pink, but there was a deep worry line etched between her eyebrows.

"You're not worried about me, are you?" She shook her head. "You don't need to worry about Sofia, either. She's fine. She's more than fine. She has Yorgos, her fisherman."

"But it can't be serious. I mean, Sofia with a fisherman?"

"I don't know. All I know is that he was there for her when I wasn't."

"She'll come to her senses. I know she will. She always does; you'll see."

"I think she *has* come to her senses, Jane. You'll see when we all sail back to Mios tomorrow."

"Then she's coming with us?"

Alex shook his head. "Not a chance. She's going with Yorgos."

"I'm . . . I'm . . . stunned. I don't understand." The crêpes arrived and Jane cut hers and chewed hungrily. "It's so upsetting to think of what she did."

"It doesn't seem to have affected your appetite," he said dryly.

"I always eat when I'm upset or tense."

He smiled and reached across the table to smooth the lines in her forehead. "You might as well. There's nothing else you can do about it."

"Are you sure? Maybe I could talk to her."

"And tell her what?" *Alex is really there for you, Sofia. You've made a big mistake by going off with a fisherman, but he forgives you if you'll forgive him. Get married as planned. You can work out your differences later.* "Thanks for the offer, Jane, but it won't work. It *is* over."

She set her fork down. "I'm sorry." Her eyes filled with tears.

"Stop," he said. "Sofia's not crying and neither am I. Why should you?" He brushed her cheek with his thumb to catch a tear. Her skin was so soft, he wanted to trace the outline of her cheek, to stroke the hollow of her throat to feel her pulse beating there. Most of all, he wanted her to stop feeling sad for something that had nothing to do with her.

"Somebody has to cry," she sniffed. "Somebody has to feel bad about all those wasted years."

"They weren't wasted. I learned a lot during those years. I learned what was important to me and what wasn't. I worked hard and I played hard, too. Both with Sofia and without. It's time for us both to move on."

She blew her nose. "You're being very mature about this. I think I'd be screaming and throwing things."

"You mean if Warren broke up with you?"

"If it happened the day before my wedding."

"Is there going to be a wedding?" Alex poured more wine for them. "When I saw you in Sofia's wedding dress, I thought maybe . . ."

"No, I'm not ready. Not yet."

He felt the knot in his rib cage start to dissolve at last, a knot he hadn't even known was there. It could have been the wine; it could have been something else. It could have been relief and hope for the future. A future that included Jane.

"Good," he said. "Maybe we can get together when we get back. You can come up and see the birds of Washington. There are some interesting ones you can add to your list."

He didn't want to put any pressure on her, and he didn't want her to think he was desperate for company. But he just couldn't let her fade out of his life again. Not after what had happened between them.

"I'll have to see how things go once we get back," she said carefully. She couldn't believe how casual Alex was being. He was acting the way he had a week ago—as if they were friends, nothing more, nothing less.

"Sure. I'll be busy, too, training somebody to take my place at the construction company, as well as getting my new business set up. My partner will be glad to hear the news."

"Do you want to go back to the hotel to call him?"

"No." He wanted to stay there and talk to Jane. He wanted to look at her across the table and watch her expressive face change from concern to sympathy to a smile.

A street musician stopped at their table, and Alex asked him to play "For the Longest Time." He smiled and nodded and played "Never on Sunday."

Alex grinned. "I tried."

"You really thought Billy Joel was in his repertoire?"

"It doesn't hurt to ask."

Her eyes softened to brown velvet, and her lips curved in the smile he'd been waiting to see. She reached across the table and took his hand, and he felt an invisible cord tighten and draw them closer together. One that had been there many years ago, but then disappeared.

Jane's smile faded and a look of longing appeared in her eyes, so strong that it made him think of that big bed in their suite, with the sound of the sea crashing against the rocks and the salty smell of the water.

Is that what she wanted? It was what he'd wanted for the past twenty-four hours: to make love to Jane again, but without the guilt or the shadow of Sofia hanging over their heads. But was it too late, or too soon, or . . .

Was she ready? Would he be just another man in her life? Or did their history make him special, make *them* special? He was afraid to ask, but if he didn't ask . . .

Her knees were pressed against his under the table. Alex held her hand in his, making lazy motions with his thumb against her palm. She was breathing hard. She stroked his lip with her fingers, and a white-hot poker of desire shuddered through his body.

"Does your mouth still hurt?" she asked, in almost a whisper.

"I don't know. Better try that again," he murmured.

He wanted her, but he didn't want to scare her off. He had to know, to be sure, before he did anything rash. The ache that had started in his gut had moved to his groin, and warning signs were flashing inside his head: Slow down. Dangerous curves ahead!

The questions hung in the air between them. *Do you want what I want? Will you go where I go? Will you be able to forget the past, forget Sofia?* She must have heard them, felt them, sensed them. So why didn't she answer? Why didn't she say *yes, yes, yes?*

"Let's go," Alex said, leaving a handful of money on the table. He put his arm around her waist, and she leaned against his shoulder as they slowly walked back up to the castle in the dark. The scent of her hair and her skin tempted him unbearably.

Keep moving. Don't stop now. Not even to kiss that tender spot beneath her ear or stop for a real kiss. Not here. Not now. Not yet. Wait till we get to the room— that room with the sound of the waves, the smell of the sea.

The streets and sidewalks were crowded with tourists hurrying to leave before the gates closed. They bumped elbows with strangers, they weaved back and forth, whether because of the wine or high with anticipation, he didn't know. He only knew he wanted her, now. Deep down in his subconscious, he knew they had to be together. Whether it was for one more night or forever, he'd couldn't say. He didn't trust himself to make those decisions anymore.

Jane was vaguely aware that the maid had turned down the bedcovers and left chocolate candies on the pillows, and that the sconces threw soft light on the woven wall hangings and on the marble floors, but nothing really registered except her overwhelming need to make love to Alex. She kicked off her shoes and went out on the balcony to stand next to him. The waves crashed against the rocks, and the moon shone on the whitecaps on the sea.

"It's magic," she said softly.

And she needed all the magic she could get, to make her dreams come true. She didn't ask for much—just one more night to spend with him. Not one like the last time; that was too wild, too brief, too scary. She wanted one whole night with the one man she'd ever really loved, and then she could return to real life. She knew he valued her as a friend, and their sexual chemistry was strong, but she also knew he was emotionally confused, rebounding from his broken engagement.

"Knowing it was all for nothing, are you sorry you came on this trip?" Alex ran his fingers lightly up the inside of her arm, and she gripped the railing of the balcony.

"Nothing?" she said with a catch in her voice. "I think it was for something. I still think—"

"Don't say you think Sofia and I are getting back together."

"Are you sure?"

"Positive. At the risk of sounding hokey, this is the first day of the rest of my life. Or the first night. And I want to spend it with you, Jane. You know how I feel about you. And how much I want you."

He planted a kiss in the hollow of her throat, and she felt as if her bones had melted. Every dream she'd ever had about Alex was about to come true, if she'd let it. If she'd accept the fact that he was on the rebound, and that this story was not going to end with happily ever after.

There was music in the distance, a fiddle, a viola, and a guitar playing some soulful tune. There was moonlight shining on their balcony, and there was the perfumed air from the night-blooming jasmine below their window. And there was Alex, the sexiest man she'd ever known, the one true love of her life,

whispering in her ear how much he desired her—
and she was going to turn him down because he
was on the rebound?

She might be stupid, she might be sorry tomorrow, but right now, she was going to grab her dream
and hold on for dear life.

Alex turned out the lights and the room was
awash in pale moonlight. A faint breeze drifted
through the open window, and the sound of the
waves splashing against the rocks below filled the
air.

Standing in the middle of the room, Jane gave a
shiver of pure delight. Slowly, dreamily, she lifted
her dress over her head. She sighed in pure ecstasy
as the soft, crocheted fabric brushed across her
overheated skin. Next came her red thong, and now
she was completely bare and feeling deliciously
sexy.

Alex kicked off his pants, peeled off his shirt, and
in a moment the moonlight was turning his bare,
muscled body to polished marble. She reached out
to touch all that warm muscle and skin, and he
scooped her up and carried her to the bed.

When her bare skin hit the satiny sheets she gave
another shiver, this time of pure, hot-blooded pleasure. Poised above her, Alex's knees pressed into the
mattress on either side of her hips. He bent down to
plant hot, hungry kisses on her mouth, then down
to the hollow of her throat and the valley between
her breasts, while her blood pressure threatened to
go off the charts.

"Enough," she whispered. "I need you now."

"Already?" he asked, a smile in his voice.

"Yes. Please. Now."

But despite his obvious stunning erection, he didn't seem to agree.

He teased, he tantalized, he brought her closer and closer with his hands and his tongue, and the tension built and built. At last he came, hot and heavy, into her slick, waiting entrance, and she clenched around him. He moaned and began the rhythmic thrusts that finally brought them to climax together in a whirlpool of action and emotion. Their voices rang out together. She threw her arms back over her head, and he rolled over and took her with him.

After an eternity, Alex covered her with the sheet and said softly, "That was amazing."

Jane fought off any niggling little questions she wanted to ask herself, like *What do you think you're doing?* Or, *This man has just broken up with his fiancée. Doesn't that bother you?* She squeezed her eyes shut, and when Alex settled under the sheet and pulled her close, she sighed with contentment, finally let go of all her thoughts and questions, and drifted off toward sleep. Tomorrow, she told herself before she lost consciousness. *I'll deal with it tomorrow.*

Tomorrow came too soon. When the faint light of dawn filtered in through the window, she was still in Alex's arms. Jane lay there quietly, wishing it could be like this forever. Wondering, dreaming . . . One thing was sure; her dreams would never come true until she talked to Sofia. And even then . . .

She eased herself out of the bed, gathering a robe around her along with her courage. With one last look at Alex, who slept peacefully, his face no longer creased by worry, she stepped out of the room and went down the hall.

She knocked softly on Sofia's door.

No one answered.

Did she have the wrong room? What would she say if Yorgos came to the door? She didn't even know what to say when Sofia came to the door. Not exactly.

Sofia did come, her hair tousled, her face soft with sleep and, if Jane wasn't mistaken, with sexual fulfillment.

"Jane, what on earth?"

"Sofia, we have to talk," she whispered urgently.

Sofia looked around the empty corridor. "It's the crack of dawn."

"I know. I just have to ask you . . . you aren't really going to call off your wedding, are you?"

"Well . . ."

Jane felt her heart sink. She knew it—it wasn't over, at all. "Everything's going to be okay once you get back, isn't it? Everything's in place for today—the flowers, the doves, the guests. If we leave now, we can be back in time. You wouldn't want to let everyone down, would you?"

Sofia smiled a giddy, little smile. "No, but . . . we'll have to see how it goes."

"How it goes?" Jane repeated blankly. "Will you sail back with us?"

Sofia shook her head. "I can't do that. But, Jane, I'm glad we've had this talk." She hugged Jane and reached for the doorknob. Jane watched helplessly as Sofia disappeared back into her room, leaving her standing there barefoot and shivering and wondering what had just happened.

Wait a minute. She had spent the last five days looking for Sofia; she deserved more of an answer. Oblivious to the other guests, she banged on the door.

Sofia opened it, her eyes wide and startled.

"Are you going to marry Alex or not?" Jane demanded. "I think I deserve an answer. And so does he."

"Yes, you do, both of you; and no, I'm not," Sofia said.

"All right. But I don't get it. What happened between Monday and today? After ten years, are you throwing away everything you and Alex had together?"

"I'm not throwing anything away, Jane," Sofia said calmly. "Things change. People change, even though sometimes they don't realize it. Like you— the old Jane would never have come all this way to find me. The old Jane would have stayed behind and let Alex do it. The new Jane is going to get the happiness she wants, what she's always wanted, if she's brave enough to reach out and grab it."

Jane shook her head. How did Sofia know what she wanted? "And the old Sofia?" Jane asked.

"She's gone, Jane. I can't marry Alex. I'm in love with Yorgos."

"What? I don't believe that."

"It's true. Just as you're in love with Alex."

Jane felt color stain her cheeks. She'd been so careful to hide her feelings, how had Sofia guessed? Sofia smiled knowingly and, once again, closed the door to her room.

When Jane returned to their suite, Alex was furiously pacing back and forth. When she came in, he grabbed her by the shoulders and glared at her. "Where in the hell have you been?"

"I went to see Sofia."

"Don't do that to me! I thought you'd run off."

"Alex! I was only gone a few minutes." She felt a stab of guilt for making him worry. "I'm sorry."

"That's what Sofia said. Sorry doesn't cut it."

"I had to see her."

"What about? It's six o'clock in the morning. Couldn't it wait?"

"I didn't know what time they were leaving. I wanted to talk to her, to ask her, to find out . . ."

"Well, what did you find out that I didn't find out yesterday?"

"I . . . she's not going to marry you."

"I could have told you that."

"I had to hear it from her. But I still can't believe it."

"Believe it. This is one thing you can't fix, Jane. You've got the tape and the medicine and the sewing kit, but nothing will fix what's wrong with me and Sofia."

"You say that, but—"

"And I'll say it again. It's over." He sighed. "Let's get out of here. There's no reason to stay any longer," he said, and began to toss his belongings into his bag.

They didn't see Sofia or her fisherman or their boat, either in the harbor or out at sea. As Alex took the helm, Jane disappeared below. The sun was warm, the seas were calm. Another beautiful day in paradise, he thought.

And now what? Just when he finally understood himself, he realized that neither Jane nor Sofia understood *him*. The next thing he had to do was to tell Nikos he wasn't going to work for him *and* he wasn't going to marry his daughter.

When Jane came up to the helm to relieve him, her eyes were red-rimmed. What did she have to cry about? They spoke only a few words. He went below, ate a few stuffed grape leaves without tasting them, made coffee, and came back to take over.

"We're making good time," he said.

Jane nodded, then disappeared.

Though they made good time, evidently Sofia and her friend made even better time, because a fishing boat was tied to their pier when Jane and Alex came in by dinghy.

The atmosphere was a repeat of the day they'd arrived: a circus. Cars parked in the driveway, delivery men carrying boxes and bags into the house, servants bustling around, and gardeners pulling invisible weeds from the wide expanse of lawn.

Alex's heart fell. Hadn't Sofia told them the wedding was off? Was he going to have to call it off himself.

Nikos and Apollonia came rushing out of the house to greet them, and Nikos threw his arms around Alex. Apollonia was crying, but they soon learned they were tears of happiness.

"She's back," Nikos said. "Our baby is back, thanks to you."

"No, we had nothing to do with it," Alex said, but they weren't listening.

"Thank God there will be a wedding after all," Apollonia said, hugging Jane.

Alex almost choked. "What?"

"Sofia and Yorgos," Apollonia said. "They're getting married tomorrow—Sunday. Sunday weddings are always lucky." She looked at Alex with a worried frown. "She said you knew, that you understood."

"I do," he said, breathing a sigh of relief.

"Smile Jane," he said under his breath as he nudged her with his elbow.

But Jane's face was pale. She looked as if she was in a state of shock.

"It's the only way, really," Nikos said. "We insisted, because of what happened. We may be old-fashioned, but we are in Greece. Women cannot run away with a man and expect the world to forget. A wedding is the only answer. And it is what she wants."

"But—" Jane began. She tried to smile, but her mouth clearly wouldn't cooperate, and her distress made Alex want to kiss all her confusion away.

After the past few days' emotional roller coaster of feeling dumbfounded, then ecstatic, then depressed, he was now determined to get what he wanted— Jane.

Chapter 16

What was he was going to say to Jane? That he loved her instead of Sofia? That they were meant for each other the way he and Sofia never were? That she was so right for him, he felt it in every bone of his body?

Would she believe that? Would she laugh in his face? It sounded improbable. It sounded crazy. But crazier things had happened.

But before he could talk to Jane, he had to talk to Nikos. Alex found him on the patio smoking a cigar. At first the older man was crestfallen to hear Alex was leaving the company, but after Alex suggested that George should inherit the business and that he'd be more than willing to train George before he left, Nikos looked hopeful.

"Thank you," the old man said. "I am sorry about . . ." He spread his gnarled hands in a gesture of hopelessness.

Alex smiled understandingly. "It was not meant to be—Sofia and I," he said, and Nikos nodded.

If only it was that easy to convince Jane.

That night there was a huge family dinner in the palatial dining room of the villa. It made Alex feel strange and awkward to see Sofia and Yorgos exchanging long, happy looks and occasional kisses. The whole scene was noisy, joyous, mind-altering . . . and somehow inevitable. Had he known all along it wouldn't work? Had he tried to make it work because he thought he owed it to Sofia?

After dinner and the toasts, there was music and dancing. This time Alex was the one to cut out unnoticed, as Jane had done only a few evenings ago. He walked down to the beach, wishing that she'd join him and they'd dance on the sand again. This time he'd tell her how he felt, and he'd try to make her believe they belonged together.

He stayed at the beach for over an hour, watching the moon rise over the sea, but she never came. Then he stood outside the house and threw stones at her darkened window, but she didn't come and open the window and offer to run away with him.

Finally he went to his room, but he was too wired to sleep. He lay there staring at the ceiling, until the musicians finally packed up and left. He listened to the voices of the guests below his window. Remembering last night, he hoped he wouldn't have to live on just those memories of these past few days and nights. But if Jane turned him down, that's all he'd have.

He was up at dawn, prowling around the house, looking for Jane in her hot-pink dress. Instead he ran into Sofia in her wedding dress. She gave him a little smile and a hug.

"Alex, are you sure you're okay with this?"

"More than okay—I have to thank you. It wouldn't have worked, you and I."

"I know," she said.

"But how . . . what . . . where?"

She nodded. "That's what everyone wants to know. Well, to begin with, we're going to live in the house daddy is giving us here on the island. Yorgos isn't just a simple fisherman, you know. He owns a whole fleet. We won't stay here forever. But first I have to teach him English, which is what I've been doing for the past four days."

I'll bet you have, Alex thought, but it didn't hurt the way he thought it would. It was over. Really over. It had been over for days, months, maybe years, though neither had realized it.

"What about you and Jane?" she asked. "I feel bad about the two of you spending all those days looking for me."

"Don't. We got to know each other again."

Sofia smiled happily. "Good. She's been in love

with you from the first day of class. Did you know that?"

Alex was taken aback. "No—that can't be. What about Professor Goodrich?"

"Who? You mean that long-haired lecher who thought he was God's gift to women? What about him?" she asked, puzzled.

"Jane had an affair with him."

Sofia laughed. "Jane? Are you crazy? Jane didn't even date in college; she spent all her time studying. And if she had dated, it wouldn't have been with Goodrich. You know that; she has principles."

"But she said . . ."

Sofia grinned. "I bet she was putting you on. You believed her?"

"Why would she do that?"

Sofia thought for a moment. "Maybe so you'd think of her as something besides the grind you saw her as?"

Alex paused. "She *does* have a boyfriend, right?"

"Warren?"

So he *was* real. "Yes, the Navy SEAL."

Sofia chuckled. "Warren is a dentist."

"Jesus."

"Yes." The look in her eyes said it all: He'd been a fool, but it wasn't too late.

"Thank you for staying for the wedding. Thank you for everything." She kissed him on the lips and left.

The next time he saw her was at the small village church. Bells were ringing, and the ceremony was mercifully short. All eyes were on the beautiful bride—all eyes but Alex's.

His were on the bridesmaid in the hot-pink dress. He thought she looked like hell. She was pale and her eyes were heavy, as if she hadn't slept last night, either.

When he went through the reception line in front of the church, he kissed Jane on the cheek. "You look terrible," he muttered.

"You, too," Jane said stiffly. She didn't seem able to hold her bouquet steady; the rose petals were shaking. The pulse in her temple was jumping, too, but she kept her voice steady. "I hear you're leaving before the fireworks tonight."

"I think I've had enough fireworks."

"I understand."

The sympathetic look in her eyes made him bristle with anger. How dare she feel sorry for him!

"You think I'm cutting out early because I can't stand to see Sofia happily married to someone else? How many times do I have to tell you I don't love her anymore? What bothers me is what's always bothered me—this is a circus. You know how I feel about big weddings. As for Sofia—"

He was interrupted as the people behind him in line nudged him forward, hugged Jane, and told her how lovely she looked.

"Thank you. You mean I don't look terrible?" she said with a pointed look in his direction.

Jane's obvious lack of understanding was because he'd failed at explaining himself. How could Sofia understand how he felt about Jane, and Jane not? Maybe he should have written out a speech and memorized it.

I love you, Jane. I know it seems sudden, but . . . If that didn't work, he'd grab her and kiss her senseless until she had to admit he was over Sofia.

The guests formed the traditional procession with the bride and groom in the lead, and walked into the town. Sofia threw flowers to the local residents and tourists who lined the road. After the wedding lunch Alex planned to catch the last ferry for Piraeus, and in Athens he'd take the first plane back to Seattle. But first he had to talk to Jane.

Just thinking about the long trip home made him tired. Or maybe it was due to the letdown, the end of the search. The end of his relationship with Sofia. Perhaps Jane was right: it wasn't easy to see your ex happily married to someone else. Not that he wanted to marry Sofia; he just wanted to find that kind of happiness.

It was so maddeningly frustrating that Jane couldn't understand that, couldn't believe he was in love with her. He saw the way she'd looked at him during the ceremony, as if he were a stranger. Sofia was wrong. She didn't love him at all.

He found himself lagging at the end of the procession, dragging his feet. He could see Jane far ahead of him, like a bright tropical flower, walking with George, Sofia's brother. He wanted to go up there and demand an explanation of why she'd lied to him about all those men in her past, but he couldn't make the effort. His shoes felt as if they were made of lead.

He dropped behind the group and accepted a ride from one of the Leonakises' cars. He climbed in back where Sofia's tiny grandmother, Yaya, was sitting in her blue silk dress and matching hat. She leaned over to kiss him on the cheek and speak to him in Greek. The only word he understood was *syncharitiria!*—congratulations. Somehow, even after the ceremony, she thought he'd married Sofia? He smiled and thanked her.

That was the last time he smiled for hours. At the wedding lunch in town, he fell into a dark mood. Everyone else was happy, laughing, talking, and making toasts. Even Jane was engaged in animated conversation with Sofia on her left. They glanced at him from time to time, and he wondered what they were saying about him.

Sofia made a beautiful bride; that was no surprise. But Jane looked even more beautiful, even with circles under her eyes. He couldn't take his eyes off of her.

When the dancing started, he cut in on Sofia and Yorgos during the second song, so he could say goodbye to Sofia.

"I'm going to catch the five o'clock ferry," he said.

"No hard feelings?" she asked.

"None," he said and meant it.

"About Jane," Sofia said as they waltzed around the dance floor.

"What about her?" he said, squeezing Sofia's hand a little harder than he'd intended.

"You have to talk to her. Tell her how you feel."

"I've tried, but she's stubborn and she doesn't listen to reason and—"

"And you're in love with her," Sofia said with a triumphant smile. "I knew it would happen if you just had a chance to get to know her. That's why I—"

"Are you saying that's why you ran away?" Alex asked in disbelief.

"Of course not. But that's why I sent you to the cave. To give you an extra day."

"And yourself. You gave yourself an extra day with Yorgos."

She didn't deny it. And he wasn't angry, just dazed as everything fell into place.

Then Yorgos cut in again. They made a dashing couple, Alex thought, standing in the doorway watching them dance. He was a good-looking hunk and supposedly he even understood Sofia. What more could she want? Her parents were happy she was marrying a Greek on a Sunday, even though he was just a not-entirely-so-humble fisherman.

Jane was dancing with George, but she couldn't tear her eyes away from Alex. He really did look awful. His eyes were the color of the Aegean during a storm; his face was gaunt. He looked as if he hadn't slept for days, though she knew he had.

She tore her gaze from him and forced herself to look at George. "I hear you're going to take Alex's place in the company."

"It would never have worked, making Alex a partner," George said. "He's a good guy, but I'm family."

"That's important," Jane said. *So why have you ignored your responsibility to the family and the company business all these years?*

"Alex just didn't fit in," he said.

"Alex fit in like no one else," Jane said fiercely. "He gave his all for the company and the family."

George's eyes widened in surprise, and Jane was relieved when the music stopped and the musicians took a break.

Sofia came bustling up to her, her white satin skirt rustling around her. "We have to talk," she said, grabbing Jane's hand and pulling her to a chair at an empty table.

"It's about time," Jane said with a half-smile. "That's what you said to me the day I got here."

"I should have told you then about Yorgos."

"You already knew?"

"I've known him since we first starting coming to the island, years ago. He was always around. He took me sailing and hiking and exploring every corner of his world, which as you might guess, is very far from my world. I refused to admit I loved him; I thought it wouldn't work. He doesn't speak English. He's a fisherman.

"And there was Alex. But when it came right down to it, I couldn't marry Alex. I loved him, but I wasn't in love with him anymore."

"And you were mad because he wouldn't work for your father, too."

"Not really. That was just an excuse."

"An excuse to run away with Yorgos?"

"Yes."

"So that's what you were going to tell me?"

"There's more."

Jane sighed and girded herself for something worse. "Go ahead."

"Alex is in love with you."

"He is not!"

"Sorry, but it's true."

"He told you?" Jane asked incredulously.

"I told him and he didn't deny it."

"He's too polite."

"No, he isn't," Sofia said firmly. "Not with me. Do you want me to give you some advice?"

"Can I stop you?"

Sofia grinned. "Don't let him get away. He's leaving on the next ferry. So tell him, tell him now, how you feel. What are you afraid of? What's the worst that can happen?"

Jane laughed raggedly. "The worst? He'll be polite and nice and sympathetic. We had some good times while we were at sea, but that's all it was. It would be wrong for either of us to mistake that for love."

Sofia threw up her hands, her new diamond ring sparkling in the sunlight pouring through the open windows. "All right, I give up. Go back to San Francisco and marry Warren if that's what you want. I'll be your bridesmaid, just like we always planned. Just don't wait until it's too late to figure out who you really want.

"Oh, and don't forget your purse," she said. "I thought you might need it, in case you change your mind. It's outside in Yorgos's car." She jumped up from the table and joined her husband on the dance floor for a slow waltz.

The next thing Jane knew, Alex was standing in front of her. His mouth set in a determined line, he asked her to dance.

She got up and joined him on the dance floor.

"We have to talk," he said, after a long silence.

Her knees buckled. He held her tight but at a distance. "What is there to say?"

"I'm in love with you, Jane."

"Five days ago you were in love with Sofia. This is a classic case of rebound." Jane was proud of how rational she sounded.

"No, it isn't. It's a classic case of arrested development: mine. I wasn't really in love with Sofia; it was you. It was always you."

"Alex, please. I was at the wedding. I saw how you looked at her, and how she looked at you."

"Then your vision is faulty. Did you also see how she looked at Yorgos?" he demanded. "I suppose you think she's rebounding, too?"

"I can't be responsible for what Sofia does. I just have to protect myself."

"From what? From me? From love? I'm asking you to take a chance on me. To give me a chance to convince you this is it, the real thing, forever."

"Forever?" Jane held him at arm's length. "We've spent five days together."

"And nights," he reminded her.

"And they were wonderful days," she admitted.

"And nights."

She blushed. "What I'm trying to say, if you'd just listen to me . . ."

"I'm listening."

"This has all been so wild, so crazy, and yes, so romantic—but it's not real life. Why don't we wait until we get back, and then take it slow. See how we really feel about each other."

"I know how I really feel about you. I love you, Jane. I feel like I've just found you, after all these years, and I want to be with you."

"I want to believe you, but how can I? You've been through an emotional wringer. So have I. Let's take some time to think it over. Then we can see each other. Or—or e-mail each other."

"E-mail?" Alex snorted derisively and dropped her hand. "After what we've been through together? Okay, you want time to think it over? You want to go back to real life? Go ahead. Be my guest. When you're done thinking, let me know. You know where to find me."

He turned abruptly and left her standing alone in the middle of the floor while couples swirled around her. She watched dumbfounded as he walked toward the door.

Before she could react, Nikos asked her to dance, then one of Sofia's cousins cut in, and when she was finally free to look for Alex, she couldn't find him. She went to the door and looked out across the town square. The ferry whistle sounded its first warning, and her heart leaped to her throat.

He was going. He was leaving on the ferry, and she'd never see him again. That separation she'd thought she'd wanted—that break, that time out—had passed in the blink of an eye, and the reality hit her like a ten-foot wave. She couldn't let him go.

Without thinking, she took off her impossibly high-heeled pink shoes and ran out to Yorgos's car, parked in front of the restaurant. She grabbed her purse and slung it over her shoulder. In her stockinged feet, she walked swiftly toward the ferry dock, a few blocks away. The whistle sounded again, and she began running.

She hardly noticed the passersby who stopped and stared and pointed at her. She realized what a sight she must be, running toward the pier in her pink dress, her bare feet, and the giant leather purse over her shoulder, but she didn't care.

The dockworkers saw her coming, and they yelled to the crew on board to wait. She was the last one to dash up the gangway before they pulled it up. Breathless and footsore, she pushed her way through the crowd to the upper deck, but she didn't see Alex anywhere.

She couldn't believe it—he wasn't there!

She'd made a terrible mistake. He'd decided to stay, and she'd rushed on board the ferry for nothing.

Leaning against the railing, trying to catch her breath, Jane watched the town gradually fade in the distance. She almost thought she could still hear the music from the restaurant, and wondered if Alex was still there.

A tear slid down her cheek. Impatiently she brushed it away. Damn Alex, anyway. Why didn't he tell her he wasn't leaving?

You know where to find me. No, she didn't. Where was he?

She had a sinking feeling that she'd blown her one chance for love and happiness.

Straightening, she looked around at the tourists— some with binoculars pressed to their eyes, others drinking coffee or lemonade, or eating hot pastries from the snack bar below. At least she wasn't seasick this time.

She decided to take some pills, just to be safe. Looking for some coffee to wash them down, she made her way toward the steps that led to the snack bar below—and then she saw him.

Alex was standing with his back to her, his hair blowing in the wind, his arms propped against the railing. She froze. Her mouth was too dry and her vocal cords were frozen.

Her heart pounding, Jane forced herself to walk over to him. Just as she reached him, he turned around.

"What are you doing here?" he asked neutrally, leaning back against the railing. In his crisp white shirt, the sleeves rolled up over tanned arms, his jacket over his shoulder, he looked like a stud on the cover of *GQ*. While she looked like a reject from a spread in *Modern Bride*.

She shrugged, but her heart was in her throat. "Heading for home, just like you."

"Home and Warren?"

"No. I'm going to break up with him."

"I don't blame you. The guy is never around, always out on a secret assignment that he can't tell you about. You have no one to talk to. No one to challenge you at Ping-Pong. It's obvious you have to break up with him."

Jane blushed. "That's not the reason."

"Then why?"

"It wouldn't be fair to him. I'm in love with someone else."

"Already?" He made a show of looking at his watch. "I thought you needed some time out, a break, a chance to get back to reality."

"I did. I took about five minutes, and I knew. I really knew all along, because I fell in love with you ten years ago, only—" Her voice broke.

Alex put his arms around her. The warmth of his touch and his voice reached inside her and soothed her heart. She burst into tears, and in seconds his shirt was soaked.

"Jane, don't cry. Please don't cry, sweetheart."

She stepped back and sniffled. "Look what I've done. First your shoes, now your shirt." She reached for her purse.

"Stop," he said. "I have another shirt in my bag

CAROL GRACE

here." His gaze drifted to her bare shoulders in her hot-pink dress. "What about you? Do you want to change?"

"I can't. I left my suitcase back at the house."

He sighed and draped his jacket around her shoulders.

Music came from the loudspeakers on the deck, and Alex smiled.

"They're playing our song," he said, brushing his lips across her ear. He put his hand on the small of her back. "Let's dance."

The look in his eyes was downright heated, and he grinned at her as he pulled her close—the same sexy grin that had first sent her heart rocking ten years ago. The sexy grin that made her feel as if she were flying instead of sailing, floating instead of dancing.

He pressed her hand against his chest and she felt his heartbeat through his shirt, even as an occasional tear still ran down her cheek.

"What is it? What's wrong?" he murmured.

She gave a watery smile. "Nothing. I'm crying because I'm happy."

Alex tilted her chin to look deep into her eyes. "I know what would make *me* happy," he said. "Instead of flying out of Athens right away, let's stay a few days. I want to show you the Parthenon by moonlight. I want to make love to you by moonlight. There's a small, quiet hotel there, and the rooms in back have balconies and a view of the Acropolis.

I want you to fall in love with Athens . . . and me."

She gave him a dazzling smile, brighter than the sun shining on the Aegean Sea. "Too late. I did that ten years ago. I love you Alex, more now than ten years ago, more now than yesterday."

"We always had great chemistry, didn't we?" He grinned back. "Even ten years ago, when we set off our first explosion. I love you, Jane. I want to marry you, and I'm not just saying that so you'll come to Seattle and work for me. I can get someone else."

"To marry you?" she asked with a straight face.

He kissed the tip of her nose, then the corners of her mouth. His eyes were brimming with amusement. "No, there never was anyone else; I just didn't realize it. You're the one—the only one. I want to marry you."

"I know—at city hall, with a bottle of champagne. No frills, no fuss, no cake."

"If you want a cake, we'll have a cake. We'll even take wedding pictures and send one to Kostos. But the honeymoon starts now, and will go on for the rest of our lives."

"Cake, photos, honeymoon, wedding," she murmured, her hands on his shoulders. "And you for the rest of my life. How can I resist?"

"You can't."

"You're on," she said. "But first . . ." She reached into her purse and pulled out the beads Kostos had given her. "Stand back," she said and tossed them overboard.

"Your worry beads?"

"And my worries—gone!"

"Forever," he promised. "Listen!"

She heard it, they both heard it, in the distance, but getting closer and louder—cheers from Zeus, Aphrodite, and Artemis, and all the gods of love on Mt. Olympus—*syncharitiria!*